FALSE CONCLUSION

FALSE CONCLUSION

Veronica Heley

This first world edition published 2020
in Great Britain and the USA by
SEVERN HOUSE PUBLISHERS LTD of
Eardley House, 4 Uxbridge Street, London W8 7SY.
Trade paperback edition first published
in Great Britain and the USA 2020 by
SEVERN HOUSE PUBLISHERS LTD.

British Library Cataloguing in Publication Data
A CIP catalogue record for this title is available from the British Library.

ISBN-13: 978-0-7278-8974-4 (cased)
ISBN-13: 978-1-78029-695-1 (trade paper)
ISBN-13: 978-1-4483-0420-2 (e-book)

This is a work of fiction. Names, characters, places and incidents
are either the product of the author's imagination or are used fictitiously.
Except where actual historical events and characters are being described
for the storyline of this novel, all situations in this publication are
fictitious and any resemblance to actual persons, living or dead,
business establishments, events or locales is purely coincidental.

All Severn House titles are printed on acid-free paper.

Severn House Publishers support the Forest Stewardship Council™ [FSC™],
the leading international forest certification organisation.
All our titles that are printed on FSC certified paper carry the FSC logo.

Typeset by Palimpsest Book Production Ltd.,
Falkirk, Stirlingshire, Scotland.
Printed and bound in Great Britain by
TJ International, Padstow, Cornwall.

ONE

Friday afternoon

Bea Abbot shut the front door on her departing guests and demanded, 'What on earth was that all about?'
Bea had intended to drive down to the boarding school that day to fetch Bernice home for the summer holidays, until the headmistress had phoned to say that a Mrs Trescott, who was collecting her own niece that day, had offered to give Bernice a lift back to London. Bea had accepted the offer with gratitude since it gave her more time to clear her desk.

When the elegantly thin Mrs Trescott and her niece arrived with Bernice, Bea had invited them in for a cup of tea by way of thanks, only to find herself on the receiving end of a series of acid remarks. What's more, the niece turned out to be a real pudding, who'd eaten six biscuits to everyone else's one and then asked to go the toilet just as Mrs Trescott rose to leave.

So, as Bea shut the door on their visitors, she asked Bernice, 'What on earth was that all about?'

Bernice was at the gawky pre-pubescent stage and never still. She'd recently had her long hair cut to a glossy, asymmetric bob but scorned make-up and most members of the human race. She'd been uncharacteristically silent during tea. Now she pushed out her lower lip and frowned, causing her black eyebrows to almost meet. 'I know you think it was very good of her to bring me back from school, and that I should be pleased to be asked to stay with them in the holidays, but I don't want to go. I realize it would be convenient for you to get rid of me so that you can get on with your work, but—'

'What? Stop right there, madam! Where did you get that idea from?' Bea put her arm round her ward's shoulders and urged her back down the hall. 'Let's start again. Welcome home. I've been looking forward to having you with me for the holidays. I've arranged with Betty, my office manageress, to take over most of my duties so that we can spend time together. I know you have plans to see various people, but—'

The doorbell rang, sharply. Someone intended to make themselves heard.

'It can't be them again,' said Bernice. 'Don't let them in!'

'Don't be silly, Bernice.' Bea opened the door and yes, on the doorstep once more stood the stylish, fifty-ish blonde with the sharp nose, and her lumpy, frumpy niece.

'So sorry,' carolled Mrs Trescott through clenched teeth. 'My niece seems to have left her pills in your toilet. So careless. May she look for them, please?' She was smiling, but cold fury emanated from every pore.

Bea managed a social smile. 'By all means.'

Without a word the niece hunched her shoulders and brushed past Bea to go down the hall to the toilet.

Mrs Trescott's expensively shod foot tapped out the rhythm of her irritation. 'These children! How one longs for the day when someone will take them off our hands. Here's my card with my smartphone number on it. I'll let you know the dates when we'd like Bernice to come to us. Next Friday for the party, obviously. And then a long weekend to follow.'

She bent closer to Bea to add, 'What a pity Bernice is such a plain child! You'll have your work cut out to make her presentable. Perhaps you should get her some padded bras? And invest in some hair extensions?'

Bea blinked. How dare the woman say such things? 'We do already have commitments for the holiday, but I will look in the diary and—'

'Splendid! Next Friday. Someone will collect her. I'm sure you'll be pleased to have a few days free.'

The frumpy girl emerged from the toilet, holding up a small packet.

'So you found it,' said Mrs High and Mighty. 'Say goodbye to your little friend. You'll see her again on Friday. Come along. You know how cross your uncle gets if dinner's late.' Still talking, she swept the girl out of the house. 'Now, we're not staying in London tonight but going straight down to the country. There's so much still to do for the party . . .'

She pushed the girl into the back of an expensive, chauffeur-driven car, and got in beside her, scolding away. 'How dare you show me up like that, eating all those biscuits. Am I glad you'll be off my hands soon! You are a very lucky girl, having someone who wants to take you on . . .' The door was slammed shut, seat belts were adjusted, and the car drove off into traffic.

Bea shut the front door, and leaned her back against it. 'I feel as if I've been run over by a train.'

Bernice stamped her foot. 'I could scream! She assumes . . .! I don't want anything to do with them!'

Bea said, 'Let's clear up in the living room, have another cuppa and you can tell me all about this new best friend of yours and why she wants you to go to stay with her.'

'She's no friend of mine,' said Bernice. 'I'd never set eyes on her till she arrived after half term and the head said I was to move into a two-bedder to look after her. If she weren't from such a wealthy family, she'd never have been accepted at our school. She's a complete dum-dum – that's what they call her. She hardly ever opens her mouth except to eat, which she does all the time. She takes no exercise and is in the bottom set for everything.'

'So why did her aunt keep saying you were her best friend? Why is she inviting you to stay with them?' Bea started to collect the used tea things. 'Where did I put the tray?'

Only a short time ago Bernice would have said it wasn't her job to help in the house, but Bea had managed to make the girl understand that if she helped with household chores, it made time for more important things, like gossiping about this new 'friend'.

Bernice found the tray for Bea and rescued a teaspoon which the dum-dum had dropped on the floor. 'The thing is, she's epileptic. They didn't want her to be in one of the dorms, but they did want someone to sleep in the same room with her in case she had a fit. The head said it would be good for me to have the responsibility – can you believe it? – oh, yes, and she also said that I should help the dum-dum with her schoolwork! I'm not sure the girl even knows how to sign her name!'

Bea could understand Bernice's feelings. Bernice was ultra-bright. She'd skipped a year at school and was still top of her class in everything. She aimed to take her exams a few years early and go off to Cambridge to study whatever she'd decided upon. Maths, probably. And more maths. Followed by extra maths or its equivalent.

Bea looked around to see if they'd collected all the tea things. 'There's no biscuits left but I've got some Dundee fruit cake in a tin in the kitchen. It's a bit worrying that you were asked to look after a girl who might have a fit at any moment. Did she have one while you were looking after her?'

'No. She seemed half asleep most of the time.' Bernice followed Bea out to the kitchen. 'The only thing she wakes up for is food. I reckon the medication she's on is too strong and could do with being toned down. Anyway, I don't think she'll be back at school in the autumn. She's got a birthday coming up, and says she'll be able to leave school afterwards. Sixteen, maybe? Can you leave school at sixteen if you want to?'

'Yes, you can.'

'She's been following me around like a lost puppy. I thought at least I'd be rid of her when we broke up for the holidays, but then you asked her aunt to bring me back to London—'

'What?' said Bea. 'No, I didn't. Your headmistress rang me and said someone had offered you a lift and was that all right by me. I asked if it were a suitable person and she said it was. So I agreed.' Bea checked on the casserole she'd put in the oven earlier and switched on the kettle. 'I'd never heard of the Trescotts before. I suppose I ought to have looked them up, but I trusted your headmistress . . . for which I apologize, Bernice. An hour in their company would drive anyone to murder.'

Bea plonked some mugs on the table while Bernice wriggled herself on to a stool and reached out for Winston, their big, furry, black cat. Winston recalled her as being a good provider of titbits and allowed herself to be picked up and stroked.

Bernice imitated Mrs Trescott. 'Who's a plain little pussy, then?' She huffed into Winston's fur. And then laughed. 'If the dum-dum had seen Winston, she'd have been all over him. She's a right softy for animals. Takes photos of them everywhere she goes. And dogs . . . she can't see a dog without falling in love with it.'

Bea lifted a heavy fruit cake out of a tin. 'How big a piece do you want?'

'Medium.' Bernice released Winston to grab a slice. 'I don't really have to have a padded bra, do I? I know I'm thin, but—'

'You have a model's figure. You're perfect for your age. Honestly, I could do that woman an injury, saying things like that.'

With a stab of pain Bea recalled another barbed remark the woman had made. At some point Mrs Trescott seemed to have come into contact with Max, Bea's only child. Max had grown up to be a somewhat self-important but hard-working Member of Parliament. Mrs Trescott had managed to work a reference to Max into their conversation, saying what a pity it was that Bea was so busy with her little domestic agency that she never had time to see her son or her grandchildren.

Phew! How dare she! It was Max and his wife who were always too busy to see Bea, not the other way round! And yet, and yet . . . couldn't Bea have tried harder to keep in touch? Perhaps she *was* a bad mother.

Winston sidled along the table. He hadn't tasted fruit cake yet, but thought he'd rather like to try.

Bea flapped her hand at him, and he pretended to cower. 'As for my not wanting you around in the holidays, Bernice, that's absolutely not true. I've been looking forward to it. I know you'll want to spend some time with your family and friends . . .'

Bernice nodded, her mouth full of cake. After a disastrous first venture into domesticity, Bernice's fragile mother had married a gentle, slightly shambolic man who had his own IT company, and who adored his wife and their toddler son. They all three loved Bernice. Of course they did. But Bea was aware – as perhaps Bernice was not – that they were also slightly in awe of the girl's sharp mind and strong personality.

Bea continued, 'Your mother suggested you might like a week with them when they rent a cottage down in Cornwall. Also, Piers, my beloved ex-husband, is due to fly in from Greece sometime today. He says that someone he painted recently – a French count, if I remember correctly – has issued an invitation for the three of us to stay for a week or ten days in his famous French chateau, swimming pool included. If that's what we fancy.'

Bernice spoke round a mouthful of fruit cake. 'That sounds good. He's taking us to the theatre tomorrow, isn't he?' She screwed up her mouth to imitate someone assaulted by a bad smell. 'Ugh! That woman! "Perhaps you should invest in some hair extensions for your ward?" I haven't come out in spots, have I?'

'No, you haven't,' said Bea. 'You know what? I feel sorry for the Trescott girl, whatever her name is. Fancy having to live with that woman's tongue!'

Winston made a move on the cake, so Bea picked him up off the table and put him on the floor.

Bernice was fast recovering her good humour. 'I was ever so restrained when the Awful Aunt criticized me. I didn't kick her in the shins, or use an impolite word.'

Bea laughed. 'You said nothing, most beautifully. I could hear your teeth grinding. If you'd been five years younger, you'd have been put over my knee and given a good spanking for dumb insolence!'

Bernice dimpled. 'I'm really proud of me.'

There was a short, staccato ring at the door and someone put their key in the lock.

Bernice assumed a world-weary air. 'Uh-ho. Look who's turned up like a bad penny. And, he's actually remembered his key.'

There were thumping sounds of a number of bags being dropped as someone made his way along the hall to the kitchen. 'I'm back.' Piers, Bea's long-divorced ex-husband, arrived in the doorway, slung around with a satchel and a travel bag, and with a cashmere sweater hung around his neck. His mop of dark hair was beginning to show threads of grey, and his dark eyes were bright with intelligence. He was a magnet for women, Mr Charm himself, dressed as usual in a T-shirt, good jeans and rather wonderful boots. 'Do I smell cake? And perhaps a casserole? Ah, the joys of home cooking!'

Bea reached for another mug. 'How did the portrait go?'

Piers took a seat, eyeing the cake on the table. 'I painted her as a Medusa, all snaky hair and bad temper. She loved it.'

Winston jumped up on his lap and fixed him with an expression of complete devotion. Piers flicked his fingers through Winston's fur, and said, 'Is it tonight we're at the theatre?'

Bernice shook her head at Bea. 'He doesn't even know which day of the week it is.'

Bea replied, 'At least he's in the right country.' She gave him a huge slice of cake and a mug of tea.

'I know it's the school holidays,' said Piers, unconcerned. 'I know I've got the summer off. What I can't remember is whether I've told my tenant I was coming back today or next Friday. I've tried ringing him but he's not picking up. So I'm hoping I can stay here tonight. I'll get it sorted in the morning.'

Bernice and Bea rolled their eyes at one another.

'I might have known,' said Bea. 'Funnily enough, I made up the spare room bed, just in case.'

Bernice, who occupied the whole of the top floor of the house, said, 'You'll be struck deaf and dumb if you try to set up your easel in my rooms.'

'Promises, promises,' said Piers comfortably, as he took another piece of fruit cake.

Piers was an internationally renowned portrait painter who flew all over the world to paint the great and the good. He didn't quibble if some of the great were not so good, provided they had interesting faces and paid the bills on time. He was something of a rolling stone, hiring studio accommodation when he needed it. He had never owned a car or a piece of real estate and was currently renting Bea's small flat in the mews at the end of her road. If he knew he would be away for more than week, he would often sublet to holidaymakers only to find himself temporarily homeless if his schedule changed unexpectedly . . . as was the case now.

Bea was ambivalent about his periodical descents on her home. He was always good company, and sometimes it seemed that their long-ago relationship might one day be resumed, but . . . Yes, there was always a 'but'. They had married too young and financial restraints plus his tomcatting around the place had put an end to their marriage, leaving Bea as a single mother with Max, their only child, to bring up as best she could.

Bea had gone on to marry her boss at the Abbot Agency, who had adopted young Max and done well by him. It was only after her second husband's death that Piers had wandered back into her life. So far he hadn't made it back into her bed, but she was aware that this was what he was aiming for.

Bea wasn't sure how she felt about that, or about him, either, come to think of it.

Bernice had taken her time to accept him. For a long time she'd referred to him as the Tom Cat, to which he'd responded by calling her 'Brat'. But by now they'd progressed to a limited acceptance of one another.

Bernice said, 'What did you bring me this time?'

Bea said, half-heartedly, 'Now, Bernice. You know it's not polite to ask for gifts.'

Piers rummaged in his shoulder bag to produce two glass snowstorms. 'I couldn't see anything I liked until these absurd things caught my eye. I think one of them plays a tune but I can't remember which one.'

Bea shook hers to make the snowflakes rise and then settle to reveal a Swiss chalet. 'I like it.'

Bernice discovered how to switch the music on in hers. 'Ghastly tune!'

They both laughed. Piers had many gifts, and one of them was finding amusing presents to give them on his return from foreign parts.

He covered a yawn. 'So, can I put some things in the washing machine?' He didn't wait for permission, but started to throw things in. 'Has anything interesting been happening in my absence?'

'Well!' said Bernice, and proceeded to tell him all about the dum-dum and the Awful Aunt and exactly how rude the Awful Aunt had been, not only to Bernice but also to Bea.

Piers set the machine going and yawned again. 'I shouldn't have jet lag, should I? It was a shortish flight. Four hours? What's the woman want? I could do with a nap. Mind if I stretch out on the settee for a bit?'

Bea said, 'Oh!' And then: 'Now why didn't I see that? It's textbook, isn't it?'

Bernice said, 'What on earth are you talking about?'

Piers said, 'I don't know about the niece, who sounds a hopeless case. But you should have realized what was up when she started on you, Brat. Criticising. Undermining your confidence.'

Bernice narrowed her eyes. 'You mean, when she said I was plain and needed the attentions of a beauty parlour? When she hinted I wasn't going to attract a man? She *wanted* me to feel unloved and unlovely?'

Bea said, 'She kept hinting that I would be glad to be rid of Bernice, and that I was a bad guardian. Worse than that, she made out I didn't care about Max. Piers, have you seen him recently? I know you keep in touch.'

'I try. He's happy enough to hear about the important people I've painted, but our meetings are few and far between. He's always so busy.'

Bernice said, 'The Awful Aunt was right on about me being plain. I suppose I am.'

Piers said, 'Bernice, you've good bone structure and intelligence. I'd never have painted you if you looked like today's vapid so-called beauties, with their Botoxed lips and tattooed eyebrows.'

Piers had painted a portrait of Bernice which had been hung in the Summer Exhibition at the Royal Academy. Bea had wondered if that would turn Bernice's head but she'd taken it in her stride, merely remarking that Piers might think she looked good in violet, but she'd never liked the colour herself.

Although, come to think of it, Bernice had recently bought herself a shirt in what she called 'dark lilac' and which could be considered violet if you wanted to be picky about it. And it did suit her. Not, of course, that Bernice would admit to being bothered about such things.

Bea looked back on what Mrs Trescott had said. 'She's clever. That woman knew exactly what she was doing when she said those things. She tried to drive a wedge between us.'

'I wonder why?' Piers yawned. 'I need a siesta.'

Bernice frowned. 'She started on that "Plain Jane" lark as soon as we got in the car at school.'

'Envy and jealousy rule, OK,' said Piers, leaving the room. 'Wake me when it's time for supper.'

Bernice looked a question at Bea, who patted the girl's arm. 'He means that it's a nasty old world out there, and people like to destroy what they haven't got themselves. Mrs Trescott didn't come across as a happy woman, did she? Well, we've had a brush with something nasty, but now we've seen what it looks like, we can avoid it in future. Finish. End of.'

As it happened, she was wrong about that.

Piers reappeared, holding a piece of paper. 'I found this in the toilet. Who's on medication for epilepsy?'

'That will be the dum-dum,' said Bernice.

Bea rolled her eyes. 'I really don't like that nickname, Bernice. What did you say her name was? Evelina, isn't it?' And to Piers: 'The child's epileptic. She used our toilet before she left. She must have taken her medication there but forgotten the packet when she left, which is why she had to come back for it.'

'Why take the box and leave the instructions?' He gave another gigantic yawn, threw the paper on the table and made off to the living room.

Bea smoothed out the list of instructions. What it was prescribed for, the dosage, possible side effects, and so on. She told herself that there was nothing sinister about Evelina having left the paper behind. She read out, 'It's called Pregabalin, and it's not for children. How old is Evelina?'

The landline phone rang. Bea was nearest and picked it up. It was Betty, her office manageress calling from the agency rooms down below. 'There's a call on the agency landline for Bernice. Someone called Evelina. Shall I put it through?'

Bea handed the phone over to Bernice, but took the precaution of switching it to speaker.

Bernice pulled a face, but dutifully said, 'Bernice here.'

A breathy, young girl's voice. 'Bernice, I'm so much looking forward to your visit. We'll have such fun.'

Bernice blinked, and Bea frowned. The hurried delivery, the forced joviality, was not something either of them had expected from the timid, almost speechless schoolgirl they knew.

Bernice said, 'I'm afraid I've got an awful lot on these holidays. It's kind of you to ask but—'

'No, you must come, you must! There's no one else who . . .

and . . .' Then in a lower voice, almost a whisper, 'You got my message?'

At the other end of the phone a sharper, older voice said, 'Give that here!'

The Awful Aunt? 'Bernice, we'll collect you at four on Friday afternoon for the weekend. Bring something suitable to wear for the party on Friday night.'

The phone went dead.

Bernice cradled the receiver. 'The dum-dum says she's sent me a message?'

Bea smoothed out the piece of paper from the box of tablets. 'I think she means this.'

TWO

Friday, late afternoon

Bernice snatched the paper from Bea and held it up to the light. 'How can that be a message? It's instructions for taking her medication.'

Bea drew her tablet towards her and went on the internet. 'Let's look it up. Pregabalin. It's for epilepsy and nervous disorders. It can cause drowsiness and weight gain and it's not for children under eighteen. Evelina's not eighteen yet, is she?'

Bernice was bored with the subject. 'So? Who cares! What's for supper?'

'Chicken casserole. Fresh veg. You thought she might be on too strong a dose. Hmm . . . I'm going to look up the Trescott family, see what's what. Why don't you go upstairs, unpack and change into civvies?'

'Want to get rid of me?'

Bea didn't reply. She was busy inputting Evelina's family name. Oh, bother. Her tablet was not big enough or fast enough to read easily. She decided to look the Trescotts up on her computer downstairs. The agency should be tidied away for the weekend by now.

Down she went. Betty, her office manager, was turning off
the lights in the big office, ready to depart. Once assured that
all was in order, Bea went through into her own office at the
back to boot up her computer. Because of the slope on which
the house was built, this room had French windows which led
on to the garden. The evening sun was still strong and she
hardly needed to put on the desk light, but did so. She liked
the light.

Now . . . Trescott.

There was a big website for an international Trescott
consortium, and another for the family itself.

Bea worked away, researching the family until Bernice
wandered downstairs. She was now dressed in a white T-shirt
and jeans which were a little on the short side for she'd shot up
that term and was now almost as tall as Bea.

Bernice handed over her school report, saying that Bea didn't
need to read it for it was all A stars. And when was supper
likely to be?

'Supper's in half an hour,' said Bea, swivelling round in
her chair. 'Listen to what I've discovered. The Trescotts came
over with the Conqueror. They are landowners with property in
the Home Counties. Their country house is a Georgian house
in Surrey, built on the site of earlier manor houses. The town
house is in Belgravia.

'The Trescotts are solid County with a capital C. They held
minor offices for the Crown in the past, went in for hunting,
shooting and fishing, doing the season, and so on. But about a
hundred years ago it seems that the Trescott money was running
out and they looked around for a wealthy heiress to marry. Enter
the Smiths, or rather the Smythes, as they became. They were
Birmingham manufacturers who had risen from the yeoman
class in the nineteenth century. They were people who made
things and brooked no nonsense. They were builders of roads
and bridges, and eventually they moved into other forms of
transport as well. And machinery. Yes, they diversified into
munitions during the two world wars.

'The marriage of the two families occurred in the late
twentieth century when a Trescott beauty – who had been
painted by Sargent – married a burly engineer from Birmingham

and they became the Trescott-Smythes. It looked like a match made in heaven; blue blood marries wealthy manufacturer and they live happily ever after. Soon after that, they extended the Georgian family mansion by half as much again, and dropped the "Smythe" part of their name. Trescott women have been famous debutantes and married well. Someone's daughter was a bridesmaid at the wedding of a minor royal.

'But as the value of farmland has taken a dive, so the manufacturing side of the family has become more important. The business side has forged ahead, gobbling up associated company as they went, diversifying at home and away. The current head of the Trescott empire is a silver fox who looks like a film star. Your Mrs Long Nose is a typical blonde Trescott, fine-boned and sharp. Either she married a cousin of the same name, or she's so like the type that she was picked because she looked like one. Did Evelina mention how they're connected? She said "aunt" but that might mean through blood or marriage.'

'If she did, I wasn't listening.'

'A pity. Information is always helpful. Now, the Smythes were stocky with firm chins. Like Evelina, who appears to be the only descendant now living who looks like a Smythe. Evelina's father, Thomas, headed up the Trescott empire until his early death. This is what he looked like.' Bea turned her computer screen round so that Bernice could see.

The man pictured was dark-haired and thickset with a strong chin. The woman beside him was a frail-looking brunette.

Bea said, 'A couple of years ago a Mr and Mrs Thomas Trescott were killed in a road accident near their country estate. Was this Evelina's mother and father, do you think?'

Bernice said, 'Uh-huh. That's the photo she has on her bedside table. She told me she only began to be poorly when they died. She was in hospital for quite a while. Then she went to a small day school and finally ended up with us.'

Bea sat back in her chair. 'I don't understand why Mrs Long Nose is targeting you. Is their money running out again, so that they're looking for another heiress to marry? No, surely not. You're far too young to be considered eligible, and the Trescott business looks to be doing well.'

'Dunno and don't care. All I know is that the dum-dum said

the family was loaded and she's the one who inherits the lot
though she can't touch it till she's eighteen. School fees are all
paid for by her guardian but she has hardly any pocket money.
I lent her a tenner to buy some chocolate, which was stupid of
me as I don't suppose I'll get it back, and chocolate isn't good
for her, anyway.'

Bea looked at her watch and got to her feet. 'I must go and
put the veg on to cook. I haven't had time to look at the wills
of her father and mother. Do you want to have a crack at it?'

'Can't be bothered. It's boring.'

'Very well.' Bea switched off her computer, made sure
everything was closed down for the night and led the way back
up to the kitchen to put the vegetables on.

Bea understood Bernice's refusal to think about the Trescotts,
for in some ways Evelina's situation mirrored Bernice's own
history.

Bernice was born with brains and personality. After a rocky
childhood in which her scoundrel of a father had almost driven
her mother to suicide, Bernice had been rescued by an elderly,
wealthy, odd-ball of a great aunt who had introduced the child
to a life of power and money before dying and leaving the girl
– not in the care of her still fragile mother – in Bea's hands.

Bernice was the heiress to a sizeable chunk of the extensive
Holland empire which, like the Trescotts, had spread in many
different and profitable directions. Although the business was
currently being steered by Bernice's great uncle through the
shoals of international trade, the girl was very much aware of
the future responsibilities that would be hers one day, if she
chose to accept them.

And yes, even though still at school, Bernice was doing her
best to prepare herself for the future, and spent some time in
the holidays with her great uncle – if he were free – or with
his finance director. Bernice was learning the ropes. As she
could read a balance sheet faster than Bea could type her name,
it seemed likely that Bernice would indeed play a significant
role in the future of the company when she grew up.

As to her social development, the girl had a tendency to get
a bit above herself but, not without a tussle now and then, Bea
and Piers between them kept her grounded in reality.

Bea microwaved some vegetables, fished the casserole out of the oven, and called Piers and Bernice to the table. Piers opened a bottle of wine for the adults and set out fruit juice for Bernice. They ate in the kitchen, mulling over various plans for the holiday. How to fit everything in? A visit to the French chateau was top of the list, and the cottage in Cornwall was a must. Bernice also mentioned the possibility of meeting up with some other school friends . . . not Trescotts!

Bernice watched Piers refill Bea's glass. 'May I have some, too?'

'No,' said Piers. 'Who's going to be the richest? You or your friend Evelina?'

'She's not my friend. When she found out I'd come top in mental arithmetic she sat there with her mouth open, and said she couldn't do maths nowadays. I told you she was a dum-dum, didn't I? She really is.'

'Who's her guardian?'

Bernice shrugged. 'I suppose it's the Awful Aunt. But there's also an uncle in the picture who has to be pandered to. I suppose it's one or the other of them.'

Piers said, 'This is Mrs Long Nose, whose aim in life seems to be to cut the girl down to size? And the uncle is the one who will be seriously displeased if she's late for supper? I feel sorry for the girl.'

Bea said, 'I'm getting a really bad feeling about this. On the surface, Evelina is an overweight child of low IQ, whom the family are trying to educate by sending to private schools. I suppose it's understandable that the aunt keeps correcting the girl if she really is such a fool, but it can't be doing her self-confidence any good. What happens if you throw a large amount of money into the mix? If, say, Mrs Long Nose and the hard-to-please uncle are in financial trouble and the girl is due to inherit a bundle, well, I'm beginning to wonder . . . no, I'm being ridiculous. What could they do about it?'

Bea laughed at herself. 'What nonsense I do talk. Of course they have the girl's best interests at heart.'

'No, they don't, said Bernice. 'And you know it. Every word Mrs Long Nose says is aimed at destroying the girl's confidence. There was this programme on the telly about the young Princess

Victoria who was kept down by her mother, who thought that that way she'd be able to control the girl when she became Queen. The girl behaved all meek and mild till she was proclaimed Queen, and then she froze her mother out. I don't think our dum-dum – sorry! *Evelina* – has the guts to do that.'

Piers frowned. 'Back to basics. Bernice, what is it that Mrs Long Nose wants from you? You were in the car with them for what, an hour or so? What did you talk about?'

'She knew a lot about me already. She knew about me being heiress to the family fortune, shares held in trust, and so on. She wanted to know how often I saw my great uncle. I didn't see why they should be asking that, so I said, "now and then". Then she wanted to know how Bea treated me, and I said "like family". She said she supposed Bea spoiled me rotten, and she laughed. So I just stared at her. I mean, what could I have said?'

'That I spoil you rotten,' said Bea, lifting Winston off the table again. Then, in a good imitation of Mrs Long Nose, she added, 'Look at what you've left on your plate! Eat your greens, girl! They're good for you.'

Bernice giggled because she always ate her greens. 'She talked a lot about the portrait. She said I'd matured since then and what a pity it was that I'd cut my hair because men liked long hair. She wanted to know if I'd enjoyed sitting for Piers and being famous, what with having my portrait in the Royal Academy and all. What was I supposed to say? So I smiled and said nothing. She said portraits by Piers were all the rage and she would ask him to paint Evelina some time. And I thought, well, that he wouldn't want to paint her, but I was ever so good and didn't say so. She said, how had it come about that Piers had painted me? I didn't think it was any business of hers, so I asked if I could open a window a crack as I was feeling carsick. Which I wasn't. But it shut her up.'

Winston's head rose above the tabletop. He leaped up on to Piers' lap and eyed a chicken bone on his plate.

'No!' said Bea.

Winston gave her a look of disgust, jumped down and made a stately exit via the cat flap to find someone who'd be only too happy to feed a deserving mouser like him.

Bernice said, 'There's only one other thing. I didn't

understand it then, and I'm not sure I get it now. After she stopped talking to me, she started on the dum-dum, wanting to know if she'd had an early birthday card from someone, and saying wasn't she a lucky girl to have someone who cared so much about her. The dum-dum smiled and nodded but didn't speak. Well, you know she doesn't talk much. Mrs Long Nose went on talking about the treats in store for the dum-dum, that her new dress had come and lots of people had accepted the invitation to her birthday party. Apparently there's going to be a marquee and two bands and lots of photographs, and the presents were already arriving, and wasn't it too, too exciting. The dum-dum didn't look excited. She looked as if she were half asleep.'

Bea thought about this as she cleared plates away from the first course and produced a fresh fruit salad for afters. 'How old did you say the girl is?'

Bernice shrugged. 'Mentally, I'd say she was five. Physically, how about forty plus? Coming up sixteen or maybe seventeen. Dunno. I'm bored with this subject. What are we doing tomorrow?'

Piers said, 'I've just had a nasty thought. At sixteen you can marry with your parents' consent. You don't think she's planning to get married so that she can drop out of school?'

Bernice said, 'Oh come on! Why would anyone want to tie themselves down so soon?'

Piers said, 'You might think it a way out of being bullied by your family.'

Bernice grimaced. 'Well, I admit Mrs Long Nose is going the right way to make her niece think like that. But she's not the only person who has a say in the child's future, is she? There's at least one uncle and some cousins.'

Piers said, 'Are they all telling the girl that she's an idiot? Setting her up to fail? If she still has no confidence in her own ability when she inherits her father's shares in the business, she could easily be persuaded to let other people handle everything for her. She could be asked to sign papers she hasn't read and wouldn't understand. That way control of all her money would pass to whoever wants it.'

Bernice was impatient. 'No, no. I know one of her uncles

looks out for her, even though he's a right pain about punctuality, and there does seem to be a boyfriend in the background. She kept a photo of him in her wallet and takes it out to look at every now and then.'

'Did you see it? What's he like?' said Bea.

'Grown up. Fair hair and blue eyes. Handsome if you like that sort of thing. He was wearing Dolce & Gabbana which was what I noticed when she dropped the photo one day and I picked it up. She went all pink when I asked who it was. Some people look dreadful when they blush, don't they? She said that he was her boyfriend. I almost laughed. I mean, why would someone who looked like a film star want to take up with her . . .?' Her voice trailed away. 'No, I see what you mean. You think he's after her money?'

Piers said, 'He's grown up, you said. Does he have a name?'

'She said it was a cousin. She said he was "in lurv" with her.' Bernice crooked her forefingers in the air to put the word in italics. 'But that's not real. I mean, it couldn't be. Could it?'

Bea said, 'Did he look like a Trescott? Fine-boned and blonde? A bit sporty but very polished?'

Bernice shrugged. 'I suppose. I'm not going to stay with them. I'm not going to see them again, any of them, so what does it matter? Now, what are we doing tomorrow? I want some new jeans. Look, I've grown out of everything!' She extended her legs to show that the pair she was wearing was now above her ankles. 'I want skinny ones, in black not blue.'

'Right,' said Bea. 'Let's forget about the troublesome Trescotts. Tomorrow morning Piers will sleep off his jet lag while you and I shop till we drop.'

Saturday morning

Trailing a teenager around department stores was not Bea's idea of fun, although the girl knew what she wanted and, moreover, had excellent taste. The prices of the items she chose were eye-watering, but the results stylish and even practical. Bernice liked to have pockets for credit cards and house keys in her jeans so that she didn't need to carry a handbag. When she'd purchased the jeans, she started on the hunt for a couple of screamingly plain but pricey T-shirts and ditto severe-looking white blouses. Each of which came from a different label.

Bea was worn out by noon, and suggested breaking for coffee and a sandwich before they tackled the purchase of some new hi-tech gadget or other which Bernice had heard about, and it was only when she seated herself with a sigh that Bea realized her phone was vibrating in her purse.

It was Piers, sounding strained. 'Bea, where are you? I've been trying to get you for the last half hour. Can you get back home straight away? We have a bit of a crisis here.'

Bernice, overhearing, stuck out her lower lip. 'This is *my* time with you, Bea. You promised, no work!'

Bea ignored the girl. 'I'm in Knightsbridge at the moment. What's up?'

'That girl, Evelina. Your office manager – she's called Betty, is that right? – woke me up saying there'd been an urgent phone call for you, Bea. She'd tried to get hold of you but you weren't picking up. The call was from your Mrs Long Nose, Mrs Trescott. There's been some sort of accident at the country house. In view of Evelina's past problems and because she's distressed, they wanted to get her out of the house till the police have been and gone. They proposed to dump the child here. I started to say it wasn't convenient, but Betty said the woman rang off after telling her that the chauffeur was already on his way with the girl. Betty tried to ring back to say she had no authority to admit the child, but Mrs Whatsit didn't pick up. I'm expecting a ring at the doorbell any minute. What am I supposed to do?'

Bea was on her feet. 'I'll get a taxi back. That will be quickest.'

Bernice said, 'No-o-o! You can't! We haven't finished.'

'I know it's hard,' said Bea, leaving money on the table for the waitress, 'but needs must. Your friend's in trouble.'

'She's not my friend. And I'm not coming with you.'

'Yes, you are, my girl.' Bea picked up their shopping bags and thrust them at Bernice. 'That was an SOS if ever I heard one. Piers doesn't panic without reason. We'll dump your purchases back at the house and then see what's what. Perhaps Piers will take you out shopping again later. He won't know anything about that hi-tech stuff you want, which means you

can feel superior to him and, with any luck, he might even foot
the bill for you.'

So saying, Bea swept the girl out of the coffee bar and hailed
a taxi. They were fortunate with the traffic and arrived back at
the house just in time to see the Trescott limousine glide away.

Bernice said, 'I am *not*, repeat *not*, going to babysit the idiot
girl. She's nothing to do with me. I don't like her. She doesn't
like me. I'm not having her spoiling my holidays.'

'It sounds,' said Bea, putting her key in the lock, 'as if
Evelina's holidays have already been spoiled.'

An overnight bag stood in the hall, and a black winter coat
had been draped over the newel post at the bottom of the stairs.

Piers appeared from the sitting room, his hands flung wide.
'She's catatonic. Won't speak. I had to help her walk in and sit
her down. There's no light in her eyes. I've no idea what's
brought this on. I asked the chauffeur, who zipped his mouth
tight and left without a word.'

Bernice rolled her eyes. 'What are we supposed to do if she
has a fit?'

Bea explained to Piers, 'She's epileptic, remember?'

Piers shrugged. 'I suppose we might be seeing the aftermath
of a fit. I'd say she's in shock.'

Bea's office manageress toiled up the steps from the agency
rooms. 'So sorry to have to haul you back, Mrs Abbot, but I
didn't know what else to do. Mrs Trescott seems to think the
girl will be perfectly all right after a good rest in a quiet room.'

Piers said, 'I was thinking of calling for an ambulance.'

Bernice said, 'Oh no! Does she always have to be at the
centre of attention?'

Bea slitted her eyes at Bernice. 'Behave, brat!' And to her
manageress: 'Betty, thanks for everything. Don't let this make
you late. I know you need to leave by one on a Saturday. I'll
have a look at the girl now and decide what needs to be done.'

Betty disappeared back down the stairs to the agency rooms,
and Bernice and Piers followed Bea into the sitting room.

Evelina was sitting on the settee, staring at the fireplace. Her
dark hair had been pulled back, untidily, into an elastic band.
She was wearing a dull red and purple flowered dress in some
slippery material. It had a cross-over bodice which made her

look matronly and on her feet were pink, fluffy, well-worn bedroom slippers.

Bea bent over Evelina and stroked her cheek. The girl didn't react. Bea straightened up, and said, very softly, 'See her eyes? She's taken something.'

Bernice huffed. 'She's like that nearly all the time. It's those pills she's on.'

Bea sat beside the girl and picked up her hands which were lying on her thighs. 'She's so cold! Poor thing. Piers, there's a rug on the back of my chair. Can you put it round her shoulders? Bernice, would you make some strong tea with sugar in it?'

Bernice flounced. 'Do I really have to waste my holidays looking after her?'

'Yes,' said Bea. 'You know you do.'

Bernice scowled, but obeyed.

Piers put the rug around the girl's shoulders. Still Evelina stared at the fireplace.

Piers looked a query at Bea, who shook her head and said, 'I looked up what those pills do, and this is it. The aunt probably thought she might have had a fit after whatever it is that has happened, and gave the girl a double dose. If that's the case, then there's no reason to worry. But I'd better check.' She reached for her bag and got out her phone and the card Mrs Trescott had given her. 'I'll see if I can reach her now.'

The phone rang and rang. Eventually Mrs Trescott answered it. 'Yes?'

'Bea Abbot here. I was called back home to find your niece—'

'Yes, yes. I must explain, such a terrible thing. My brother Constant made a mistake with his pills and took an overdose . . . dreadful, dreadful! It was Evelina who discovered him and roused the household. The police are asking questions which is only right and proper because my brother Cyril said he thought he heard someone arguing with Constant in the night, but of course he was dreaming, and of course Evelina had nothing to do with it but, given her problems, which I know you are aware of, her reaction to the terrible tragedy of my brother and his wife all those years ago, we needed for her own sake to get her out of the way to some safe place in case she said something, admitted something . . . You understand?'

THREE

Saturday afternoon

Bea said, 'No, I don't understand. The girl seems catatonic. I wondered if she'd taken something—'

'Yes, of course. I made her take double the usual dose, which will keep her quiet. Please see that she continues to take the pills. It's most important. For now, let her sleep it off and then give her carbohydrates, plenty of them. If all is well, we should be able to collect her tomorrow morning.'

There was no question of 'would you' or 'could you' – Mrs Trescott expected to be obeyed.

Bea said, 'May I ask why—'

'I must go. There's so much to be done. Oh, by the way' – an even sharper note in the cut-glass voice – 'my chauffeur says there was a man at your house when he delivered Evelina. Who is he? I didn't know you had a man living with you.'

'No, I don't. A friend flew in yesterday, dossed down here overnight, but—'

'He's not interested in young girls, then?'

'No, of course not. Look, I don't understand why—'

The line went dead. Bea said, 'I could scream! What's going on? She says one of her brothers has died of an overdose and another brother said he'd heard him arguing with someone. So now the police are involved and Mrs T thinks it best to get Evelina out of the way. Why? Is it because she might have a fit if she were questioned by the police? Or was she involved in her uncle taking an overdose of whatever it was? Are we harbouring a criminal?'

Bernice stood in the doorway with a mug of hot tea. 'She's in trouble with the police?'

Bea flung her arms out. 'I don't know! How dare that woman dump her niece on us! Piers, are you with me on this? Ought we to phone the police and say we've got Evelina here if they would like to interview her. Only . . . no, that won't do. I think she ought to be in hospital.'

Piers rubbed his chin. He hadn't shaved that morning. He had very designer, very attractive stubble. 'I haven't the foggiest.'

Bernice said, 'Leave it to me.' She went to sit beside Evelina. She placed the tea in Evelina's flaccid hands, folding them around the mug. She made her voice soft. 'Look, you're quite safe here. Drink up. It'll make you feel better. Have you eaten today? I can see you got dressed in a hurry. Did you have any breakfast this morning? Perhaps I can get you something to eat when you've drunk your tea?'

Evelina's eyes focused on Bernice, and then went back to staring at nothing.

Bernice gently raised the mug and held it against the girl's lips. Evelina's eyelids fluttered, and she gave a little sob. She opened her mouth and drank a few sips. Then she took hold of the mug and drank the lot.

Bea and Piers froze.

Evelina's eyes focused on Bernice with what that young lady had previously described as dum-dum's 'puppy dog' look.

In the same gentle voice Bernice said, 'That's better. Want some more? And perhaps some egg and toast soldiers? You must be hungry.'

Evelina's mouth twitched into an attempt at a smile. She nodded.

'Good girl,' said Bernice, sounding much older than her years. 'Now, would you like to lie down here while I rustle up some food, or come with me into the kitchen?'

Evelina's eyes skittered to Bea and Piers, and then went back to Bernice. The puppy dog look was firmly pinned to her face. She pushed back the rug Piers had put around her and got to her feet by inches, pulling herself up by the arm of the settee. Keeping her eyes averted from Piers and Bea, she took Bernice's outstretched hand and was led out to the kitchen.

Piers and Bea looked at one another.

Piers said, 'The brat's growing up.'

Bea pushed her fingers back through her hair. 'I don't like this. Ought we to tell the police that we've got the girl?'

'If the death was due to natural causes or an accidental over-dose, then we don't need to do anything, and the Awful Aunt did the right thing in whisking the child away from the scene.'

'But surely, however fragile she is, if the girl discovered the death then she ought to tell her story to the police? They would make allowances for her, wouldn't they? And, as she's underage, she would have an adult present to safeguard her interests.'

'You're right. But she's a poor little sausage, isn't she? I suppose they fear that even being asked gently what she knows about her uncle's death might cause her to have a fit.'

Bea was restless. 'I see that, but I can't help thinking that we've been put in a difficult position. Madam may well have been acting in the child's best interests by removing her from the scene of the crime, but . . . I don't know . . . was it the right thing to do? The assumption is that we'd hide the child from the police and I don't understand why it's necessary to do so. Am I overreacting? What do you think?'

Piers cracked his fingers. Nodded. 'Agreed. It stinks. You can say the family are protecting the child and yes, they have a point. But the police ought to know where she is in case they need to interview her.'

Bea tried to rationalize her position. 'We took her in out of common humanity because she was in trouble and we will look after as best we can. I agree she is not in any state to be inter-viewed in formal circumstances at the moment, but the authorities need to know that she is currently staying with us.' She hesitated. 'Perhaps I should warn the Awful Aunt that this is what we think should happen?'

She picked up her phone again. She thought Piers would probably tell her not to warn Mrs Trescott. She rather hoped he would. But he didn't. Instead, he shut the door so that the girls in the kitchen wouldn't hear.

Bea tried to get through to Mrs Trescott, but was diverted to voicemail. Pushing herself to feel brave, Bea left a message to say that she did not feel comfortable about the position she was in. She said Evelina seemed to be in deep shock, but if the police wished to interview her, then they should be told where she was to be found.

She clicked off, feeling limp. 'Maybe the police don't need

to contact the girl. They're so stretched that a death by natural causes or by accident must be low on their list of priorities.'

'You did the right thing. You always do.'

Perhaps they both thought about a time when he had done the wrong thing several times over, and it had ended their marriage. She knew he regretted it now. But if he were to have his time again, he'd probably act the same way. Wouldn't he?

Bernice led Evelina by the hand into the room, and guided her to sit on the settee once more. Bernice said, 'She's eaten two scrambled eggs and had half a pint of milk. I said that if she were up to it we'd like to know what happened, and she's agreed to tell you. Come on, girl! Piers and Bea will look after you, but you must tell them what happened for your own sake.'

Evelina lifted her eyes as far as Bea's hands, and dropped them again. She shook her head, wordless.

Bernice actually patted the girl's shoulder. 'Be brave. You'll feel better, after. Get it off your chest.'

Evelina nodded. She held Bernice's hand fast in hers, and spoke to that. 'I found him. Lying in bed.' She lifted frightened eyes to Bernice, seeking reassurance, and then dropped them again.

Bernice encouraged her. 'You can do it. You know you can. You're a lot stronger than you think. So what did you do?'

'I screamed. They came. They shouted at me. They sent me to bed.' She began to rock to and fro.

Bernice said, 'Did he have a bad heart?'

'I suppose he must have.' A dull tone of voice.

'Did he take too many sleeping pills by accident?'

'I suppose.' The girl's eyes went out of focus, and she was silent.

Bea glanced at Piers. Evelina had agreed that her uncle might have had a bad heart, or taken an overdose, but she'd not done so in a way that convinced.

So was either of Bernice's suggestions the truth?

Bernice seemed to have caught up with this line of thought, too. She frowned, and frowning, tried to pull her hand away from Evelina's. The girl let Bernice's hand go. Her eyes stared into the past. She was helpless. Defeated. Resigned to whatever happened to her. Or . . . doped out of her mind?

Bea said in a brisk, no-nonsense voice, 'Now, you've had a perfectly dreadful day and hardly anything to eat. Suppose I show you to our guest room and you can unpack, have a shower and a lie-down till supper time.'

Piers made a sharp movement, and Bea remembered that he'd slept in the guest bedroom on the first floor the previous night, and might well expect to sleep there tonight as well. She looked him a question. Where was he sleeping tonight?

He said, 'I can't get back into the mews cottage till after the weekend. No problem. I'll move out to a hotel.'

Bernice gave a resigned sigh. 'No, it's quite all right. She can have the spare room in my quarters at the top of the house. After all, I've been dossing down with her for weeks at school. Her snoring doesn't really bother me. Come along, Evie. Let's get you upstairs and settled in. You'll like it up at the top. It's nice and quiet, and I know you like it quiet. You can hear the birds singing in the garden below. Don't worry, I'll carry your case up for you.'

She eased the girl out of the room, and up the stairs. As they went Bea heard Bernice say, 'What have you got in your case? Bricks?'

Piers went to the door and shut it behind them. He said, 'Bernice asked a couple of leading questions there. The girl ran with Bernice's suggestions, but I'm not sure she told us what really happened. Agreed?'

Bea put her hand to her head. 'Half of me thinks the girl is off her trolley and not responsible for her actions, whatever they might have been. Evelina doesn't seem to know what happened last night. But one thing is clear: she's out of her mind on the medication she's taking and she is in no condition to be interviewed by the police.'

Piers started to pace the room. 'I think we can trust what she did say of her own accord. She said they shouted at her. Not at each other. Not for help. They shouted at her. Why? Were they afraid she'd somehow caused the uncle's death?'

'The other uncle apparently said he'd heard someone arguing with Constant. Auntie says he was dreaming. What if it was Evelina who was arguing with her uncle?'

'Is she capable of arguing with anyone? I don't think so.'

Piers stared out of the window at the back, then started to pace the floor again. 'Say it was an accidental overdose. The Trescotts were right to get the girl out of the way, weren't they?'

'I'm biased because I've taken against the Awful Aunt. I wish I could be sure she was acting for the best of all possible motives.'

Piers rubbed his eyes. 'Do you really think there's something sinister in it?'

Bea hesitated. 'How can we possibly tell?'

Piers went to stand by the window at the back, looking out on to the garden. He fiddled with the cord of the blind. Thinking. Eventually he said, 'On balance I think that it's up to the police to make enquiries in the case of an unexpected death, and presumably that's what they're doing. We know nothing ourselves about the manner of the death. Only what we've been told. We've informed Mrs Trescott we think that the police must be told where the girl can be found if they wish to interview her, and that's all we need to do. We will look after the girl while she's in our care, but we don't need to do anything else. We don't need to be involved.'

Bea wasn't so sure. 'We could take the girl to a specialist to see if she's on the right medication.'

'We can't do that. We have no legal right. And if we did, wouldn't it take time to evaluate the girl's condition? She'd have to be placed as an in-patient in hospital, wouldn't she, in order to undergo tests and psychiatric assessment and so on? It might take weeks, not days, to get an answer.'

He was right. Of course he was. The voice of reason.

Bea felt restless. 'And yet, and yet . . . I feel that something is horribly, nastily, nightmare-of-the-worst-kind of wrong.'

Piers set the cord rattling against the window. And didn't contradict her.

Bernice came into the room, treading lightly, but with a heavy frown on her face. 'I put her to bed with my old teddy bear and she went out like a light. Honestly! Her clothes! It's all very well at school to go around in sagging underwear but the family's supposed to have money, so why don't they get her a bra that fits, and some suitable everyday wear? Everything she's got looks expensive but as if it were bought for an old woman who walks with a stick. No one our age wears clothes in those colours and made in that horrible, slippery fabric. The only other clothes they've sent for her are a navy-blue woolly jumper and skirt. Both are the wrong length and for someone much larger. She hasn't a single pair of jeans or a T-shirt or an outdoor jacket. And no shoes. None. She's got a pair of pyjamas with cartoon animals on, packets of medication and a half-empty box of biscuits. A toilet bag but no Tampax. We need to take her shopping.'

Bea and Piers both looked at their watches. The shops were still open, but . . .

Piers exclaimed, 'Ouch! I quite forgot! The theatre tickets we've got for tonight! Bea, do you want to take Evelina in my place?'

Bernice folded her arms at him. 'Don't be stupid. She's not going anywhere. She's asleep and I'm not having her woken up. Someone has to stay with her. I'll stay if you like. You go with Bea, and see if you can get a refund for my ticket.'

Bea put her hands on her ward's shoulders – they were almost of a height now – and said, 'You came good there, Bernice, but I wouldn't dream of leaving you here by yourself to look after Evelina.'

Piers said, 'Ditto. I'll contact the theatre and see if we can get the tickets exchanged for another date.'

'Sure,' said Bernice, impatient as ever. 'Book them for some time after we've been slobbing it out in the French chateau, right?'

Bea was about to say they must ask the Awful Aunt what to do about the girl's clothes when the landline phone rang, and yes, it was the dreaded madam herself. Bea switched it to speaker mode as the woman began. There were no preliminaries.

'I got your message. There is absolutely no need for you to inform the police where Evelina is staying. I get your point that you are in loco parentis, so to speak, but if you were aware of the facts you'd agree that the girl, with all her fanciful ideas, might make the situation even worse than it is if she were questioned before she's calmed down. There is no need to complicate matters by suggesting she was involved in any way.

We have to bear in mind that stress might tip her into another episode. In a couple of days' time, maybe—'

'A couple of days?' Bea echoed. 'You want to leave her here that long? Look, I understand she's very fragile, and I agree she's in no condition to speak to the police at the moment. But if she's going to be here for that long, I do think the police should know where she can be found.'

A pause. Then: 'Very well. I'll see that they are informed and hope they won't need to act on the information. Now, is that all?'

'There's one other matter which I wanted to ask you about.'

'What?' Sharp and to the point.

'May we take her shopping for toiletries, undies and such? And she'll need some shoes. There weren't any in her overnight bag.'

'Didn't the housekeeper put them in? She's absolutely hopeless. Well, I suppose there wasn't all that much time to . . . well, never mind. I'll ask the boys to bring some things over for her tomorrow. Now, if there's anything she needs, please get it for her, keep the bills, and I'll reimburse you later.'

'The boys? Who are they?'

'Her cousins. They want to see that she's all right, so they'll drop in to see her tomorrow morning. I'll send her party dress over as well because it might need letting out for Friday. Also, she needs some evening shoes. We were going to buy them on Monday but as things are . . . if you could see to that for me, I'd be obliged.' It was an order, not a request.

Bea grimaced. 'Are you sure she needs to be hidden away like this?'

'Hidden away? What on earth are you talking about. A couple of nights away, spent with a friend from school . . . what could be wrong with that?'

'If the police come asking for her, what am I to say? Do I just refer them to you? If I knew what happened, it would help.'

A deep sigh. 'Well, I suppose you do need to know. Evelina behaved very badly at supper. Constant was justifiably annoyed that she'd made us late and told her off for it. That reduced her to tears. As usual. But then – I can't think what got into her – she started kicking the table and shouting it wasn't fair.

As if life were ever fair. I can only suppose she hadn't taken her pills that day. And yes, things were said in the heat of the moment and yes, my brother did say it was all too much for him to cope with. No one thought he was that depressed, but he must have been, mustn't he?'

Bea glanced at Piers and Bernice, to find they were also wide-eyed with amazement. What exactly had been going on? A family quarrel?

Madam continued, 'Then this morning neither he nor she came down to breakfast and we couldn't understand why until we heard Evelina screaming and found my brother dead in his bed. Can you imagine! The shock! He'd been drinking heavily, of course, but we didn't realize he was so confused he'd double up on his medication.'

Bea couldn't take it in. 'How did he . . .?'

'Sleeping pills. A bottle of whisky. But no note. The autopsy will prove it was an accidental overdose, of course. The thing is it was nothing to do with Evelina. It's true that my brother said her school report was atrocious and he did go off the deep end with her about it. It also true that she did scream at him to let her alone, but honestly, that was just a teenager's normal response to being criticized, wasn't it? She didn't mean it when she said she wished he were dead. Only, when she did find him dead this morning it must have tipped her over into having another of her little episodes. She hasn't had one for months, and we did think she'd grown out of it. I'm sure she had nothing whatever to do with his death. We called the doctor and he said he had to report the death to the police, and that's when we decided to get Evelina out of the way. Now do you understand? We have to protect Evelina at all costs. Nothing must jeopardize the big event on Friday.'

Bea said, 'Poor girl. I have to think about this.'

'What is there to think about? Your course of action is clear. Keep the child safe until we can bring her back here for the party next weekend.' She rang off.

Bea looked at the others. 'Did you get all that? She's saying that Evelina's uncle was confused after a family quarrel and took an accidental overdose plus a bottle of whisky. At least, I think that's what she was saying. Accidental overdose. In one breath Madam says Evelina had nothing to do with her uncle's death, and in the next she says that they had to get the child out of the house because . . . Because why? Because they think she might have helped him take an overdose and then forgotten about it or because she had a fit? Am I imagining it, or is the family hoping the police will agree the death was an accident, but that if they don't, they are prepared to lay the blame for it at Evelina's door?'

Bernice shrugged. 'It's not our problem. Her clothes are. So, can we take her shopping tomorrow? Look, I get a decent allowance and if you won't stump up for some decent clothes for her, then I will. I don't care if I don't get paid back.' She struggled with tears, brushing them off her cheeks with angry movements. 'Oh, she's such a victim! It makes me so cross! And yes, I know it's her own fault, and if she'd been brought up differently she wouldn't let them push her around, but it just makes me so mad!'

Bea put her arm around the girl's shoulders, and drew her close.

Piers did the same thing. They held the girl between them till her tears were under control.

Piers said, 'You're right, Brat.' And now the word was definitely a term of endearment. 'I'll tell you what, if your stern guardian here won't stump up for some better clothes for Evelina, then I'll go halves with you.'

Bernice sniffed. 'You don't want to paint her, do you?'

'What?' A long moment of consideration. Piers took all such questions seriously. And then: 'Heavens, no! There's nothing there to paint.'

'That's all right, then.'

Piers went off to see if he could exchange the theatre tickets and Bea tried to work out what they'd have for supper. They'd planned to eat out but now they had to babysit and she had to rethink. Bea was sorry for Evelina. Of course she was. But she wished she'd never seen her.

FOUR

Saturday night

The three of them ate round the central unit in the kitchen and returned to the living room afterwards.

Bernice was still worrying away at the problem of their uninvited guest. 'You know, the dum-dum did take her pills after breakfast at school yesterday. She must have done, because she was still zonked out by the time we got back here. I buy it that she was reduced to tears because her school report was so awful, but I don't buy it that she kicked the table and shouted because of a disagreement with the family.'

Bea rolled her eyes. Did they have to talk about it? They should have been at the theatre by now . . . Oh well.

Piers took Bernice's point seriously. 'You can drive weak people into a corner and nine times out of ten that's where they'll stay, weeping and wailing and not daring to fight back. But the tenth time, a cornered rat might turn round and bite.'

Bea lay back in her chair and looked up at the ceiling. Her house had been built in early Victorian days and there was a rather beautiful plaster rose around the chandelier. Ah, was that a cobweb? She decided it wasn't, because there was no way she was going to get up on a stepladder to look. She made a note to tell her cleaner about it next week. How long would they have to house Evelina?

I am not, definitely not, going to get involved.

Despite her best intentions, one part of her mind kept thinking about the girl. She said, 'The autopsy will give the approximate time of death. Presumably he died sometime in the night. It was hours later, next morning, that Evelina got up and found him. She has a history of epilepsy. She's on medication for it. She finds her uncle dead and has a fit. Yes, I go along with all that. What I can't get my head round is that the poor creature we saw on Friday afternoon was capable of working out how to kill her uncle by feeding him an extra lot of sleeping pills. That is what we're being asked to believe, isn't it?'

Bernice said, 'Not even if she'd been shaken up by the row at the table? Suppose her uncle had threatened to dock her ration of chocolate . . .? No, sorry. That wasn't a nice thing to say, was it?'

Bea went on: 'If the epilepsy is something she's grown out of, and it resurfaced when she found the body, then that's one thing. I'll go along with that. Otherwise . . . am I imagining a conspiracy and if so, what is the point of it?'

Piers reiterated, 'It's not our problem. The police have been called in by the family. Let them deal with it. Meanwhile, we look after the child, and return her to sender asap. Now, is there anything we want to watch on the telly?

Half past ten. Time for bed.

Bea had showered and was attending to a broken nail when Piers tapped on her bedroom door and entered without waiting for permission. He was wearing a short towelling robe and nothing else. He made as if to lie down on the bed until she said, 'Don't even think of it.'

He grinned and sat on the bed instead. He said, 'You told Bernice everything was going to be all right but you're worried.'

Bea used her nail file, hard. 'I'm annoyed with myself and with you and everyone. We've fallen into the habit of calling that poor child a dum-dum. That's not nice. She's got little enough self-worth as it is.'

'You feel sorry for her.'

Bea slammed the nail file down. 'She irritates me. I tell myself that if I'd been put down by my relatives all the time, I'd have done something about it. But she's so passive!'

'According to Madam Trescott, the child flared up at the dinner table so she can't be all that passive. Are you afraid she'll have another fit while she's with us?'

Yes, she was. Her breathing quickened. She told herself there was absolutely nothing to be afraid of. But, suppose Evelina attacked Bernice while they were asleep at the top of the house . . .?

She said, 'No, ridiculous. However, we must bear in mind

that, according to Madam Trescott, the child had a fit when she
found her uncle dead, but they didn't take her to a doctor for
a check-up. Why not?'

Piers shrugged. 'If it's a fairly frequent occurrence, they
wouldn't need to. They'd know what to do. Lie her down on
her side, see that she doesn't swallow her tongue, and wait for
her to recover.'

Bea spread her fingers out. Did she need another manicure?
Should she try to take Evelina to a good hairdresser, to see
what they could do with the girl's neglected mop of hair? How
could the Trescotts allow the child to go around looking like
Orphan Annie?

No, what good would it do to give the child a makeover, if
she were mentally damaged and needed appropriate care? On
the other hand, perhaps that's when she needed it most?

Bea said, 'I admit I'm angry with myself. That child is about
my height and shoe size. I know perfectly well that I ought to
lend her some shoes or even a pair of my good boots till we
can get her to the shops to buy some for her, but . . . well, you
know how I feel about my boots. I'd rather have one good pair
of boots than a whole new outfit.'

She swished to her feet and shed her negligee. For some
reason she had chosen to wear one of her most attractive silk
nightgowns and was aware she looked good in it.

Piers grinned. A shark-like grin. In a moment he'd make a
move on her.

She fended him off by saying, 'I hate the thought of lending
her anything of mine. I know it's illogical. I know it's selfish
and I know I've got to do it!' Saying which, she threw back
the duvet, got into bed, and closed her eyes. 'Turn the light off
when you leave, right?'

Piers bent over to kiss her forehead. And left.

Her eyes opened. She stared into the darkness long after she
heard him enter the guest room and close the door behind him.

Sunday morning

Breakfast was a little later than usual. Bea rose early and went
to the church on the corner of the road for an eight o'clock

communion, because she felt the need to get back in touch with basics. To put the present difficult situation into perspective. Sometimes Bernice came with Bea but that morning the girl hadn't risen in time so Bea left her to have a lie-in.

The age-old service did bring Bea peace and she returned to the house in time to find Piers in the kitchen setting the table for breakfast, with the cat Winston trying to trip him up at every step he took.

And here came Bernice, wearing one of her new outfits: a severely plain white blouse over skinny black jeans, plus a violet silk scarf.

Bea did a double take. 'That's my scarf! Bernice, you've been in my drawers? How could you? Why didn't you ask? I don't mind lending you something, but I do like to be asked first.'

'Sorr-ee.' A fraction off insolence. 'I didn't think you'd mind, but of course if you object strongly, I'll put it back and never ask again.'

Piers held up a jug of milk. 'Don't push your luck, Brat. We're all feeling fragile today.'

Evelina hesitated on the threshold. 'Is it all right if I come in?' She was wearing the navy blue skirt and jumper which Bernice had estimated correctly would be too large for her and which did nothing for her skin tones. Her hair had been roughly gathered into a ponytail with an elastic band, and she still wore the pink bedroom slippers she'd arrived in. She held herself badly, probably because her bra was barely containing her assets. Bernice had been right about that, too.

'Come in,' said Bea. 'Piers produces wonderful breakfasts, which will set us up for the day. Then we can go shopping for some bits and pieces that you need.'

Evelina edged her way on to a stool. 'Auntie said the boys are going to bring everything else I need, so I'd better not go out.'

Bernice poured herself a bowl of cereal and pushed the packet to Evelina. 'Help yourself. Who are these "boys"? Was it one of them who sent you that early birthday card?'

'Yes.' Eyes down. 'Benjy and Joshua. They're brothers. My cousins. They're ever so clever, and they know everybody. Josh is going to be prime minister one day and Benjy is going to run Trescotts.'

Bea said, 'Are they your uncle's children, or your aunt's?'

'My aunt's. My uncles don't have any children. And it's my uncle Constant who . . .' The girl hiccupped, and fell silent.

'Oops,' said Bernice. 'I didn't think. I'm so sorry for you.'

Bea patted Evelina's shoulder. 'Eat up. Think about something nice. I'll loan you a pair of boots to go out in this morning, shall I? Do you like boots? I love them. I think we're about the same size. Just till we can get to the shops and buy you something to wear.'

'Oh, no.' The girl's eyes went all shiny. 'I can't. I don't have any money, you see. Not till the weekend when I'll be able to buy anything I like.'

'What's happening at the weekend?'

'I'll be sixteen and there's going to be this wonderful big party and I can marry and have lots of nice things. Anything I want. Within reason, of course. They'll see to the money and Joshua will look after me. And I won't have to go back to school.'

Bernice suspended operations on her cereal. 'You don't really want to get married at sixteen, do you? Before you've seen anything or done anything?'

'Of course. It's been planned for ages.'

Bea said, 'They might have to cancel your birthday party, because of the death in the family.'

'Oh, no. Auntie says not. She says, "Life must go on." There'll be a private cremation for Uncle and a big thanksgiving for his life later. She says I can stay here for a couple of days to be quiet and the boys are bringing me some money so that I can buy some evening shoes to match my dress while I'm here. Auntie buys my clothes from Harrods in Knightsbridge. I've never shopped in Kensington before. Do you know where I ought to go?'

Bea said, 'I'll take you.' She thought that Evelina now looked awake even if she wasn't yet firing on all cylinders. Also, she was answering questions in a normal fashion.

The morning sun was streaming through the windows which overlooked the garden at the back of the house. Bea made her way round the table to put some bread in the toaster. 'Brown bread all right for you, Evelina?'

The girl turned to look at Bea, who was behind her, and nodded.

Bea was satisfied. The girl's pupils looked normal. She was not under the influence of any drugs. Conclusion: she hadn't taken her pill that morning. Was that a good thing, or a bad? She'd had a good night's sleep. She seemed brighter in herself, but . . .?

Bea decided not to remind Evelina to take her pills but resolved to watch her closely. The first sign of the girl having a fit, and she'd be off to the doctor's, and no delay!

Winston the cat deserted Piers to wind around Bea's legs.

'Oh, the beautiful kitty!' cried Evelina. She slipped off her stool and dived for Winston, who decided he wanted food and not a mauling by a stranger, so high-tailed it out of the cat flap at the speed of light.

Evelina looked as if she might cry. 'He'll be back in a minute, won't he? Will he let me feed him? I love cats, and dogs, too. One day I'm going to have one of my very own.'

'Of course you will,' said Bea, feeling sorry for the girl.

Piers produced a proper English breakfast, and turned the radio on low for some background music. No one seemed to want to talk much. What was there to be said?

Well, what had the family been rowing about that had caused Evelina to kick the table in distress? A poor school report or some family problem?

Had the uncle really meant to kill himself? No. Why would he? There'd been no suicide note. It had been an accidental overdose, surely. If only the other uncle hadn't said he heard arguing in the night. Who had Constant been arguing with? And why?

Would he have been arguing with Evelina over her bad school report in the middle of the night? No. Why would he?

Was Evelina a hapless victim of circumstances, or a wily psychopath?

And if the latter, were Bea and her family safe from harm?

They were clearing the table after breakfast when the front doorbell rang.

Bea opened the front door and blinked.

Two golden lads stood in the porch, bearing gifts. Or rather, the taller of the two was carrying a bulky zippered travel bag, which presumably bore Evelina's party dress, while the other's hands were empty.

Two blindingly white smiles. Two handsome, upper-class, well-dressed, young men, with floppy fair hair, exuding privilege and money. And a whiff of exclusive toiletry.

'You must be the famous Mrs Abbot.' A note of condescension, almost of derision. This young man didn't really think she was famous, and he was making it clear that he didn't. He had a private-school-and-Oxbridge-educated voice, and a wide smile showing perfect teeth. 'I'm Benjy.'

'And I'm his elder brother. I'm Joshua.' Joshua was slightly taller and heavier than his brother.

'Do come in,' said Bea. 'My condolences for your loss.'

'Thank you,' said the taller of the two. Joshua? The one who was going to be prime minister one day?

'No great loss,' said his younger brother. So he wasn't in deep grief at his uncle's passing? Was he the one who was going to run Trescotts? Benjy?

Benjy said, 'How is Evelina today? Recovered from her fright, I hope?'

Bea pinned a meaningless smile on her face. 'How kind of you to bring some things for Evelina.'

The taller of the two – Joshua? – handed over the zippered bag. 'It's her ball gown. That's all we were given to bring.'

So they'd not brought Evelina's shoes, a change of undies, or any extra clothes. No money, either. Oh well.

Doing the polite thing, Bea showed them into the living room. 'We've just finished breakfast. Would you care for a coffee?'

'No, thanks. We're on our way out of London for a lunch party. Possibly going on the river later.'

'How exciting,' said Bea, matching their false smiles with one of her own.

Evelina appeared in the doorway. 'Hello. I'm here. I'm all right. Did you bring my shoes?' She was as wooden as a doll.

'Hi, there. We're on our way out of town, but we brought

you your party dress.' Joshua put his arm around Evelina's shoulders, and gave her a hug. A brotherly gesture?

The girl didn't object, but she didn't react, either. She said, 'Thank you. I hope you have a nice day.' She spoke in the voice of a well-schooled child who had been taught that manners rule OK.

'Wow!' That was Benjy. He was looking beyond Evelina at Bernice, who had followed her friend into the room. By contrast with the badly dressed Evelina, Bernice made a striking appearance: tall and slender with a well-cut mop of glossy hair, clear skin and eyes which looked violet to match her scarf. And a welcoming smile.

Joshua turned to look at Bernice, and let his arm drop from Evelina's shoulders. He and his brother both stared at Bernice, who coloured faintly under their gaze. She said, 'You are the dum-dum's cousins?' Then suddenly caught herself. 'Oops! Shouldn't have said that.'

'The dum-dum?' Benjy and Joshua glanced at poor Evelina and sniggered. They actually sniggered! Both of them!

Bea wanted to kill them both. How dare those two nasty-minded, superior bits of trash think it was amusing that their cousin had been nicknamed the dum-dum?'

Evelina blushed an unbecoming scarlet. 'It's what they call me at school.'

Bernice reddened. 'I didn't think you knew. Actually, I didn't think full stop. It was stupid of me.'

Bea tried to calm the situation down. 'It was a silly nickname, wasn't it? Suitable perhaps for eight-year-olds. I suggest we forget it. Evelina, my dear, would you like us to call you "Evie" in future?'

Evelina struggled with tears. '"Evie" would be nice. Thank you.'

Benjy caught Joshua's eye and twitched his head in the direction of Evie. Bea noted the gesture and wondered what it meant.

Benjy moved in on Bernice. 'You're the wonderful girl who's been so kind to our little cousin?' He breathed his admiration all over her.

Bernice was almost as tall as Benjy. She looked at him with doubt in her eyes, her colour fluctuating from pale to pink and back again. 'We were room-mates at school. Was it you or your brother who sent her an early birthday card?'

'Joshua's always taken a special interest in her.' Benjy sent his brother another sharp look . . . to remind him that he was supposed to be looking after Evie and not making eyes at Bernice?

So the younger brother was the one who called the shots in that relationship?

Benjy turned his charm on Bernice. 'If only we weren't expected for lunch in the Cotswolds today! But there's plenty of time for us to get to know one another better.'

He had got within Bernice's personal space, and the girl was not comfortable with that. She tried to move back a step, only to come up against the wall behind her. Her body language said she wasn't sure what to make of him.

Bea wondered if she should interfere. Bernice was at an all girls' boarding school, and this might well be her first experience of a man coming on to her. Did she know how to handle it? Possibly not. No, she didn't, for she now shot a glance at Bea asking for advice. Or help?

Bea spoke for Bernice. 'I'm afraid she's no time for socializing during the holidays. She's preparing for important exams.'

'All work and no play. We have to remedy that, don't we?' He leant a fraction closer, and for a moment Bea thought he was going to try to kiss Bernice.

Eyes wide, Bernice reared her head up and back. 'Come any closer, and I'll bite!'

Benjy thought that was hilarious. 'Oh, by God! A shrew! A real, honest-to-God shrew! I like it!'

Joshua brayed out an uneasy laugh.

Bea made ready to intervene but it was Evelina who acted, by pushing Joshua away from her side and moving closer to Bernice. 'You leave her alone, Benjy. She's my special friend, and she's only fourteen.'

'Only fourteen!' Benjy held back his amusement. 'Well, at fourteen she should be experimenting with everything life has to offer. That's what teenagers do, isn't it?'

Bea recovered her wits. 'I think that's enough, and more than enough. Gentlemen, you should be on your way. Thank you for bringing Evie's dress, but please don't call again without an invitation.'

Benjy smiled. 'Oh, take that frown off your face. I was only joking.'

He hadn't been joking. No.

Piers appeared in the doorway, sketchbook and pencil in hand. Who was he sketching now? Answer: it could be anyone from her office manageress to someone he'd glimpsed in the street. Meanwhile . . .

Joshua turned on Piers. He was an impressively built lad. 'Who the devil are you?'

Piers stepped aside from the doorway. 'A friend of the family. I believe your car must be double-parked outside. Traffic is building up. Careful you don't get a parking ticket.'

It was the right thing to say. The boys might be cavalier in their attitude to women, but they had learned to respect parking attendants.

'Until Friday!' said Joshua, taking Evie's limp hand and kissing it.

Benjy said to Bernice, 'We'll meet again. And that's a promise. I'm looking forward to it.'

And they were gone.

Bernice was ashen. She was trembling but didn't want to show it. She even tried to laugh. 'Evie, I'm sorry to say it, but your cousins don't have very good manners.'

Evie produced an uneasy smile. 'Oh, lighten up. They're all right, really. Boys will be boys.'

Bea guided Bernice to the settee and sat beside her. The girl was rigid with nerves. In a moment she might well start a crying jag. Would it be best to let her cry? Her stiff shoulders precluded any possibility of being given a hug.

Bea said, 'Bernice, are you all right?' She knew that was a silly thing to say, but still said it.

'Of course she is,' said Evie. 'She has to learn about boys sometime.'

Piers squatted down in front of Bernice. 'You might like to learn the art of self-defence. Kickboxing, or kung fu. Which do you fancy?'

A touch of colour crept back into Bernice's pale face. 'A knife. A sharp little penknife.'

Piers shook his head. 'You could do too much damage with a knife. You don't want to spend time in prison for killing him, even if he is an asshole.'

Evie said, 'He likes girls. He's so charming, and such a flirt. He keeps on and on till they give in. Even if they start off by saying "no", he always wins. It doesn't last. When he's got them going crazy for him, he drops them.'

Bernice stiffened her back. 'Kickboxing, then. I fancy that.'

Piers' fingers flew over his phone. 'I'll see what I can find.'

Bea said, 'Self-defence classes. There must be some on the internet. We could start today. I'll take them with you, Bernice. I have never been threatened with rape but I'd like to know how to—'

'It's not rape,' said Evie. 'They always consent. And don't worry about being impregnated. He uses a condom nowadays.'

Bernice reached out and gripped Bea's hand. She didn't say anything. She didn't need to do so.

'Well, my dear. If this young man calls again, we are not going to let him in. And if he makes a nuisance of himself, we'll get the police to remove him.' She sought for something to lighten the mood. 'And now, let's have a look at Evie's party dress.'

FIVE

Sunday, noon

E vie unzipped the bag and pulled out her dress. It was a violent pink, with tiers of tulle over a full skirt. The word 'fluffy' came to mind. It was suitable for someone playing at being a Disney princess. There was a stiff bow at the back, and the bodice was dotted with tiny pink bows, each containing a sequined heart. The dress had been cut with a low V-neck and full, see-through sleeves. As she held it against her, they could all see that the bodice was far too small for Evie's full bosom and that the colour made her look sallow.

It was a disaster. It was pricey, yes, but it didn't fit and it wouldn't do anything for the girl.

Evie looked around for a mirror. 'I'll have to try it on. Auntie said she thought I'd put on weight again, and it was going to need letting out. The shop will do it for me, won't they? And I need to get some silver sandals to go with it.'

Bernice closed her eyes. 'Oh, Evie! It's hideous. You can't like it!'

'Auntie picked it out for me. She said everyone would be looking at the dress because I'm going to be the star of the show. She said it would be very suitable for the occasion.'

Bea was shocked. She looked at Piers. 'I don't think that shade of pink is quite right for you, Evie. What colour should she wear, Piers?'

Piers took the dress away from Evie and set it aside. He looked the girl up and down. He turned her around. 'It's a special occasion in her life. She has to stand out in a crowd, like royalty. I would suggest ivory. No, cream. Something that looks simple, unfussy. It should show off her arms and shoulders but not be too low in front. No tricks, no extremes of fashion. She has to be able to look at the photographs in five years' time and not wince. Her hair should be up to show off her long neck. Pearls? Yes, she could wear pearls. Real flowers for her hair. Cream court shoes with a low heel. Make everything easy to wear so that she can enjoy herself.'

Evie's mouth drooped. 'I'm supposed to be making a big impression, not blending into the background.'

Bea read the label on the dress, which was from a designer boutique. 'We understand that, but Piers is always right about what we should or should not wear. Your aunt has gone to a lot of trouble to rig you out for your special day, but this dress is going to have to be let out to fit you. Will the shop be able to do that in time? Suppose we take it back to them and see if they've got something else in your size. You can try several on, and see which you prefer. Is that all right?'

Evie twisted her hands round and round. 'I don't know. What would Auntie say if I picked something different?'

'That you are growing up and experimenting,' said Bea.

Experimenting. That was an unfortunate word to use, wasn't it? It reminded them of Benjy's threat to Bernice.

Evie looked at Bernice with what looked like a mixture of irritation and triumph. 'Bernice has to have a dress for the party, too. Has she got to wear cream as well?'

'No,' said Piers. 'Her colour is violet. Or she could wear ivory, lilac or a misty grey. With silver. And diamonds. No, she'd not old enough yet to wear diamonds.'

Evie said, 'I'm to wear a tiara. A family piece that goes back generations. Have you got some decent jewellery to wear, Bernice?'

'Dunno. My uncle Leon did say there was some stuff in the bank and we'd look at it some time, but I'm not coming to your party. I hope you have a wonderful time, but it's not for me.'

'Of course you're coming! That the whole point of . . .' She stopped short. Then added, 'I want you to come. I've never had a girlfriend to go around with before. It'll be like we're sisters. I've always wanted a sister.'

Bernice looked at Bea as if to say, *Is the girl mad? Why would I want to be her sister?*

Bea looked at her watch. 'It's Sunday and the boutique won't be open today, but the big stores will. Retail therapy is just what we need to take our minds off recent events. Bernice is only halfway through the list of what she wants to buy and you, Evie, need all sorts of things. Shoes, for a start. It's too hot to wear boots, but you can borrow a pair of my sandals till we get to the shops. Do you want to come, Piers, or will you give it a miss? We'll eat lunch out but perhaps you could organize some food for supper later?'

Piers said he'd stay at home, so Bea took a handful of credit cards and the two girls to go shopping.

First they bought some better bras for Evie, and then underwear. Evie gradually overcome her diffidence in order to express an opinion about what she'd like to wear, and proved to have excellent if slightly old-fashioned taste. She also proved to have a good if slightly ample figure under her nasty navy outfit, and it wasn't difficult for Bernice to persuade her to try on some jeans.

And yes, because of the new bra and shapely jeans, Evie actually began to hold herself more upright. T-shirts followed with Bea vetoing ones with rude messages on them. Then two denim jackets, one with lots of glitter on it for Evie, but a plain one for Bernice.

Evie got out her smartphone and asked Bernice to take a shot of her in the new clothes. Bernice obliged, and then it was her turn to be photographed. The girls really got into the swing of it in the shoe department and turned the place upside down looking for, well, they weren't quite sure what, but they would know it when they saw it.

Evie clicked happily away. Bea was pleased, seeing the girls enjoying themselves.

Finally they found a quiet restaurant in which to rest amid a pile of shopping bags. And ate, and ate. Bea passed on the dessert but the girls had two enormous sundaes. Finally, when they reached the coffee stage and were able to all lean back in their chairs, Bea asked, oh so casually, 'You decided not to take your pills today, Evie. Do you manage without them often?'

Evie put her hand over her mouth and giggled. 'Don't tell Auntie, or she'll be cross with me. I've been trying to cut down on them, but she doesn't know that. I'll have to take one tonight, I suppose. Just in case.'

Bernice said, 'They make you awfully sleepy. Are you sure you need such strong ones?'

'I asked Uncle Constant that, and he asked the clinic if I might reduce the dose, but the doctor said it wasn't advisable.'

'Is that the uncle who died, or a different one?' said Bea, and then wondered if she'd been wise to bring the subject up.

Evie stilled, her eyes on her empty plate. Then she shook her head and was silent.

Bernice leaned across and patted Evie's arm. 'Your uncle dying like that must have been horrid. Let's talk about something else.'

'I'd like to tell you,' said Evie, speaking more to Bernice than to Bea. 'But I can't explain properly. I mean, I thought I heard . . . but they said I didn't. Perhaps I dreamed it.'

'Your aunt said you'd had a dream? Or was it your uncle who had the dream?'

'They should know. They were all of them there. Nunkie and the boys and Auntie.'

Bernice wrinkled her nose. 'How many of them are there? Are they all Trescotts?'

'My father was the eldest, but he and my mother died in a road accident. He was the one who ran the company and made it international and everything. When he died Nunkie took over. He was christened Cyril but he hates that name so the family all call him Nunkie. We say it with respect, if you see what I mean.'

'Do you like him?' Bernice picked up on the ambivalence of Evie's words.

'Like him?' As if the idea of liking him was unthinkable. 'Well, he's old and not interested in children, which is understandable, isn't it? He's been married twice but he hasn't had any children and he's single again now. He comes and goes as he pleases. He might be in Australia one minute and Scandinavia the next. He has his own private plane, of course. It isn't usual for him to be with us for more than a couple of days at a time, but there was some business or other he had to attend to last weekend and of course he's going to stay over for the party.'

'So there's one more uncle?' said Bernice, scribbling names on her paper napkin.

'Uncle Constant was the youngest. He is . . . he *was* a director of the firm but he didn't like London so he lived in the country house and collected stamps. He's the one who made a fuss if anyone was five minutes late for anything. He was my guardian, but he never took much of an interest in me except to tell me try to make an effort. That's about the only thing he ever said to me . . . "Make an effort, girl. Pull yourself together."'

Bernice said, 'He sounds horrid.'

'Not really. Just a bit distant. He never married, which Auntie says explains everything. That's Auntie April, whom you've met. She was next to the youngest. She was married for ages but then something happened that I've never understood and she got a divorce and brought the boys back home for good. She's a director of the firm, too, and unlike Uncle Constant, she does go to meetings and stuff. She's important to the future of the company because she's the only one who has children. Well, apart from me, and I'm not exactly up to it, am I?' A brave smile. 'Auntie looks after me because Uncle Constant is not . . . was not . . . interested.'

Bernice put her elbows on the table and her chin in her hands. 'Your aunt told us there was a horrible row at supper the night before he died. They think your uncle Constant was upset enough to take too many sleeping tablets by mistake. Do you think that, too?'

Evie blew her nose on her paper napkin and sniffed. 'That's what they said. And they ought to know, oughtn't they? Auntie and the boys, and Nunkie.'

Bea said gently, 'What did you actually see and hear, Evie?'

'I thought I heard . . . but they said it was nonsense. They said I'd had a fit and they gave me two pills and sent me back to bed.'

'What did you think you heard?'

Down went her head. 'Nothing. I mustn't think about it or I'll get upset and have another fit.'

Bea exchanged glances with Bernice, who rolled her eyes. They would have to leave it at that, wouldn't they?

Evie spurted into speech. 'I woke up. I saw the time was nearly nine. I was scared I'd get into trouble. They don't like me to miss breakfast because of taking my pills regularly. I saw my bedroom door was open, so I thought someone must have opened it and called my name because I was going to be late for breakfast if I wasn't careful. So I went out on the landing to explain that I'd overslept but I'd be down in a minute. That's when I saw that Uncle's door was open, too.

'Uncle was lying in bed. Asleep. I thought he was going to be late for breakfast, too, and I was pleased because he couldn't shout at me for being late if he was, too. I called his name but he didn't move and that was odd because he sleeps so lightly and is angry if anyone wakes him in the night but he's always up really early in the morning, saying the early bird catches the worm and stuff. I didn't know what to do and I didn't want to go in and touch him because . . . I don't know why. So I called out for help, not very loudly at first and then more loudly, and they came, all of them came.'

She snuffled. Bea handed the girl another paper napkin, which she used. Then she said, 'I'm a wicked girl. Do you know, the first thing I thought of when they told me he was dead was that he wouldn't ever say, "Pull yourself together, girl!" again. Sometimes I have such thoughts, hating people. I know it's very wrong of me.'

Bernice asked, 'So who came to the rescue?'

'Auntie first. Then Nunkie and the boys. They closed the door to Uncle's bedroom and told me I'd had another fit. Auntie gave me two pills and I went back to bed and slept for ages and then she came in and woke me up, and she said I was to get dressed because I was going away for a bit and I said "Why?" And she said that Uncle had done something stupid and taken too many sleeping pills, and the police would be asking questions and they didn't want me to have another fit, so I was better out of the way. She packed a bag for me while I got dressed, but I was feeling so stupid and so upset that I didn't change my slippers and that's why I didn't have any proper shoes with me.' She ducked her head and reversed herself into childhood.

So that was that. All was explained, and Auntie had been quite right to get the child away. Bea called for the bill and paid with a card. Eyeing the mountain of shopping they'd accumulated, she decided to take a taxi home.

They were all quiet on the return journey but, as they drew up in front of the house, Evie's mobile went off and she answered it, leaving the others to ferry their purchases into the house. Bea could only hear Evie's side of the conversation, which consisted mostly of the words: 'Yes, but . . .' spoken at intervals. Evie was being urged to do something she didn't want to do.

Finally Evie clicked her phone off and joined them in the hall. 'That was Auntie. The boys rang her after they left here. She says they're really concerned. They didn't mean to upset Bernice. They didn't realize she wasn't used to boys and didn't know how to talk to them yet. I tried to say that Benjy was out of order, but Auntie, well, she didn't listen. She says that if they frightened you, Bernice, they're both very sorry and want to make it up to you.'

'No need,' said Bernice, in a tight voice. 'Forget it. I have.'

Evie shook her head at her. 'You have to learn how to accept a compliment, Bernice. Benjy likes the look of you, and that's quite something. He's very picky. He'll look after you at the party and give you a wonderful time. You've got to loosen up a bit. Relax. There's more to life than swotting for exams. When you've been introduced to the right sort of people, you'll find that life can be a whole lot of fun.'

Bea froze. Evie was regurgitating what she'd just been told to say by the Aunt. Was this . . . could it be . . . were they trying to groom Bernice for entry into their world? Bea dithered. Was this a good thing, or a bad? When she grew up Bernice would come into a lot of money. She'd been sent to a good boarding school where she might not only have an excellent education, but also form relationships with other children from a similar background. Educationally, the school had done well by Bernice. Socially, Bernice had only really made one good friend, but when puberty hit the other girl they'd drifted apart. Bernice hadn't seemed to have made any other close friends. Socially, she was a loner. Well, perhaps it might be good for Bernice to mix in wider circles?

Bernice had no doubts about rejecting Evie's ideas. 'Evie, I know you've had a hard time and your education has been all over the place. I've heard you talk about your future, about getting married early to a man who aims to be prime minister one day. It sounds fine at first sight, but what are *you* going to do with *your* life? Sit around in a pretty dress and do what? As the wife of an up-and-coming politician, you will be asked to entertain important people. Do you know how to run a weekend event, or a dinner party? Are you familiar with the politics of yesterday, today and tomorrow? Can you converse with guests easily, remembering which is a banker and which a newspaper magnate? What value will you be to your husband, if you can't pull your weight in that world?'

'Joshua will always look after me. He says I'll never have to worry about anything.'

'You want to hand over control of your life to your cousin? Why? Adults are supposed to be responsible for their own lives. If you let Joshua take responsibility for everything, then you'll be turning yourself into a doll, a soft toy without any brains.'

'I don't need brains!'

'No,' said Bernice, folding her arms at Evie. 'Not as long as you've got money coming in. But you haven't been learning how to take control of the money, have you? You don't even have a clue about budgeting for yourself. You keep saying that Joshua will look after you so that you don't have to bother about anything, but I ask myself why he'd want to do that?'

'You don't understand. I'm such a lucky girl. He picked me out when I was young and he's stuck by me through thick and thin.'

Bernice zipped her mouth shut. She looked at Bea, who shrugged.

Bea recalled that when Joshua had looked at Evie, he hadn't seemed to be entranced by what he saw. He hadn't kissed her or held her tightly when he came in. He hadn't shown any sign of concern about what she might be feeling.

The girl was no beauty, and mentally she seemed young for her age. All she had going for her was the prospect of money. But it would be cruel to point that out to her, wouldn't it?

Piers appeared from the living room, sketchbook in hand. 'I nearly rang you earlier. Some woman arrived with a pedigree puppy for Bernice. I told her you were out and refused delivery. She said she'd be back.'

Bernice's expression! A mixture of horror and fascination.

'A puppy?' said Bea. 'But Bernice can't possibly look after . . . She's at boarding school! Who would have—'

Evie's smug face told Bea who might have thought up such a thing. The girl gave a little bounce of pleasure. 'Oh, I wondered if he might! I told Benjy you'd love a puppy.'

'What?' said Bea. 'When did you tell him that?'

'When he rang me last night. And early this morning, too. He wants to know everything about Bernice, what she does, what she likes, everything.'

Bea raised her hands in frustration. 'But, Evie, no one would be so thoughtless as to give a puppy to a girl at boarding school.'

Bernice's eyes were wide. 'A puppy for me? Really and truly? That would be . . .! But no! I can't, can I? Bea's right. I can't take it to school. I've never thought of having a pet myself. I mean, it's not sensible. When I'm grown up, perhaps. When I have my own place.'

The doorbell rang again. Followed by the others, Bea waded through bags of shopping to open the door. A chunky woman in a leather jerkin over stout trousers stood there, surrounded by a small mountain of boxes. She was holding out a wriggling, appealing bundle of light brown fur. Bright eyes looked hopefully around.

The woman said, 'Which is Miss Holland? I have a present for her from a Mr Trescott. A puppy. His name is Copacabana et cetera. Copper for short. Pedigree, naturally. Plus bags of food, basket, lead, et cetera.'

Bernice reached out a finger to touch the puppy's head, and to scratch behind its ears. The woman thrust the dog into Bernice's arms. 'That's right. I need a signature.'

Bernice cuddled the puppy, her expression soft and pleased. Then she blinked, hard, and looked up at Bea with a plea for understanding.

Bea didn't know what to say or do. It wasn't possible for her to take a dog in. What would their tyrannical old cat, Winston, say or do if they tried to introduce a puppy into the house? And if they did accept him, hours would be needed to train him, he'd have to be taken for walks twice a day and fed and wormed and . . . No, it was impossible!

Well, if Bernice was around she might take on responsibility for the dog. On the other hand, she'd not been brought up to look after animals and it was odds on that she'd enjoy the cuddling but not the training or the cleaning up after dog poo.

Bea knew herself well enough to realize she wouldn't enjoy the cleaning up after dog poo and the necessity for taking the dog for walks and training it, either. She could see that Bernice was falling in love with the scrap but . . . no, it was out of the question to take it in.

Bea said, 'That's a very expensive present, Bernice.'

Bernice understood and her mouth tightened. She blinked, hard, twice. She kissed the dog's head. 'No, it's not possible for me to accept. I can't have a dog while I'm away at school.'

Evie was jigging up and down. 'Isn't he adorable? Isn't he the most wonderful, cuddly thing! You can't refuse him. You can leave boarding school. You can go to a day school. There's plenty of room here and you've got a garden.'

Bernice cuddled the puppy against her cheek. It licked her face. Would she give in, accept the dog and agree to change the plans for her future?

'No,' said Bernice. She handed the dog back to the woman. 'I'm sorry. There's been some mistake. I can't accept a puppy. It would be quite wrong to have one when I can't look after him. I'll pick one out for myself when I'm grown up. Please return him to the breeder.'

'My instructions,' said the woman, 'are to deliver the puppy et cetera to you, and to get a signature. I cannot take it back.' She put the puppy down on the floor, where it whined and held up a paw, looking lost. It really was a most appealing little mite.

Bernice put her hands over her face. 'Take it away. Please!'

Evie was stricken. 'You can't mean to refuse him!'

Bea looked at Piers. What should they do? The consequences, if they did give in and take it, were considerable in time and money. And there was no way Winston would tolerate another pet in the household.

Piers picked up the puppy and put it out in the porch. 'We cannot accept it. If you won't take him back, then I suppose someone passing by may take pity on him and dump him at the Battersea Dog's Home. Or he'll get run over.'

The woman blenched. 'You can't do that. It's a pedigree dog. I have all the papers here. You can show him at Crufts.'

Bernice put her hands over her ears and fled for the stairs. Up and up she went. They heard her bedroom door slam at the top of the house. Then there was silence except for the whimpering of the puppy in the porch.

Evie wept. 'Oh, the poor little thing. You can't leave it out there. Mrs Abbot, surely you could take him in? I'll pay for his food and things, if you like. Then I can come and visit him and take him for walkies.'

Bea stiffened her backbone. 'If Joshua wants to give you a puppy, then that's up to you. I can't take a puppy in here. It's not practicable.'

The dog woman said, 'It's not Mr Joshua. It's Mr Benjamin who ordered the dog. For Miss Holland. What am I to tell him? That you put the puppy out in the street to be run over?'

Piers said, 'You will do whatever you think is right by the dog. We are not able to accept him. Now, please go.' He ushered the woman out and closed the front door on her.

Bea thought, Piers is bluffing. Of course he is. Isn't he?

SIX

Sunday afternoon

B ea held her breath, afraid the woman might really leave the puppy in the porch; in which case she would have to take it in and, oh . . . the problems which would then arise! She hurried into the living room to look out of the window overlooking the porch. From there she'd be able to see what had happened to the puppy.

Fortunately for Bea's peace of mind, the dog woman picked the puppy up, stowed it in a special travelling cage in the boot of her car, piled in all its 'et ceteras' and drove off into the traffic.

Evie followed Bea into the sitting room. She stamped her feet, moving fast into a two-year-old's tantrum. 'Oh, the poor little puppy. How could you! You are horrid, horrid people and I hate you!'

Piers came in, too. Ignoring Evie, he spoke direct to Bea. 'Why are they targeting Bernice?'

A good question. Bea ignored Evie to go after Bernice. On the top floor Bea took a deep breath before tapping on the door to the girl's bedroom.

Dear Lord, give me the right words to say.

Bernice was lying full length on her bed with her head under a pillow. She hadn't bothered to remove her trainers first which irritated Bea, though not to the point of making a scene about it. Bea sat on the bed beside the girl. 'Have a good scream. Bite the pillow. It might help.'

Bernice convulsed with harsh laughter. She withdrew her head from under the pillow. 'I've already done that. Didn't you hear me?' She half turned to Bea.

Bea lay down beside Bernice and held her tightly, risking a rebuff. Which didn't come. Bernice even laid her head on Bea's shoulder.

She'd been crying, great gobs of tears. Her cheeks were scarlet. 'I wish I were grown up, and had my own place and could have a dog . . . except that I prefer cats, really. It's going to be years and years before I can do that. Life has suddenly got complicated, and I'm all in a whirl. I'm having to grow up too quickly. I don't know where I am or where I'm going. I thought life had settled down with you here, and school . . .'

'There, there. There, there.'

A gulp. 'I wasn't loved when I was little. Don't try to pretend that I was, because I know I wasn't. I remember feeling lost and angry all the time. I used to make myself small and hope I wouldn't get shouted at. Mummy tried to love me but she was so afraid of Daddy she couldn't manage it, and when he died Mummy went to pieces and couldn't look after me. Then my great aunt came and oh, she was so old and she looked so funny, didn't she? Wobbling around on those skinny legs of hers and smoking like a chimney. But she did love me, didn't she? She scolded me and she loved me and I could tell the difference. It was only then that I began to feel safe.'

'Yes, she did love you, very much.'

'And when she died you came and you said I was a little soldier, and I've always remembered that. It helps a lot.'

'You are a little soldier, and I do love you. Your mother does, too.'

'I know. But she's not particularly clued up about anything, is she? Sometimes she seems more like my little sister rather than my mother. I'm so glad she found someone to look after her. It's like she had a second chance at life when she met Keith. He's great, isn't he? I mean, he's not a power in the land or even a rich man, but that's not important, is it? He loves her and looks after her and she adores him. And the baby, my little bro, he's so cute and maybe he's going to be clever, though you can't really tell at this age, can you?'

'Yes, yes. They all three love you. They know you're going down a different path in life but that makes no difference. They love you, no matter what.'

Bernice gulped. 'I don't think I'm very loveable. I'm spiky and self-centred and sometimes I just want to scream and shout and I don't really know why.'

'It's part of growing up.'

'When my great aunt died and Uncle Leon told me I had to come and live with you, I thought it would be terrible, because why would you want to take me on when your own son was grown up and important and married and had children of his own and you hardly bothered to see them?'

Bea said, 'That's not true, about not wanting to see them. I do love them and I do ask to see them, but they live busy lives and it's not always easy for them to make time for me. It's true I hadn't thought of taking on a teenager at my age. You've driven me round the bend occasionally, but you've brought new life into my days. It wouldn't have been right for your Uncle Leon to take you. He's a wonderful man but—'

Bernice sat up and rubbed her eyes. 'He's a commitment-phobe. That's the right word for him, isn't it? He's charming and clever and he's a brilliant businessman. He makes all that look easy and I'm going to learn a lot from him as I grow up. But if you try to pin him down to doing something for the family, he sort of slides away. I thought at one point that you and he . . . but then I worked it out that he gives you an expensive present one minute and forgets your existence the next. You're not like that, so it wouldn't work.'

Bea crowed with laughter. 'You're right. I'm very fond of him, but I don't think he'll ever change.'

Bernice ran her fingers back through her hair. 'You know what? I think I've been lucky, landing up with you and Piers. At school, some of the girls with money in their backgrounds think that just having money makes them special. Not all of them. I'm beginning to be friends with two girls in the year above me, and we've been getting together lately because we all three like playing table tennis and no one else much does. We talk about everything, politics and art, and books. I didn't tell you about them in front of Evie because it might make her feel bad, but I do like them. I feel comfortable with them. One of them said she'd like me to go to stay with her and her family this summer and she's going to get her mother to contact you about it. Her family are landowners in a big way but also into banking. I'd like to go . . . But then there's Evie, and seeing the family, and the chateau in France and I don't know if I'm on my head or my heels.'

'Evie won't be with us long. I'll have a chat with your friend's mother when she contacts me and we'll see what can be worked out.'

Bernice got off the bed and ran her hands down her body, looking at herself in the mirror. 'I haven't got any shape yet. I think I'm the only one of my age at school who hasn't.'

'Everyone develops at a different rate. I was a late starter, too.'

'You and Piers aren't alike, but you fit together like . . . two pieces of a jigsaw puzzle. You're not into banking or high finance or . . . or things. You work with people and you value them not by how much money they have, but how they live and what they do. It does my head in, sometimes, how good you are at understanding people.'

'We're very middle class, I suppose.'

Bernice snorted. 'It's not caste that counts. It's class. You and Piers have class in spades.'

A tap on the door and Piers came in. 'Are you all right, Brat?' His tone was warm, and his smile was even warmer.

Bernice responded with a teasing, 'Sure. Tom Cat!'

They exchanged high fives. He said, 'You did good, there.'

Bernice allowed an anxiety to surface. 'You were bluffing, weren't you? You wouldn't have let the puppy be run over, would you?'

'No, I wouldn't. I would have taken the pup in myself, even though I know I can't possibly look after it. Fortunately I was saved from a life of picking up poo. However, your soft-in-the-head friend seems hell bent on it. She's on the phone to the aunt, begging to have the puppy for herself. The aunt isn't playing, if I've interpreted Evie's reactions correctly. What is the matter with that family?'

Bea sat up. 'Three unexplained deaths so far. And I'm not sure that's the last of them, either.'

Bernice stared at Bea. 'Three deaths? What do you mean? Evie's uncle is the only one, isn't it?'

'No, it isn't. Her father and mother were killed in a road accident some years ago. I could bear to know more about that. Also, we've had a number of stories about that family fed to us by different people and I'm beginning to wonder if some of them are more fiction than fact. I thought at first that these little inconsistencies didn't matter, that they were nothing to do with us. I bought their story that we should take in the girl for a couple of nights because a tragic death in the family might tip her into a medical emergency. Yes, I did think the Trescotts were being rather overcautious, but I gave them full marks for caring so much about Evelina. Now, I'm not happy about the situation. The girl hasn't shown any signs of having been affected by her uncle's death, has she?'

'Well, no,' said Bernice. 'But those pills deaden her reactions so that she behaves as if it didn't matter.' She thought back over Evie's behaviour that morning and shook her head. 'But she wasn't deadened, was she? She enjoyed going out and shopping with us. She got upset about the puppy in a silly little girl way, but not as if she were about to have a fit. Honestly, who'd believe she was nearly sixteen?'

Bea said, 'I think I'd like to do some research on the Trescotts. I want to check every single bit of data they've fed us.'

'Why bother?' asked Bernice. 'We can shoot her back to her family tomorrow, can't we? And that will be the end of it.'

Bea said, 'Will it? What about their invitation to you for the weekend? What about Benjy's threat to you?'

A shrug. 'I don't like him. I'm not going to the party. End of.'

Piers said, 'I've come across people like Benjy before. They have a sense of entitlement which can lead to a feeling of invincibility. They think they have a right to whatever takes their fancy. His wish to impress Bernice might be a passing phase. His eye might light on someone else this afternoon and he might forget her completely, but I wouldn't count on it.'

Bea said, 'The moment those two boys walked in, I smelled trouble. For a start, why did they come at all?'

Bernice stared. 'To bring Evie's dress.'

'Their chauffeur could have done that. Madam promised to deliver some other things Evie needed: outdoor shoes and some money for a start. They didn't arrive. They only brought the dress. So that could have been an excuse, and it wasn't the real reason why they came.'

Piers frowned. 'You have a point. They were on their way out for a day in the country and dropped in on their way to deliver Evie her dress, but . . .' He clicked his fingers and concentrated. 'Let me think this through. They came in. Joshua put his arm round Evie's shoulders in a brotherly fashion but he didn't look at her. He didn't ask if she were feeling all right. She didn't respond to him in any way. She didn't look up at him and smile, she didn't pull his arm more closely about her as if she wanted his embrace. Then Bernice came in and both boys – not just Benjy – focused on her. Joshua's arm dropped from Evie's shoulders. He forgot about her to stare at Bernice.'

'At that point,' said Bea, 'Benjy shot his brother a sharp look, signalling that he keep his eye on Evie. Joshua obeyed, which tells us something about the two brothers. Joshua may be the older, but Benjy is top dog. Which left Benjy free to target Bernice. He frightened her.'

Bernice bridled. 'I wasn't frightened. I was . . . taken aback.'

Piers said, 'You threatened to bite him. I must say that I cherish that moment. Bea and I stood there like dummies, but you threatened to bite him.'

'Upon which,' said Bea, 'instead of apologizing, Benjy upped the stakes, making it clear he was stimulated by your rebuff. Today he's sent you an expensive present. Can he not bear to be turned down? What is it to him, a grown man from a moneyed background, who is socially adept and moves in circles where there are plenty of eligible girls, if a fourteen-year-old turns him down? He knows how old you are. If he didn't know when he arrived, Evie put him straight. He must know he shouldn't come on to a fourteen-year-old. I find Benjy's behaviour alarming.'

Bernice rubbed her arms. 'So we don't let them into the house if they come again. And I'm not going to their party.'

Bea said, 'I'm looking at the Joshua and Evie arrangement. Even when she's not half asleep on her pills, she doesn't strike me as being very bright, and she's no raving beauty. What has she got to attract Joshua? Answer: she's got money coming to her when she's eighteen. She's an orphan and at sixteen she can be married with her parents' or guardians' consent. Am I right in thinking that she's being groomed to accept Joshua as her husband in order to keep the money in the family? He's the one who wants to be prime minister, right? Hmm. I don't think he's got enough steel in him for that, but he could go far with money and influence behind him.'

Piers said, 'Looking into the future, by the time the girl's eighteen she'll probably have produced an infant or two to secure the future of the dynasty, and unless she grows a backbone between now and then, will have been persuaded to hand over everything she has inherited to her husband. He doesn't strike me as being madly in love with her. I wonder if he thinks he can play the part of loving husband for a couple of years or so, make sure he's got an heir and a spare, and then dump her for a more intelligent, better-looking woman . . . taking the loot with him.'

Bernice gasped. 'That's evil!'

Bea said, 'We don't *know* that that is the case. It would be interesting to find out what Benjy's prospects in the firm might be. Is that branch of the family so strapped for cash that Benjy needs to look out for another heiress to marry? Is he looking for someone young and impressionable, who would be swayed by his charm and his knowledge of the world? Some friend of Evie's, perhaps? Someone Evie is at school with?'

Bernice let herself down on to the bed. 'Me? He's picked me out because I have money coming to me when I'm older?'

'Mind you,' said Piers, 'you've got a lot more to offer than poor Evie. You've got brains and you will be a beauty one day. Your intelligence is probably something he hadn't bargained for. If he's wise he might appreciate that and treat you well. But if he's so convinced he's God's gift, he might find it a challenge to browbeat you into submission. He called you a shrew. I hope he doesn't fancy himself as a Petruchio, a young gallant who sets out to break a lively girl's spirit in order to get himself a wealthy, compliant wife.'

'No, no. I'm not old enough.'

'If he fancies you, he might be prepared to wait for you to grow up.'

'Yeah, if I fancied him. Which I don't. I do have opportunities to mix with some boys of my own age, you know.

At school we team up with senior boys from the college down the road for dances and to stage plays. Some of them are quite decent and one or two have hung around me looking as if they want to ask me something but I've not been interested. I've never been tempted to see them outside school, though some girls do.'

'Benjy's clever,' said Bea. 'He's got more brains than Joshua. He tried throwing his good looks at you, and you ducked. So he went one better. He tempted you with the gift of a puppy. You were tempted for a minute or two, weren't you? Do you think he'll stop now? I don't think so.'

Bernice spread her hands. 'What else can he do?'

Bea's head was filled with scenarios of what a determined young man might do to a slip of a fourteen-year-old girl, but she pushed them away. No need to frighten Bernice . . . yet.

There was a wild whoop from down below and Evie came pounding up the stairs, screaming with joy. 'I'm going to have a puppy, I'm going to have a puppy.' She danced into the room, cheeks flushed scarlet and hair flying, a hyped-up young miss in an ecstasy of happiness. 'Benjy's going to give me the puppy for a birthday present! Isn't that wonderful! Oh, Bernice, I'm so happy I could die!'

Bea realized that the Trescotts were giving Evie something to love and something that would love her in return. The poor girl probably hadn't had anyone to love or to love her since her parents died.

Evie seized Bea's hands. 'Say it's all right! You don't mind if I have him here till I go home at the weekend, do you?'

'Yes,' said Bea, trying to keep calm. 'I do mind. I have a cat. I cannot have a dog here.'

Evie's lower lip wobbled. 'Oh, but you wouldn't be so unkind as to refuse me. He won't be in the way, I'll look after him myself all the time.'

'You didn't tell your aunt that I'd let you have the puppy here, did you?'

Evie's lower lip came out. 'She said I was to ask you and then get back to her.'

'Sensible woman,' said Bea, with a briskness she did not feel. 'Tell her that you are looking forward to having the puppy on your birthday. Now, we must think about food for tonight. You two girls haven't yet unpacked all the lovely things we bought this morning. Evie, we'll have to find you a holdall to take them back home with you when you go. Do you know when you are being collected?'

'Oh. Yes. Thursday afternoon, I think. But I have to have my dress altered first. Can we do that tomorrow?'

'I don't see why not. Now, I know it's Sunday, but I still have some business to attend to. Piers, will you organize supper for us all?'

'Half an hour?'

Bea made her way down the stairs first to the ground floor, and then down again to the agency rooms. Her office was quiet, and peaceful. She went in, shut the door and leaned against it, trying to think what she must do first.

There were a number of people who might be able to give her information about the Trescotts. The Awful Aunt had made reference to Max, Bea and Piers' grown-up son. She would try him first.

Max was a Tory MP in a safe seat, had managed to capture a wife with money and to produce a couple of children who were the delight of their mother's wealthy parents. Bea loved him dearly while deprecating the fact that he always thought he knew best. Perhaps because she didn't automatically take his advice about everything, Max rarely found time in his busy life for them to meet. In fact, Piers probably saw Max more often than she did.

It had crossed Bea's mind once or twice that Max considered his father, that internationally famous portrait painter, more socially acceptable than a mother who worked at an agency providing domestic help for the upper classes. Bea was ashamed of herself for thinking this, but there it was, the worm in the bud or whatever, which sneaked back into her mind every now and then.

The last time Bea had spoken to Max, he'd promised to give her a date when they could all go out for a lunch to celebrate his birthday, but hadn't done so. She hadn't wanted to be seen as a nagging mother, and so hadn't reminded him about it. Now was the time to remedy that.

She tried his mobile, and by good fortune he was able to take the call, which wasn't always the case. As he reminded her, he was a very busy man. Now, though, he seemed pleased to hear from her.

'Mother? Yes, I hadn't forgotten we'd planned to meet up, but things happen, you know. I have to put my duties first. However, I have been thinking about you. We really must get together again. I was only saying so to Leon the other day when we met at the Summer Exhibition. My word, how time does fly. It must be three months or more since and—'

'Leon? Leon Holland? You mean, Bernice's great uncle?'

'Who else? We were admiring Bernice's portrait, and of course I told them about Piers being my long-lost father, and then the Trescotts came up and well . . . we all said what a small world it was and—'

'You know the Trescotts?'

'Of course. One meets them everywhere. They were very taken with the portrait of Bernice. A fetching little thing, isn't she? But with a temper, I shouldn't wonder. I had to explain the link between Leon and you and Piers. Do tell Piers I gave them the introduction. It might get him another commission. Every little helps, doesn't it?' He turned away to speak to someone for a moment. Then he came back to Bea. 'Sorry, Mother. Must go. Needed on the landline.'

'I was hoping we could make a date to—'

'Yes, yes. Must do that. I'll see you at the Trescott party on Friday. We'll fix something up then.' And he clicked off.

Bea thought, Well, that explains how Bernice and Leon came to the attention of the Trescotts, and maybe that's why they thought it a good idea for Evie to board and share a room with Bernice? A casual meeting at the Royal Academy could lead to all sorts of connections being made, and clearly had done so.

But now . . . Max couldn't find time to meet his mother for lunch but would be attending the Trescotts' party. Hmm. Well, by the sound of it, all the great and good would be there. But not Bernice.

Bea began to wonder what Leon's take on this connection with the Trescotts might be.

Leon Holland, Bernice's great uncle, ran the international and highly successful Holland Holdings. He was a man of about her own age with a strong personality, well-built, fair of hair and skin. Almost handsome. Suave. A very private man.

He'd been in her life for years, always a touch more than a friend but never advancing to a deeper relationship. She'd wondered several times, in a not-caring-over-much kind of way, if they might one day get married. But he really wasn't the marrying sort and then there was Piers, always hanging around, often annoying the life out of her, but still sexually active. She'd never been able to rely on Piers for long as he travelled all over the world to paint the high and mighty. And yet, and yet . . . if she had to decide between the two . . . Which would she choose?

She didn't want to answer that question.

She scrabbled around for Leon's private phone number, which he'd given her ages ago, asking her to use it only in an emergency. He did have a London base, but at this very moment could be anywhere in the world: Germany, Japan, or Fiji. He could be in his private jet somewhere over America, or in a board meeting in Kuala Lumpur. Maybe, with luck, he would be in Europe.

He was in the habit of ringing her once or twice a month, when they would talk about their lives in general and in particular about Bernice and how she was getting on. If he were in London, he might well ask Bea to accompany him to a formal dinner when he needed a partner, or an informal supper for two in quiet surroundings. She was always happy to accept his invitations. He could be amusing company. It was a restful relationship for both of them.

Bea found his private number. Her call went to voicemail. 'Leave your number and I'll ring back.'

He'd be in a meeting and wouldn't wish to be disturbed. She rang again. Left another message. And again. Five times. However busy he was, even if he'd muted the sound on his personal phone, he'd soon notice that it was vibrating and would understand that someone was leaving urgent messages for him.

Now all she could do was wait for him to respond. She switched on her computer to look up the details of the Trescotts' fatal road accident. She read it through again and printed it off. It had been written up as a genuine accident, but without giving any details. She must enquire further. But where?

Her phone rang. Leon came on the line. 'What's the emergency? Is Bernice all right?'

'She's fine. It's the Trescott family. You know them?'

A long pause. 'I'll ring you back in five.' The phone went dead.

Bea fidgeted through five long minutes, thinking hard all the time. Finally, the phone rang again.

Leon said, 'Trescotts? What's the problem? What have they got to do with Bernice?'

She made a wild guess. 'You know them? You're having business dealings with them?'

'I know them, yes. Everyone does.'

Bingo. She said, 'No, this has to be more personal. You're having talks with them? I wonder . . . is a merger in the offing?'

'What have you heard?' He was annoyed.

'Nothing. It's the only thing that makes sense. Why else would they want to get close to Bernice?'

'What on earth are you talking about?'

Bea explained. Evie had been placed in school, to be looked after by Bernice. The lift back from school with the aunt, and her treatment of both minors. The Trescott child being dumped on Bea, and the invitation for the weekend. The invasion of the two young men.

Leon said, 'So, there's been a social contact through school. There's nothing in that.'

'What about the three deaths?'

SEVEN

Sunday afternoon

'What three deaths?' Leon was sharp.

'Evie has been dumped on us supposedly because her Uncle Constant's death – which is said to be from an accidental overdose – had triggered an epileptic episode and they don't want her harassed by police. She doesn't seem in the least upset about it to me. The aunt hinted that Evie might have had something to do with her uncle's death, and the girl herself doesn't seem to know whether she's coming or going. And I'm stuck with her.'

'Constant. I don't know any Constant. I'm sorry if a Trescott relative has died, but it's nothing to do with me.'

'Ah. The Trescott you know is Nunkie? Cyril.'

'Well, yes. The Silver Fox. Well-named. A canny businessman, not to say tricky. Yes, there have been some preliminary talks about our joining forces in one or two divisions where our interests match. This is top secret. We don't want the markets to start reacting until we're ready.'

'Right. So it's not generally known that you are talking to the Trescotts, and you didn't know about Constant's death. Wouldn't it have been natural for the Silver Fox to mention his brother's questionable death?'

'Is it questionable? And why should he burden a stranger with such a thing?'

'Constant was a director of the firm. He owned a chunk of shares but never bothered to attend meetings He was Evie's guardian and she's due to inherit her father's estate. I don't know who Constant has left his shares to, but don't you need to know if his death affects the balance of voting rights?'

Silence.

Bea said, 'Leon, I think the Trescotts are jumping the gun. If the deal is straightforward and you have all the facts on the table, why are they keeping quiet about Constant's death, why has Evelina Trescott been dumped on me, and why do they want Bernice to attend their birthday party next weekend?'

'Ah, well. I know about that. The two girls are at school together, so it's a compliment to me to invite her. It's about time Bernice was introduced to people who matter.'

'Ah. So you knew about the invitation? You don't think it's unsuitable? She's fourteen, not eighteen.'

'A little young, I agree. But I'm told it's going to be a small family party—'

'With two bands and a marquee? A family party to which you and Max have also been invited? You are on those sort of terms with them? Do you know why the two younger Trescotts, Joshua and Benjy, are making moves on Evie and Bernice? I'm told Joshua wants to be prime minister one day. I doubt if he's got the bottle for it, but with money and contacts behind him, he might do well enough. He seems to have elected himself as Evie's beau, even though in my view he doesn't care much for her, or she for him. The one I'm concerned about is Benjy. Evie says he's aiming to run the Trescott business one day.'

'Mmm. Yes. I've come across him. So . . .?'

'He's handsome, brainy and in my view, psychotic. He knows Bernice is only fourteen, but that's not stopping him. At the moment he's being charming to her, but with a hint that he'd use force if he had to. He frightened her, Leon. If he were to get her alone somewhere, then what chance has a slightly-built, fourteen-year-old girl got against a hunk in his twenties?'

'Now you're being absurd. Why would he risk assaulting my niece?' Leon was amused.

'He wouldn't think of it as "assault". He believes he's so charming no girl could resist him, no matter her age. There's more to this than a young buck fancying a milkmaid and wanting to have his wicked way with her. There's three unexplained deaths in the family so far. And the two youngsters are targeting young girls who will both come into money. My question is why? Don't the Trescott clan have enough money to forward the ambitions on their young hopefuls?'

'That's ridiculous. They're as safe as the Bank of England.' Leon was getting angry. 'Look, Bea. Normally I respect your opinion, but you are making too much of a purely social contact. A possible merger has been discussed, yes. It isn't dependent upon a dynastic alliance between the two families, if that is what you're hinting at. Yes, the Trescott child is at the same school as my great-niece. But we met entirely by chance one evening at the Royal Academy. The Trescotts were very taken with Piers' portrait of Bernice and mentioned that they'd probably ask him to paint Evelina at some point. That's it, period.'

Bea changed tack. 'If you're thinking of a merger, you must have researched the Trescott background?'

'Naturally. They will have done the same for me.'

A tingle went up Bea's spine. The Trescotts had researched the Holland family . . . including Bea and Piers? 'They know I'm Bernice's guardian?'

'Bea, admit it. You are way out of your league here. How can you, running a small agency from the basement of your house, understand international finance?'

Bea was shocked. 'Do I hear the fine voice of the Trescotts denigrating everything I am and do?'

'My dear, you're overreacting. Trust me. I know what I'm doing. I'll get you an invitation to the party, too. That way you can see for yourself there's nothing untoward going on. It's going to be quite a do. I understand the birthday girl is getting engaged to her cousin on that day.'

'Isn't Evie too young to commit herself? As for Bernice, she's already been given a verbal invitation and doesn't want to go.'

'She'll go to please me. I don't want her teenage lack of social graces to upset our negotiations. I'll be back in town tomorrow night and we'll make arrangements then. Get yourself a new outfit, and make sure the girl is appropriately dressed, too. I'm relying on you, Bea.'

On which note, he rang off.

Sunday, early evening

Bea put the phone down just as Piers threw the door open and came in. He looked harassed, but before he could explain, she unloaded her worries on him. 'Leon is having talks with Cyril

Trescott about a merger. Leon says the invite to Bernice is a complimentary move to him, greasing the wheels of commerce. He wants me to get us both appropriate outfits and turn up, ready to do the social.'

'Bernice doesn't want to go. Do you?'

'No, but Leon thinks it might jeopardize the talks with the Trescotts if she refuses. I don't know if he's right or not. Leon doesn't know the young Trescotts and doesn't want to believe me when I say they're trouble.'

'If you're there with her, surely nothing can happen.'

Bea pushed back her chair. 'Leon also says that Evie is supposed to be getting engaged to her cousin at the party. Do you think she knows a proposal is coming so soon?'

'Does she even know which year it is?' He gestured backwards with his head. 'I came down to get away from the jollity. She's up there, dancing around, making plans for her future with her puppy. She's driving Bernice mad with envy, but fear not: our Bernice is tamping down her temper in a most admirable fashion.'

'Do you think Evie's anywhere near ready for marriage? I don't.'

'If she's proposed to in front of all their important guests, would she have the nerve to say "no"? And is it our problem?'

'I think it's *my* problem,' said Bea. 'But not yours.'

'Your problems are my problems.' He seemed to mean it, and that made her feel all warm and fuzzy. She half smiled and turned away to hide it.

'Of course,' he said, smoothing out a grin. 'I can't really help you if I'm exiled to that cold and lonely flat in the mews . . .?'

What should she say? *Welcome back?* Or: *Not yet?*

She couldn't decide. She said, 'So long as you observe the decencies and sleep in your own bed next door to me . . .'

'For how long? Haven't I served my sentence?' He was serious.

She could say, *Perhaps, soon?* She was veering towards, *Give me a little more time,* when Bernice came racketing down the stairs. 'Food's up and Evie's driving me mad. I'll kill her if you don't take her off my hands!'

'Point taken,' said Bea, switching off her computer and getting to her feet. 'Your uncle Leon is organizing an invite for the party for me as well as you. He wants us to get all kitted out, prepared to do the social.'

'I don't want to go.'

'Neither do I. Unfortunately your uncle is having talks in secret about a merger with Trescotts, and wants us to fly the flag for him. So I suppose we must go.'

Bernice did her frown thing. 'A merger with Trescotts? I usually spend some time in the holidays with Mac, Hollands' finance director. I know I have to learn about the business from the ground up and I am trying to do so. Mac's a brilliant teacher. I've learned more from him than from a dozen lessons in business studies at school. He's taught me how to read a balance sheet, and what to look for in the business columns of the newspapers. When we last met we talked mainly about my learning Mandarin and what's happening in the Far East. He didn't mention the possibility of a merger at half term when I saw him, but I suppose he thought I was too young to be trusted with the knowledge. Or it might not have been on the cards then.'

Bea said, 'I don't think a merger had crossed anyone's mind till the principals met at the Royal Academy at the Summer Exhibition, and that was early in June, after half-term.'

Piers said, 'Not that I know much about it, but a merger of two big organizations like Holland and Trescotts would deliver a whacking great bonus to the shareholders of each, because of the consequent rise in share prices.'

Bernice waved her hands around. 'Leon doesn't need money. He's rolling in it.'

Piers said, 'The richest men can always do with another yacht or penthouse or a more up-to-date private jet. Once you move into that level of society, the temptation is always to go one better.'

Bea said, 'My impression is that Leon didn't look for this, but that when the Trescotts swam into his life, it started him thinking about a merger.'

The door burst open and in bounced Evie, her untidy mop of hair flying around, and real colour in her cheeks. 'Supper's up. What are you all looking so serious about? Isn't it wonderful about my being given a puppy? I'm so glad his name is Copper. It's so easy to remember. But he's not really copper-coloured. He's brown with a bit of white.'

Bea said, 'Fine. Let's eat before we drop dead from hunger. Bernice . . . a moment?'

'What now? I'm ravenous,' said Bernice. But she shut the door as the others left.

Bea said, 'If the Trescotts have done their homework, they will be aware of your mother's existence. It's a long shot but I'm wondering if they might try to get to her, try to convince her that it's time you went out and about more. They could make out a case that it would be in your best interests to go to stay with Evie. Your mother is a lovely woman, but . . . I don't know how to put this, but . . .'

Bernice got it. 'You're right. Mummy's still a bit fragile though not as bad as she used to be. She doesn't want high society life for herself but she might worry herself into a state thinking that perhaps this is an opportunity I ought to take. Why don't you explain it to Keith? As my stepfather, he's got every right to protect her, and if they tried to put pressure on him, it would slide off like water off a duck's back.'

'I'll brief him, then. And we'll hope Leon hasn't mentioned that part of the family to the Trescotts.'

Bea sighed. She saw that this 'arrangement' with Keith paralleled how the Trescotts might arrange to spare Evie from difficult situations. Of course, Bea and Bernice were acting in the best interests of the girl's mother, weren't they?

As were the Trescotts for Evie?

Bea said, 'Bernice, have you talked about your mother to Evie?'

'No, why would I? Evie's not a proper friend.'

Piers had organized a delivery of some Turkish food, which they all liked. While they ate, Bea considered the information that had been fed to them by different people. There were inconsistencies here and there. What did she know, for a fact?

Evie's father and mother had been killed in a road accident and the date had been given as late July. Perhaps when Evie stopped burbling about the puppy, Bea might get a word in edgeways about her parents' deaths?

Eventually she managed to do so, saying, 'Have you ever owned a puppy before, Evie? Do you know how to train him?'

Evie lost all her animation. 'Daddy had a King Charles spaniel. It went everywhere with him. It was sent away to be re-homed . . . after.'

'After your parents died?' Bea collected the dirty plates. It might be helpful to get Evie to talk about that, provided it didn't tip her over into an epileptic episode.

Evie looked down at her hands. 'I mustn't think about that time. It's bad for me, and I might have to take a double dose of pills tonight.'

'I understand,' said Bea. 'You've been feeling all right today, haven't you?'

'Yes. I suppose.' There was no colour in her face or voice.

Bea decided to push a little more. 'A dreadful thing to happen to your family. How old were you?'

'I don't remember. It hurts to remember. Fourteen, I think.'

Two years ago, then.

Evie held on to her head with both hands, breathing deeply. Everyone else froze. Was she going to be ill?

No. She took her hands from her head and looked up. 'I'm all right. I'm not going to be ill. It's like it was meant, that I should be getting another brown and white puppy. It's a sign that life goes on. I'm going to have a lovely little dog of my own, and learn how to look after it and it will be with me forever and ever.'

Bernice looked grim. She knew she couldn't have a puppy herself, but it took an effort of will for her to be happy that Evelina should have one instead.

Bea tried to be encouraging. 'There's a manual for everything nowadays. I'll get you one from Amazon tomorrow, so you can look up what you have to do.'

Evie produced a blinding smile for both of them. 'Oh, you are so good to me. I'm so glad Bernice is my special friend.'

Bernice's brows drew together in a frown, but she caught a warning look from Bea and bit back words of rejection.

Evie's colour was almost normal again.

Bea dished out some vanilla ice cream and handed round a
bowl of soft fruits. 'What was your father's dog called?'

'She was called Snoopy. Well, that wasn't her pedigree name,
of course, but what Daddy called her. After the accident they
found her lying next to Dad, licking his face. She wasn't hurt,
but nobody could bear to keep her, after. So Auntie found a
good home for her. When I was better, I did ask if I might go
and see her but they said it would be too upsetting for her, and
me. I had to be so careful, you see, afterwards.'

'The shock of the accident made you ill?'

'Yes. I was in hospital for ages. Everything hurt. And then
I was moved to the clinic. I don't really remember much about
that time. I had counselling, of course. I couldn't stop crying
and they were at their wits' end what to do with me till they
put me on these special pills and I'm all right now, provided I
keep taking them.'

Bea said, 'Is that the pills you're on now? They're pretty
strong stuff. They make you sleepy?'

'And hungry. But the doctor said I must take them or I'd
have a stroke and be nothing more than a vegetable, able to
think but not to speak or do anything but lie in a chair all day
and be moved to a bed at night. I have to take them, twice a
day. If I don't, Auntie says I'll have to go back to the locked
ward.'

A locked ward! The child had been sectioned?

Bernice was round-eyed. 'Really, a locked ward?'

'Well, sort of. Yes. It wouldn't have been safe for me to
wander around alone. It's a lovely place, the clinic. It's a
Georgian mansion which has been converted to a clinic for
people with mental health problems. They're very strict. When
I first went there I wasn't allowed to leave till I'd been on the
new pills for a couple of months. Then I went home and attended
a small day school for a while. But I'd missed a lot of schooling
and I felt so tired all the time that I couldn't keep up. The other
girls started to call me names and make out I was totally stupid.
And, it turned out that it was a bit of a bind for Auntie, because
it tied Carlo up – that's our chauffeur – because he had to take
and fetch me every day. Actually he was nice about it. He used
to ask me how I was getting on with my schoolwork, which

was more than anyone else did. Anyway, my aunt heard about this school that we're at now, and I became a boarder and was lucky enough to be with you, Bernice, and I feel much better.'

Which explained a lot.

Bernice said, 'Well, you *are* a bit behind at school. I suppose it's because you were ill for so long. Do you know how many terms you missed?'

'Three, I think. No, it was four, what with the hospital and the clinic. Just over a year, I suppose. I was quite all right before I was ill. Daddy used to say I was his little abacus, because I could do mental arithmetic so quickly, and Mummy used to get me to check all her household bills. But that's all a long time ago. I can't do that now.'

Piers chipped in. 'What exactly is wrong with you, Evie? Are you epileptic, or not?'

'Well, I was. I think. But I seem to have grown out of it. I haven't had a fit for ages and ages. I can't remember when I last had one. Before this last weekend, that is.'

Bernice said, 'You hadn't had a fit all that time? But I thought you were still having them. That's why they put me in with you, so that I could call for help if you felt ill.'

Evie shook her head. 'I don't think I've had a real one for ages . . . years, I think. Till I found Uncle dead. At least, not a proper fit, though there's been times when I've sort of cut out and don't remember what's happened, but that's just nerves. I know the pills say they're for epilepsy but they're also for severe nervous conditions, which is what I've got.'

Bea was beginning to understand. 'You'd worked it out that the pills were too strong and asked if the dose could be reduced. When that didn't work, you took the instructions out of the pack and left them for Bernice to find. As a message. What did you hope to gain by doing that?'

Evie lowered her eyes. 'I was confused. I didn't know what I was doing.'

There was a collective sigh around the table. The problem was should they or should they not continue to question a girl with a background of nervous breakdowns? Or whatever it was that was wrong with her?

Piers said, 'You know very well what you're doing now,

Evie. You've stopped taking the pills and you're getting quite sharp. Not all the time, but most of it.'

Evie said, 'You mustn't go on at me or I'll start crying, and when I start crying I can't stop and have to go back to the clinic and I don't want that.'

'No,' said Bea. 'Of course you don't. Now, it's getting late and we've all had a long day. Let's clear the table, find a television programme we can all bear to watch, and have an early night. Tomorrow we're going to hit the shops again.'

Piers came into Bea's bedroom as she was taking off her earrings and putting them away. She opened her mouth to tell him to get out, and closed it again. She felt ambivalent about having him there. In some ways it was oh, so comfortable to have a before-bed chat with him in intimate surroundings and she was beginning to think that yes, she might allow him into her bed at some point, but . . .

He'd hurt her so badly in the past.

Yes, but that was years ago and perhaps they'd both grown up enough by now to forgive and forget.

But not tonight. She felt too uneasy, too concerned about Evie and Bernice and the future. She couldn't relax.

He sat on the bed. 'You need to know something. Ages ago I arranged for my website to send all queries to my agent. We've always got on well and I've been with him for years. Before I went on my last jaunt, I told him I wanted the school holidays off. I've just received an email saying he wants to see me urgently. Tomorrow. Guess why?'

Bea suspended operations on brushing her hair. 'The Trescotts want you to fit in a portrait of Evie?'

'They want me to do one of Cyril, the one Leon says is the Silver Fox. He's the current head of Trescotts. After that they want a second one, a group portrait of April Trescott, her two sons and Evie. One happy family. To start work in two days' time.'

'They consistently play down Evie's importance, don't they? Will you go?'

'A big fee has been offered. Double my usual. My agent is sure I'll want to go for it, even if it means working in the summer holidays. Oh, and an invitation for the party is waiting for me at my agent's office.'

Bea said, 'We're being corralled into the Trescott corner. I don't like it.'

'Neither do I. The money's good, but that's not the be all and end all.'

'Take care. Take precautions. I don't know what else we can do.'

'I could refuse to comply and so could you.'

'On what grounds? That we think the Trescotts are not acting in the best interests of a girl who has been sectioned at some point? I'm not her guardian.'

'No, but you are Bernice's. You have the right to decide whether she should go to the party or not.'

Bea stood up and slipped off her negligee. 'Off my bed, you! Leon says there's no ulterior motive in the invitation.'

He rolled off the bed. 'I don't like it.'

She turned back the duvet, shed her slippers and slid into bed. 'Neither do I, but I don't see how I can refuse. After all, if this merger means more money for Bernice in the long run, then surely that's all right?'

'Are you selling out to Mammon?'

She flounced. 'Are you?'

He shook his head and left the room. She switched off the light and closed her eyes. She was not selling out. She was being practical. Neither of the girls was going to come to any harm at a birthday party. Piers would paint the Silver Fox. Leon would be pleased. Bernice would have her first experience of an adult party. Evie would get her puppy and be happy. All would be well.

She wondered if she ought to buy a new outfit for the occasion, or if she had anything in her wardrobe which would do . . .

Evie said that when she was in hospital, everything hurt.

Now why would everything hurt when she hadn't been in the car at the time of the accident. Or had she? If that were the case, then she might well have been injured, too.

Yes, that was probably it. Nothing to worry about.

The tragic accident. The double strength pills.

Everything hurt.

Bernice saying she didn't want to go to the party. Understandable in a way, but if she were chaperoned she'd be perfectly all right.

Wouldn't she?

EIGHT

Monday morning

B ea summoned a taxi to take them to the exclusive boutique from which Evie's dress had come. Piers joined them saying he'd look at what they might have on offer, but then go on to see his agent. Today the girls were identically dressed in white T-shirts and black jeans. Both were bright-eyed and bushy-tailed, which probably meant Evie hadn't taken her pills again.

All Bernice could talk about was the various methods of self-defence she'd looked up on the internet. She was keen to try them out with Piers, who refused to be a guinea pig, saying the very idea made his eyes water.

When they were halfway to Knightsbridge, Bea's mobile rang.

Mrs Long Nose, in person. 'Where are you? I tried your home number and your office number. Finally some woman in the agency deigned to give me your mobile number. It would be helpful if you kept in touch with me.'

Bea's gritted her teeth but returned a soft answer. 'We're on our way to see what can be done about Evie's dress. If they can't alter it in time, and she decides to have something else, will that be all right?'

'What? Oh. Yes, I suppose. So long as she's suitably turned out. You understand it's going to be a very important day in her life. You'd better get her some shoes, too.'

Bea grimaced at the woman's hectoring tone, but managed to say, politely, 'We'll see to it.'

'That's not why I rang. You are making sure that Evelina is

taking her pills, aren't you? She talks such nonsense when she misses even one. The thing is – though perhaps it's better not to tell her that at the moment – there has to be an autopsy for my brother. So tiresome! We could have done without that, with the family's big day coming up at the weekend. An autopsy is standard procedure, they tell me, because Constant hadn't seen his doctor for a while. One more thing, there's been very little in the newspapers so far about his death, and we hope to keep it that way, though there will be an obituary in *The Times* eventually. Make sure the girl doesn't see it. No need to stir things up. Make sure she takes her pills, that's the important thing.'

'Yes, but—'

'We've decided to leave her with you for the time being. Oh yes, I nearly forgot. Leon says Evie's little friend will be more comfortable if you accompany her to the party, so I'm arranging for an invitation to be sent to you as well. I think that's all. Let me know immediately if Evelina is unwell, as we'll have to take her back to the clinic straight away.'

Off went the phone.

Mrs Long Nose's voice had been so sharp it had cut through the traffic noise, so both girls and Piers looked at Bea to find out what the call had been about.

Bea did her best to produce a reassuring smile. 'Mrs Trescott is worried about Evie, that's all. She says that if the dress doesn't fit and can't be altered in time, Evie can choose something else.'

'Oh, good,' said Bernice. 'That pink stinks.'

Evie giggled. 'Pink stinks.'

She really was subnormal, wasn't she?

Actually, the pink did stink. It hadn't looked right on the girl in Bea's sitting room, and it looked even more ridiculous when Evie tried it on in the salon. It glittered, it shimmered, it screamed 'bad taste'. The strong fuchsia pink did nothing for Evie's complexion, and the skirt was both too long and too wide for her to walk around in. Oh, and it didn't fit.

Fortunately the mention of the Trescott name made it possible for the top assistant to attend to them. She seemed to know all about the forthcoming weekend and how important it was that

Evie should look good. She twitched at the fabric of the pink horror, and commented that she'd been concerned it might not fit, but . . . and she shrugged.

Bea could see her thinking that the customer was always right, however crazy they might be.

'Now.' The assistant tapped her teeth. 'What shall we have instead? White?' She shook her head. 'Cream, perhaps?'

The room was lined with deep, glass-fronted cupboards containing dresses short and tall, each in a cellophane wrap. The assistant brought out a sheath dress in cream with a short train. It fitted Evie and the underpinnings gave her an hourglass figure. It looked wonderful on her, except . . . it wasn't right.

'No, I'm afraid not,' said the top assistant, exercising tact. 'She needs some colour.'

Evie admired herself in the mirror. 'It makes me look grown-up. If I have my hair done up, wouldn't it be all right?'

'No,' said Bea. 'It makes you look matronly.'

'Exactly,' said the top assistant, and bustled away to look for something else.

Bea wandered over to where Piers was thumbing away at his mobile. When she was close enough, he said, out of the side of his mouth, 'She shouldn't wear anything that makes her look too voluptuous. It sends the wrong signals. I'm beginning to wonder if she could be pregnant.'

'I'd wondered, too,' said Bea. 'You think Joshua has been busy?'

'Poor kid. She's hardly compos mentis enough to know what she's doing in that department.' Piers frowned at his mobile. 'I have to go soon. Where shall we meet and at what time?'

'Let's try these,' said the assistant, sweeping back with an armload of more important looking dresses with big skirts. Evie tried them on. None looked right.

Meanwhile Bernice had been poking around to see what else there was on view. She pulled a dress out and held it up against herself.

'Ah,' said the assistant, with a note of genuine enthusiasm. 'Those dresses have just come in from a designer new to us.' She took the garment from Bernice and held it up against the girl.

Piers abandoned his phone to consider the result.

This dress screamed simplicity of the most expensive kind. On the hanger it was a mere tube in ivory silk georgette over an ivory silk slip. The top was patterned with splashy roses and lilac flowers whereas the skirt was plain. The neckline was not too low and there were cap sleeves.

The assistant was ruthless. 'Off with that top and jeans. Let's see it on you.'

Bernice cast a look of panic at Bea, but obliged. Once on her body, the dress flowed around the girl's slender form. Bernice turned to look at herself in the full-length mirror. 'No,' she said. 'No, no and no!'

The assistant smiled and nodded. Bea smiled, too. They could both see that the dress was perfect for Bernice at this time of her life. It said, 'I'm still young but I'm going to be quite something when I grow up.'

Bernice moved this way and that, swaying, watching herself in the mirror, hardly able to believe what she saw. Despite herself, she was beginning to come to terms with looking good.

'That's the one,' said Piers, returning to his phone.

Bea nodded. 'Yes.'

Bernice said, 'Oh, all right, then.'

Evie clapped her hands and danced around. 'It's lovely, Bernice! You're going to be the belle of the ball.'

'No, I'm not,' said Bernice, frowning. 'That's you. Now, what are you going to wear?'

Evie, said, 'I want what she's wearing.'

'Ah, yes,' said the assistant, 'That might well do. Now, I think we have another garment from the same designer. Not identical, but in the same style. A larger size, of course.'

Piers said, 'Catch up with you later,' and disappeared.

The assistant returned with another soft column of a dress, this time in the palest of pink georgette over silk. It wasn't quite the same style as Bernice's dress but clearly it came from the same designer. It had an Empire line high waist and short sleeves, and a low neckline which showed off Evie's pretty bust to perfection without making it too obvious. It was patterned over the sleeves and bodice in greens and blues, which picked up the colour of her eyes, and the skirt was short enough and wide enough to dance in without tripping over the hem.

'I like it,' said Evie. 'Now we really can be sisters.' She pulled out her smartphone and took a snap of Bernice . . . and then made Bernice take one of her.

Bernice walked around Evie and poked her tummy. 'You're a bit soft looking here and there.' This was true but no one had been going to mention it, had they? Bernice nodded to herself. 'We'll have to firm you up at the gym this week.'

Bea mentally adjusted her estimate upwards of what she'd have to pay for Bernice's dress. She thought these two shift dresses would each cost far more than the pink horror which they were returning to the boutique. Granted, the Trescotts would pay for Evie's dress, but Bea would have to pay for Bernice's. Well, that was all right. The Hollands could afford it.

'And now for Madame?' The assistant was on a high.

'Oh, no!' said Bea.

'Oh, yes!' chorused Evie and Bernice.

'Something from the same designer, so that we all look as if we belong?' said Evie.

Bernice walked around Bea, looking her up and down. 'Something simple and classy. Not black. She looks too severe in black. She can wear something silvery, perhaps? Very, very plain. She's got some good jewellery that would go with it.'

Evie squealed with delight. 'I like it. Oh, I didn't know shopping could be such fun. I feel so . . . so . . .' Tears sparkled on her cheeks, and she brushed them away.

Is she going to have a medical episode? Oh, dear God . . .!

Bernice was equal to the occasion. 'Have you got a tissue? I expect Bea has. She's always got some in her handbag.'

'It's just that I'm so happy,' said Evie. 'I'm not going to look a fright at the weekend, and I've got you for my special friend, and I'm going to have a puppy and . . . I've never been so happy since . . .' She wound herself down, remembering the last time she'd been so happy.

Before her parents had died?

Evie's head drooped, and she gave a little hiccup. But she didn't cry any more.

Bea said, 'All right. I don't mind trying something on, but

we're not going to spend long looking for it, and if the first one isn't right, I've got something at home that will do. Don't forget, we have to find some shoes to match your dresses before we relax over a snack lunch, and then we can go home for a rest.'

'I don't need a rest,' said Bernice. 'I vote we go to the gym. All right with you, Evie?'

Evie said she'd never been to a gym and wouldn't know what to do. So Bernice said, 'Leave it to me. I'll show you.'

Which was an advance on Bernice saying she didn't want anything more to do with her new friend.

But when they arrived home in a taxi, burdened with parcels and making plans to visit the hairdressers and the gym, it was to find a chauffeur-driven limo double parked in front of the house. Illegally.

Evie's face went blank. 'Oh, that's Nunkie's car. Don't tell him I haven't taken my pills, will you?'

'No, I won't,' said Bernice.

'The subject won't come up,' said Bea. 'If it does, I'm not lying for you, but I will sidestep the question.'

She let them into the hall and was met by her office manageress, hurrying up the steps from the basement. 'Mrs Abbot, you have a visitor. He came down through the agency rooms to see you. I said you were out and he said it was urgent and he'd wait for you. I put him in the room at the back downstairs, the one we use for interviews. I hope that's all right.'

Bea got the subtext. The caller had not been allowed in Bea's office where he might have poked around for this and that. In the opinion of her office manageress, the caller wasn't to be trusted.

'Thank you,' said Bea, 'that's perfect. Any agency problems?'

'Nothing that can't wait.'

The visitor came up the stairs into the hall, smiling.

The two girls turned dumb at the sight of him.

Bea took one look and understood why.

He was indeed a silver fox, barbered and upholstered to perfection, with strong features which just missed being handsome. This was the man who ran the Trescott consortium, who was talking mergers with Leon. He was not only a man of power but foxy with it. Cyril Trescott. Nunkie to Evie.

'Mrs Abbot? Good to meet you at last.' He turned the full force of his personality on her. He was tall; taller than Piers; taller than Leon. And heavy-set. He was a Trescott but there was plenty of Smythe blood in there, too. A powerful combination.

He exercised charm. He lifted her hand to within an inch of his lips. 'Ah, but they didn't tell me you were such a beautiful woman.'

Bea responded to his charm with a smile for two seconds until she realized that this was the way she was meant to respond. Without thinking too much about it, she went into overdrive as a slightly silly woman who knew about clothes but left business matters to other people.

'Oh, Mr Trescott! You make me blush. Come into the living room, do. Take a seat.' The room had been shut up all day, and the sun had been beating down on it. She threw open the French windows that overlooked the garden at the back, to get some air. The windows led out on to a balcony which linked the living room with the kitchen, and from which cast-iron stairs twisted down to the garden below. She stood there for a moment, looking out over the garden, wondering how best to handle the forth-coming interview. She decided to continue to be a slightly silly woman of limited intelligence.

She fluttered back into the sitting room, saying, 'Girls, isn't it lovely that such a busy man can find the time to drop in on us like this? I do hope we haven't kept you waiting, Mr Trescott. Such a lot to do. Oh, and I do hope your sister isn't going to be too upset by the amount we've spent on Evie's dress. I must thank her for bringing Evie into our lives. It was such a pleasure to take her shopping. I think, I hope, that she will do you credit on her great day.'

I'm overdoing it. I can feel Bernice going into shock at my shenanigans. Surely he'll see through the charade.

He didn't. He accepted it that this is what the majority of women were like.

Bea gushed, 'May I introduce my ward, Bernice Holland?'

He turned a meaningless, unfocused smile on the two girls, who were still standing by the door, surrounded by shopping. 'Bernice, yes. I know your uncle well. And Evelina – you've been behaving yourself, I hope. Not giving this delightful lady a hard time?'

Bea decided he didn't know anything about teenage girls. Bernice in particular hated to be talked down to as if she were an idiot. Would the girl restrain herself from telling him what a fool he was? Because he was very far from a fool, even if he hadn't realized how bright she was.

Evie replied in the dead voice she had been accustomed to using in the past, 'Yes, Nunkie. I'm fine. We've been shopping this morning.'

Bernice said, in a close imitation of a nicely brought-up child, 'Would you like to see what we've bought?'

Bernice has worked it out that he won't be interested. She realizes he thinks she's a nonentity and he doesn't have to bother to charm her.

'No, no. That's fine, that's fine.' Another warm and completely insincere smile. 'Off you go, you two, while I have a little chat with your charming hostess.'

The two girls skittered up the stairs, carrying their bags of shopping with them.

Bea shut the door on them and turned on the fluttery act again. 'Some coffee, Mr Trescott? Or perhaps tea? I do hope you haven't been waiting for us long. I'm afraid we're all at sixes and sevens, what with this and that, but it's the holidays, you know. So much shopping to be done and—'

'Yes, yes.'

He's not come for chit chat. He didn't come to see if Evie was all right. Why has he come?

He looked around, noting the comfortable mix of antique and modern furniture, Adam ceiling and fireplace, large Chinese-style side lamps, and the portrait of Bea's second husband, which Piers had painted some years ago. 'Delightful little place you have here. You even have a small garden outside? Charming. And the park nearby for fresh air.'

Bea maintained her smile with an effort and waved him to a chair.

Delightful little place, indeed. It's worth a few million. But well, I suppose he's used to something more palatial.

She said, 'To what do we owe the pleasure of your visit?'

'Ah, yes.' He took the winged armchair by the fireplace, the one Bea usually sat in, and stretched out his legs. 'I have heard so much about the charming Mrs Abbot from my friend Leon, and about how good you've been, taking care of our poor little Evelina, that I had to make your acquaintance. I do hope the girl hasn't been causing you too much trouble.'

'Not at all,' fluted Bea, who wasn't sure what attitude to take on the subject. 'My ward has taken quite a shine to her. They do everything together.' She seated herself opposite him on the settee.

He inclined his head with another of his gracious, condescending smiles. 'And you have your little hobby downstairs. The agency. It must take up so much of your time. I understand from your son – what a delightful couple, he and his wife – I gather you don't see much of them? But perhaps, when you retire . . .?'

Bea told herself not to grit her teeth and held on to her smile. 'Such a busy boy he is. What a relief to know that someone is working so hard in the House of Commons for the rights of us poor working women.'

I'm definitely overdoing it. If he's researched me at all, he'll know the agency is on a sound footing and makes me a very good living.

He took out his phone and silenced an incoming call. 'Forgive me. Business follows wherever I go.' He continued to hold on to the phone and look down at it while talking to Bea. She considered such behaviour the height of bad manners but decided not to say anything.

He said, still looking down at the phone and not at Bea, 'Then you have all the extra problems of dealing with your difficult ward, Bernice. You have been considering some counselling for her, I gather. Perhaps I can give you the name of the doctor we use for Evelina. It's made all the difference to her. We thought at one time we'd lose her, you know.'

He managed to tear himself away from the phone long enough to look up at Bea and to shake his head, indicating the seriousness of the problem of his niece.

Bea carolled, 'Oh, Bernice may be a little wayward at times, but she responds to a little TLC. That is, to tender loving care. Children usually do, don't they?'

Now she'd definitely gone too far. His brows twitched. It was clear he'd never considered that TLC was the answer to anyone's problems.

He looked down at his phone again, hesitated, but finally decided to put it down for the moment. Instead, he leaned forward to get within her personal space. He smelt of something spicy and expensive. He himself was exactly that: spicy and pricey.

He said, 'To be frank, my friend Leon asked me to call. He felt that you might be out of your depth when it comes to matters you've never had to deal with before. Being in charge of a young girl who's on the cusp of womanhood, with such expectations . . . it's not to be wondered at that you have been cautious about introducing her to the wider world. Even if it is one in which she will be expected to take part in due course.'

Oh, that's clever. He's making out I'm a poor choice of guardian for Bernice because I don't swim in international waters.

She said, 'Oh, you are so right, Mr Trescott. I have such fears for her. She is young and feisty. I dread her falling into the wrong company. Suppose she were introduced to drugs or even – such a dreadful thought – find herself at some young man's mercy and become pregnant? I wake up at night worrying about this. She's been fine so far, being at boarding school. But when she's sixteen or seventeen . . . what will happen then? At least we have some years to go. She's only fourteen now, you know. And not . . . not fully a woman, if you get my meaning.'

It wouldn't hurt to emphasize Bernice's age. Ah, it wasn't news to him. He knew her age already. Which means . . . what?

Another of his avuncular smiles. He had decided that Bea was a harmless sort of female and had ceased to concentrate on her. His hand strayed to his phone and away again. He was only going through the motions of being charming now.

'Ah, Mrs Abbot, my dear Mrs Abbot . . . may I call you Beatrice? Now we've met and I can see for myself why my friend Leon raves about you. I'm sure we're going to be great friends, you and I. You must allow me to teach you a little about the ways of the world. When you and I were young, we never thought of experimenting with what life had to offer while we were at school, did we? Oh, there was the occasional . . . of course some did. I seem to remember that they were the ones who went further and faster than their more prudish friends. They certainly came to no harm. And in today's world, well . . .'

He knows that Evie has been 'experimenting', and he doesn't care!

He nodded, pleased with himself. 'My dear Beatrice, I think you will agree that you have led a somewhat cloistered life. Your second husband died young, I believe, and your first . . . well, a bit of a nomad, never putting down roots . . . I daresay he's been experimenting all over the place . . .'

This man is poison! How dare he say that about Piers . . . even if it is true!

'And it does you credit that you worry about such things. But I'm sorry to say that the young things of today will go ahead and experiment whatever we do or say. We love them dearly. Of course we do . . .'

This man doesn't know what love is!

'But all we can do is provide a good home and look after them as best we can if they come to grief out there. I'm sure your Bernice will take the usual precautions. I imagine you've talked to her about this already?'

Bea put a hankie to her eyes, keeping up the act. 'Oh, Mr Trescott. You have no idea. Such a wilful child she is.'

'There, there.' Again he looked at his phone, to read a text on it. He nodded, considered replying to the message but finally put it away. He stood up, taking an envelope out of his pocket. 'I know you'll make sure the girl is nicely turned out for Friday. I brought invitations for you both. There's been a spot of bother back at the country house, which I believe you know about. My sister and I think it would be as well if you kept Evelina with you until Friday.' A slight hesitation, then, with some reluctance: 'My sister says the girl has a vivid imagination. You wouldn't credit the things she comes out with! Attention-seeking. I believe it's a teenage thing. Such a shame. Her father, my brother, had such a fine head for business.'

'What are you saying? Is there something I ought to know about Evie?'

'No, no.' Again the avuncular, meaningless smile. 'Nothing for you worry about. Now, about Friday, we'll send a car for the three of you in the afternoon.'

Bea tested the waters. 'I'm afraid you'll have to excuse Bernice. She doesn't feel she's old enough to attend.'

'I'm sure you'll persuade her otherwise.' Another meaningless smile, but this time with a trifle of iron in it. He was accustomed to having his slightest wish granted, wasn't he? 'I am so glad to have met you at last. I feel we have so much to talk about. Perhaps you'll have supper with me one evening? Now I'm afraid I must leave you. Business calls.'

He moved to the door, assessing the room and its contents as he did so. He said, 'A pleasant enough neighbourhood, this. I believe the prices around here have rocketed recently. I'm in the market for something like this little place for my secretary. You'd consider an offer, wouldn't you? You could well afford to retire, and perhaps move out of town? Before you are too old to enjoy retirement?'

'You are too kind. Let me show you out.'

Bea held on to her smile until she'd waved him off into his limo and shut the door on the outside world. Then she said several very bad words. Loudly.

Bernice appeared from the kitchen, followed by Evie.

'Well!' Bernice exploded. 'What a performance!'

Bea twisted her lips in a smile. 'Mine? Or his? Am I right in thinking you and Evie didn't go far up the stairs? That you dumped your bags on the landing, crept back down to the hall and went out through the kitchen on to the balcony? You wanted to overhear what that man had to say?'

'Of course,' said Bernice. 'Evie didn't think it was right to eavesdrop at first, but she did see the point when he started on her. What a piece of work is that man! I think that—'

Bea put up her hand. 'First I want to know what Evie thinks.'

Evie pushed back her untidy mop of hair. Tears stood out on her cheeks. 'What do you want me to say?'

Bernice pushed at Evie's shoulder in a gesture of affection.

'What you yourself think, Dum-Dum. You're not on your pills now. You can even string a couple of sentences together without doing yourself an injury. So, tell!'

'He's my Nunkie. I mean, everyone does what he says.'

'Does nobody else in your family think for themselves? Come on, Evie. Does it hurt to use your brain?'

'Yes,' said Evie. 'It does. Everything hurts.'

Evie said that 'everything hurt' after her parents died. Was she injured in the crash or . . . No, I don't want to go down that rabbit hole.

'Spit it out,' said Bernice. 'You heard what he said. What did he mean by that crack about you telling porkies?'

Bea did a double take. '"Porkies" meant lies, didn't it? It was rhyming slang. "Pork pies" meant "lies", didn't it?'

Evie gaped, and didn't reply.

NINE

Monday afternoon

Bea thought Evie needed time to think. When the girl had arrived, she'd been doped to the eyeballs. She seemed to have stopped the medication of her own accord and a new personality was emerging from the old. She was no longer parroting the Trescott party line every time she opened her mouth but it was still there, embedded in her brain, fighting with the new ideas she'd come across since moving into Bea's orbit. It was no wonder the girl was confused.

Bea said, 'Come on, girls. Let's have a cuppa and a sit down. If Evie wants to talk, she will. If not, not.'

'I do want to. I do.' Evie wrung her hands. 'But you won't believe me. No one does.'

Bernice turned Evie round and pushed her into the kitchen. 'Try us. You can have tea, mind. But no cake. You're on a diet from now on.'

Bea made tea, and they sat round the central unit.

Evie wept a little. She made a couple of attempts to speak and failed.

Bea said, 'Evie, we do understand that you must miss your father and mother terribly. Tragic. But what about this third death in the family? Can you bear to tell us how your uncle Constant came to take an overdose? You said there was some kind of scene at supper the night before?'

'Yes, he was cross with me for making supper late, and then he read out my school report and of course it was awful and he said I was a disgrace and he couldn't think why I'd been sent to such an expensive school and I tried not to listen because he was going on and on, and then the others joined in and yes, I did get upset.'

'You kicked the table and shouted.'

A wince. 'I did kick the table, but I didn't shout. They did. All of them. I didn't even finish my supper but went off to bed early.'

'You didn't see your uncle again that night? He didn't come in to talk to you later?'

'No. Not that I know about. But . . .' Her chin wobbled. 'Maybe I just don't remember. That does happen with epileptics, doesn't it?'

'Are you really an epileptic?' asked Bernice. 'I haven't noticed you having a fit.'

A shudder. 'There's no other explanation, is there? It's why they're all so worried about me, making sure I'm safe and looked after.'

Or someone wants you to think it. In which case . . . no, I really don't want to go down that road.

Evie said, 'I'm a bad girl. I was tailing off my medication the last week at school and I haven't taken any since Saturday. I ought to take double tonight and go to bed straight after supper, or I'll be ill again and have to go back to the clinic.'

Now she's back in Trescott mode. I can hear her aunt saying those very words.

Bea was brisk. 'I think you're perfectly all right, Evie. If you decide to take a pill so that you don't have a fit, then that's what you should do. Do you know what to look out for, if you feel a fit coming on?'

'No, I don't get any warning. It just happens.'

'How often?' said Bernice. 'The head asked me to look out for you going all weird, but I didn't notice anything in particular.'

'It's only happened twice that I know about, but they tell me there have been other times that I don't remember.' She drooped. 'I'm awfully tired. Do you mind if I go upstairs and rest for a bit?'

'Of course.' The girl disappeared and Bea started clearing the table. Bernice made no move to help but sat there, stroking Winston who had arrived from nowhere, hoping for a titbit or two.

Bea said, 'Bernice, do you want to go after Evie? Will she be all right on her own?'

Bernice heaved a great sigh. 'Bea, would those pills stop her having periods? I asked her if her period was due because Mrs Long Nose hadn't packed anything for her, but she looked at me as if I were crazy. Apparently she hasn't started yet.'

'It happens to some girls,' said Bea. 'They don't start till much later. Yes, the pills may have slowed down her development.'

'I suppose that's why she's not interested in boys. Did you see, when Joshua put his arm around her, she went all stiff?'

Bea would have gone into this further, but at that moment a key turned in the lock of the front door and Piers walked into the kitchen, wearing a horrendous scowl.

One look at him, and Bea slid off her stool. 'What's up?'

'Don't ask. I'm in a foul temper. I was going to drown my sorrows in drink but came straight home instead.'

He came straight home? He considers this his home? Yes, of course he does. He hasn't any other.

Piers took Evie's place at the table. 'Anyone got a cyanide pill handy? Or a gun? Not that I know how to fire one. If I tried to kill someone, I'd probably miss. And if I took a cyanide pill it probably wouldn't kill me but give me the runs instead.'

Bea put the kettle on. 'Coffee coming up. I assume your meeting with your agent didn't go well?'

'He thinks I should be pleased to forgo my summer holiday in order to paint the Trescotts. He can't understand why I should even think of turning down their very kind offer, which is for double my usual fee, you understand. And that, if you haven't worked it out already, means my agent gets double his fee as well. I could spit!'

Bernice looked worried. 'Hang about. You promised you'd keep the holidays free so that we could go to France and stuff.'

'You really think I'd turn down spending quality time with the two women in my life for a fistful of dollars? No way.'

The two women in his life? Bernice and Bea?

Bernice was puzzled. 'But can you afford to turn work down? I thought that being freelance meant you had to take what you could. I mean, you don't even have a flat of your own or a car.'

'Sweetheart,' said Piers, 'I have never found a place in which I wanted to settle after Bea threw me out, and I have never wanted the bother of owning a car in London, which is almost totally gridlocked seven days a week. I have an excellent accountant and stockbroker, and if I never get another commission – which is what my agent has threatened me with – then I shall retire happily on the pension I've been paying into for donkey's years. I'll sit in the sun and doodle on scraps of paper and I'll still have enough to take you two to the ball or wherever else you wish to go.'

Bea put a mug of strong black coffee in front of Piers. She placed her arm around his shoulders in a rare gesture of affection. 'Your agent tried to pressure you into agreeing the Trescotts' terms?'

He managed a grin. 'He almost wept when I refused to give up my holiday to paint them. He hinted that people don't cross the Trescotts and live to tell the tale. I said that in that case I was a dead man walking, which he didn't find amusing. He said he personally would sue me if I didn't do as I was told, so I pointed out that I'd included a clause in my contract which gave me the right to pick and choose my commissions.

'He asked if I wanted to break our contract and I said, "No, of course not". I was going to say "Yes", but fortunately I remembered just in time that if I did that, I'd have to pay him a whacking great fee. I reminded him that he could break the contract if he wished, but then he'd have to pay me said fee instead. I'm a hard-headed businessman, I am.'

Bernice inched her stool nearer to Piers, and put her arm

around his waist, so that the three of them were linked. 'I wish I'd been there to hear you. So, did he sack you?'

'He said he'd have to consult his client. I said that was fine, and I'd go down the road for a coffee while he did so. I'd no sooner taken my first sip than he joined me, trying out the old hearts and flowers approach. Would I please reconsider, because his office is in a building owned by the Trescotts through some multi-national corporation. When he'd phoned Cyril Trescott to say I wasn't playing ball, Cyril had reminded him of this inconvenient fact. The poor man could see his rent doubling overnight, or his lease being terminated. So would I please, just for once, etc.

'I kept my temper. With an effort. I said that I regretted I was unable to accommodate him. I said I looked forward to our next meeting when we could rough out dates for the commissions I do wish to accept. I've had plenty of offers for the next two years already. I thought he'd have apoplexy. He wanted to tell me to get lost but common sense prevailed and informed him that he couldn't do that, either. Sacking me meant he'd be even more out of pocket. I am sorry for him. A little. But I'm also feeling somewhat uneasy as to what happens next.'

Bernice said, 'But what could happen? You've said no. They tried to make you change your mind and failed. So they'll have to accept what you say.'

Piers was calming down. He sipped coffee with appreciation. 'First the velvet glove. The charm, the smiles, the offers of money from an unlimited purse. If that doesn't work, they hint at the power they have to crush you like an ant. Unfortunately for them I have no hostages to fortune, except for you two.'

Bea cut him a slice of heavy fruit cake and added a wedge of Wensleydale cheese, a combination he particularly liked.

He took a large mouthful of each and relaxed. Almost smiled. He said, 'I suppose we're all vulnerable to a certain extent. I am uneasily aware that I have annoyed a man who isn't used to being denied whatever he wants. I looked him up on the internet last night. An interesting face. I wouldn't mind painting him some day, though I don't know that he'd be pleased with what I might come up with.'

'Mmm,' said Bea. 'Having met him myself, I tend to agree. You wouldn't like him. And, I think you're right about the way the Trescotts work. Mrs Trescott was slightly condescending to me at first, as if I were an acquaintance who might be useful one day, though of course not of equal standing to her. When she needed me to take Evie out of circulation, she clicked over into imperious mode, ordering me to look after the girl without so much as a please or a thank you. There was an underlying assumption that I should be delighted to fall in with her wishes. When I said it wasn't suitable for Bernice to attend an adult party, she brought in the Silver Fox, Cyril Trescott, to persuade me to do as she wished. He was ultra-charming on the surface but equally sure I'd fall in with his wishes. But, as I didn't do so he added a nice touch or two of his own. He insinuated I wasn't savvy enough to steer Bernice through to adulthood, and that I should retire to the country and let her get on with life in the fast lane. He even suggested he might buy my little house for his secretary.'

Bernice protested, 'But this house is just right for us and you don't want to retire yet, do you?'

'No, I don't want to sell up and retire. Far from it. So what will they think of next?'

The landline phone rang, and Bea answered it. It was Betty, her office manager from the agency downstairs. Betty was not exactly in a panic but did need some advice. A problem had arisen with a placement that had gone wrong. The client was a valued client, so could Bea find a few minutes to sort everyone out?

Bea pushed the Trescotts and their problems to the back of her mind and went down to deal with the crisis.

Only when the agency closed for the day was Bea was able to relax; whereupon all her hopes and fears for Evie came flooding back. Bea told herself she was imagining things. And yet . . .

Cyril Trescott had said that Evie was a fantasist. Bea had seen no evidence for it. According to Evie's own account, she'd been a normal, bright teenager until at fourteen – the age which Bernice was at now – her parents had been killed in a shocking accident and she'd been hospitalized. A long convalescence had followed in which she'd been taking strong medication. Unsatisfactory attendance at two schools had followed. Then she'd woken up one morning to find her uncle dead . . . and suffered a relapse. Bea thought that if you put that all down on paper and looked at it, then it made sense.

Evie was a fragile youngster with big prospects. She was going to become engaged to her cousin, so that he might look after her. The parallels with Bernice's fragile mother were obvious. Families looked after their own.

Evie would sign whatever her family wanted her to sign. After marriage her future – and her money – would continue to be controlled by the Trescotts. That all made sense. Surely her family was right to take care of her in the way they thought best?

The Trescotts had now turned their attention to Bernice. Why? What would the Trescotts have to gain by courting a fourteen-year-old? Bernice was far too young to marry. Even if Benjy fancied her, surely he wouldn't wait two years for a bride. Would he?

Bea had every right – in fact, she was duty-bound – to look after Bernice to the best of her ability. Which she would do. As for Evie, Bea told herself that the Trescotts knew exactly what they were doing and she, Bea Abbot, had absolutely no right to interfere. Indeed, how could she interfere, even if she had wished to do so? How could she, a middle-aged widow who ran a domestic agency, protect somebody else's child from predators? If in fact they really were predators and not kindly people looking after a fragile youngster?

Well, there was one thing Bea could do, and that was to talk things over with Leon.

She reached for the phone, and it rang. Marvellous to tell, it was Leon, trying to reach her. 'Bea, are you free for supper tonight? I've a table booked for eight o'clock. I'll send the car for you at half seven, shall I?'

'Why, yes. I'm glad you rang, Leon. It would be good to talk. So much has—'

He clicked off. He was in a hurry, wasn't he? Well, that's what happened when you were a Captain of Industry. Still, they'd have time to talk over a meal tonight.

She blocked out of her mind that Leon might be thinking more of the possible millions he might make from the merger than of his great-niece's welfare.

So, what should she wear? A little black dress? She didn't feel like wearing black tonight. She had a rather good grey silk top, embroidered with pearls. That would do, teamed with her favourite black skirt over boots. Or was it too warm for boots? She did love boots. But no, perhaps not tonight. High heels it would have to be.

She would arrange for Piers to give the children pizza for supper.

Monday evening

The chauffeur-driven car arrived on the dot, with a message that Leon would meet her at the restaurant. The sounded fine, until Bea discovered the table had been booked for four and that she wouldn't have him to herself. Another woman was already seated beside him, a sharp-faced blonde in a designer evening dress cut so low at the front that it gave Bea vertigo to look at it. April Trescott!

Leon was also wearing black tie. The two of them were going on to a function together?

Wha-a-a-t?

Leon half rose to meet her, and then sank back into his chair. 'Bea, I think you've already met my friend April?'

April showed her teeth. 'Delighted to meet you again so soon, Beatrice.' She didn't sound delighted. She sounded annoyed that someone who was so far her social inferior had dared to appear at *her* table. She looked Bea up and down. 'I'm so glad you didn't feel the need to dress up.'

She was sitting close to Leon, and hadn't shifted when Bea arrived.

Bea manufactured a smile, thinking that April's remark was putting her in her place, wasn't it? What on earth was Leon playing at? Did he wink at her? No. He was far too busy patting April's arm which was lying on the table next to his.

Leon petting a woman's arm in public? He was not a touchy-feely person. He never had been. What was going on?

Bea seated herself where indicated and took her time to consider her opponent. Conclusion: April Trescott had spent a considerable amount of time and money in keeping herself trim.

Hair, skin and bosom were not as nature intended. She wasn't the type of woman Leon usually admired. Or was she? Bea was beginning to think she didn't know anything about anyone.

Leon unfolded his napkin. 'Well, Bea, we're going on to a private do later, but I felt I must make an opportunity to see you as I'm off again tomorrow afternoon, back for the party.'

Bea tried to work out what this development meant. She hadn't seen Leon with another woman before. He'd told her shortly after they met that he'd had a loving partner for many years, but there'd been no children and he'd not wanted another relationship after she died. Bea had always thought that he liked women, but not well enough to marry them.

April firmed her shoulder against Leon's, and he didn't recoil. April laid her left hand – on which several diamonds glistened – over Leon's right. April was laying claim to him.

Bea felt as if she'd made a false step in the dark.

The waiter handed her the menu. She took it and then laid it down. Was Leon really involved with this woman? Was a relationship developing because of the projected merger? What did that mean for his relationship with Bea? Did it mean he wanted to cut his ties with his friends from the past?

'Did you forget your glasses, Beatrice?' asked April. 'My grandmother couldn't read the menu without glasses for years before she died.'

Was April Trescott wearing contact lenses? No, she's had that op that means you don't need glasses.

Bea said, 'Leon knows what I like.' She looked at Leon and saw, with a twinge of alarm, that he was looking tired. 'Are you quite well, Leon? All this dashing around the universe.'

Leon opened his mouth to reply, but April got there first. 'He's had such a rough time, poor dear. I'm sure he doesn't want to worry you with his little problem. We're in the process of sorting it out, aren't we, my love?'

My love? And he's smiling back at her. In the old days he'd have cut her off at the knees. What's going on here?

April summoned the waiter and ordered for herself – and for Leon. Bea ordered something simple for herself, telling herself that it wasn't done to throw a tantrum and chuck the cutlery at another diner in public.

Leon removed his hand from under that of April's and made a play of straightening his tie. 'Well, Bea. You're looking good, as ever. I'm glad you've seen sense and have persuaded Bernice to attend the party. As I told Cyril, you've always had plenty of common sense.'

How did he know Bernice had agreed to attend? Ah, Evie must have been on the phone to April. April has told Cyril, who has told Leon . . . and Leon is behaving totally unlike himself. What is the 'little problem' April was talking about? Leon's not well? Is she feeding him some medication that . . .?

Oh. Oops. Like Evie? If that is so, what can I do about it?

Bea said, 'You're under the doctor, Leon? What's the problem?'

April answered for him. 'An allergy. Most unfortunate. We were having tea together and oh dear! It suddenly came over him. It's so easy to pick these things up abroad, if you're not careful. You don't travel much, do you, Beatrice? I suppose you can't when you have to scrape a living. You don't mind my calling you Beatrice, do you? And you must call me April.'

Bea ignored that provocation to concentrate on Leon. 'Leon, we need to talk about Bernice some time. If you're in such haste tonight, perhaps you can ring me tomorrow?'

'Well, I'm sort of in transit tomorrow. Meetings.' He took out his phone and fumbled with it, frowning slightly. He didn't seem to be able to find what he wanted on the screen.

'Oh, don't worry about business now,' said April, taking his phone from him. 'Beatrice must know how busy you are, and she won't worry too much if she can't speak to you tomorrow. Dear Beatrice, you must have so many calls on your time, too. Family and so on.'

With a touch of fake embarrassment, April added, 'I didn't mean you don't have a wonderful relationship with your son and his wife, although I understand you haven't seen them for quite some time. I didn't mean to imply that you didn't care. It's difficult to find time for family when you're so busy with work, isn't it? I always say family comes first, but there . . . that's the way I was brought up.'

Bea felt acid hit the back of her throat. This woman knew about Max and his wife and that they had not made time to see

Bea for quite a while. Had April made friends with Max, too? Had Leon been telling her about them?

If April had got close to Leon, then what did that mean for Bea and Bernice?

The food came. Luckily Bea had chosen something light and fishy, which was easy to eat. She thought of Piers treating the girls to a pizza each, and wished she were back with them.

April was wearing diamond earrings. They glittered as she chattered on about the glories of Rome or Miami . . . or whatever. Bea lost track of the important names that were dropped. Leon ate a little, but not as if he enjoyed it. He refused wine and drank water. Well, if he was on some kind of medication, it wouldn't be a good idea to drink wine.

April drank two glasses of wine.

Bea wondered if she could decently leave after the fish course. She could say Bernice was ill and needed her. No, she couldn't. April would find out that was a lie because Evie would tell her the truth.

April gestured to the waiter to fill up Bea's glass.

And then . . . Bea realized she ought to have foreseen it . . . Cyril Trescott, the Silver Fox, arrived at their table and put his arm on Bea's shoulder. He said, 'Ah, we meet again,' in a warm tone, and took the fourth chair. The one beside Bea, hemming her in.

His hand on her shoulder had been heavy. He'd meant her to feel the weight of his hand, and to remind her of the power behind it.

He was smiling, but his eyes glittered, needle sharp. He had ceased to dismiss her as a pawn in the game. She guessed he'd been asking around about her. He must have discovered that she had a reputation as a shrewd businesswoman and that she was not the fluttery creature she'd pretended to be when he visited her at home. He was annoyed because he'd miscalculated earlier, and he was now going to take it out on her.

'My very dear Beatrice.' He continued to smile, but spoke softly . . . oh, so very softly . . . but the words came out through clenched teeth. Yes, he was pretending to do the social, but he was very angry.

She almost quailed. Then she stiffened her back and managed a smile. 'Mr Trescott, I didn't expect to see you again so soon.'

'You should have done.' Still smiling, he beckoned to the wine waiter. 'Take that slop away and bring us something decent. Bring me . . .' And he reeled off a name which Bea recognized as being the most expensive red on the wine list.

Bea looked a query at Leon. 'Leon, you didn't tell me you had invited Mr Trescott as well?'

Leon produced a shadow of his usual tight smile. 'He thought it would be a lovely surprise. You two really must get to know one another better.'

Leon had betrayed her.

Bea wanted to remind Leon that she'd once saved his life, but the man sitting beside her was no longer the person she knew. She concluded that he'd sold out to the Trescotts for the sake of what . . . more money, more power? And sacrificed Bea and Bernice to get it?

She was on her own.

Still smiling, Cyril Trescott ignored the others to speak directly to Bea. 'I understand my sister is taking Leon on to a private party, which gives us the opportunity to get to know one another better. We can go on somewhere quiet where we can talk.'

'What a lovely idea, but I'll take a rain check if I may. I promised my ward I wouldn't be late home tonight.'

The wine waiter was about to pour her another glass of wine though the old glass sat almost untouched on the table. She reached out to prevent his doing so.

Cyril Trescott grasped her forearm and forced it down to the table. In that soft voice of his, so soft that no one but her could hear, he said, 'I don't take "no" for an answer.' He was very, very determined. And let her feel it.

She refused to show pain but met his eye full on. She said in a normal voice, 'Using force is no way to make friends with me. Release me, if you please.'

TEN

He released her but continued to hold her eye. One side of his mouth twitched into a smile of satisfaction. He didn't need to say it. His hold on her arm was a foretaste of what he had planned for her later that night.

Still in that soft voice, he murmured, 'Mrs Abbot, your speech is slurred, your behaviour far too loud. You have obviously had too much to drink. You will leave with me when I am ready to go. You can choose to go quietly or, if you try to make a scene, I will tell the waiter that I am taking you away to a safe place where you can sober up.'

She had had only one sip of wine all evening, but if he claimed she was drunk and incapable and insisted on dragging her out to his car, then any protest she might make would be put down to the drink she'd supposedly taken.

She leaned back in her chair and considered her options. She saw now that Cyril was exactly like Benjy – or rather, that Benjy was like his uncle. They both believed in force if charm didn't do the job. If Bea left in Cyril Trescott's car she'd be completely at his mercy and she didn't like to think where he might take her or what he might do to her. If she used any of the self-defence methods Bernice had mentioned, she'd probably just fall over her own feet, because she'd never seen them done in real life.

Her arm was on fire. She wanted to rub it, but wouldn't give him the satisfaction of showing that he'd hurt her. He gestured to the wine waiter to fill Bea's glass with the replacement wine. Bea shook her head. 'I prefer white when I've eaten fish.'

'You will drink it to please me.' Again, the words were only meant for her to hear.

She could do just that, of course. No, she couldn't. He'd

regard it as a victory for his side, and she refused to give him even that much ground. She said, 'I regret. No.'

He said, 'I hear you've been a very naughty little girl. Naughty little girls need to be smacked and stood in the corner till they apologize and promise to behave in future.'

What exactly had brought this on? From being charm itself, he had turned into a bully. Why? She tested a theory. 'You seem to be upset about something. Is it because Piers can't fit you into his schedule at the moment? You can't dictate when and where an artist will work.'

'Oh, I think *you* could manage it.'

Could she? She thought about that. Could she really make Piers do something he didn't want to do? In everyday life, possibly. In his artistic life, no. She said, 'I don't say it's impossible for you to make him work for you, but I think you'd be sorry for it if you did. At the moment he sees you as a hungry wolf, and he wouldn't be able to paint you any other way.'

'A hungry wolf?' He was amused. A little. But still angry and still intent on getting his own way. 'Oh, believe me, I can think up several ways of getting him to do what I ask. I understand he doesn't own any property or even a car, and dosses down on other people's beds . . .'

And here he narrowed his eyes at Bea. So he knew Piers was sleeping at her house?

He said, 'There are always methods one can use, if one wants it enough.'

Was that a threat of physical harm? What a pity this conversation was not being taped!

She considered the meaning behind the words. 'You are threatening to arrange for someone to beat him up? How very obvious. I thought better of you than that. And there's a problem. If Piers were attacked physically he'd lose his ability to paint, and then you'd have lost him for good. There are other portrait painters, some better known and more . . . more malleable. Why not try one of them?'

He grinned. 'He's the one I've chosen. I like the idea of being painted as a hungry wolf . . . in which case, my dear, you will have to substitute for . . . who? Little Red Riding Hood? No, that role has already been assigned to Bernice. You can be the granny, who meets with a sticky end.'

Bea winced. 'I bet your Nanny used to tell you, "Now, Master Cyril, don't you eat that unripe pear, because it'll give you tummy ache." I bet you went ahead and ate it anyway, and denied you had tummy ache afterwards. Surely by now you've learned from your mistakes? Not everyone will roll over and play dead if you frown at them.'

'I don't make mistakes. However, I understand that you've made plenty in your time. You haven't kept a close enough eye on your toy boy. You do realize he's still playing around with other men's wives?'

She felt a shock run through her. Could it be true? No, no and no!

Or . . . could it? No. Piers wasn't like that. Yes, in the past he'd been promiscuous and she knew why and to a certain extent could understand and forgive. But he hadn't been like that for some considerable time. For years, if not months.

She didn't know what he'd been up to on his forays abroad, did she?

Oh, no! No. No! Surely not! She clutched at the edge of the table to steady herself. Suspicions whirled around in her head . . . and settled.

She took in a deep breath and let it out slowly. Even supposing Piers was still at it – and she was pretty sure, almost sure, that he wasn't – then it really didn't alter the situation between them. He loved her. He wanted to be back in her life.

And she? She loved him, and she wanted him back in her life.

She turned a radiant smile on Cyril Trescott. 'You are a clever man, but perhaps not quite clever enough to understand people like me and Piers. Perhaps you only see what you want to see? Perhaps that single-mindedness has made you what you are. I don't suppose you have ever trusted anyone long enough to get them to love you.'

Here she looked across at April, who was holding a glass of the rich red wine to Leon's mouth, and coaxing him to drink. April was acting on Cyril's instructions, to ensure that Leon was as putty in their hands. Bea averted her eyes. Leon was a lost soul. She couldn't help him. Or could she?

Bea spoke across the table to April, but made sure Leon and Cyril were listening. 'They tell me that poisoning is a woman's game. Leon, did you know that April uses drugs to control her niece? Don't you worry who she might target next? What she might put in your food?'

Cyril Trescott's voice rose. 'That's an actionable statement.' But his eyelids fluttered. He knew – or perhaps it was better to say that he guessed – Bea had spoken the truth. For the first time, she had pierced his armour.

She felt a moment of triumph. She said, 'That statement is not actionable if true. Mr Trescott, I don't think you murdered your brother—'

'What?' A deep flush rose up from his neck. 'WHAT!'

'No, I don't think you yourself would kill someone who stood in your way. But you might recall King Henry II who, having quarrelled with an old friend, said to the world at large, "Who will rid me of this pesky priest?" One of his trusty knights went forth and slew said pesky priest as he stood in front of the altar in the cathedral at Canterbury. Henry never laid a finger on the man but everyone knew he was responsible and he had to do penance for it.'

Now Cyril was coldly furious and containing his rage with some difficulty. 'You cannot possibly be accusing me of murder!'

'Certainly not,' Bea picked up her handbag and tried to rise.

He grabbed her arm again, forcing her back into her seat. He kept his voice low, but the words were spat out. 'Enough! I will give you twenty-four hours to persuade Piers to report for duty. In the meantime, I'm going to look into the Hollands' crazy notion of making Bernice your ward, because you are so clearly unfit for the job. The girl will be better prepared for her future in other hands, and I am going to set proceedings in motion to do just that. You understand?'

His grip on her arm was excruciating. She told herself to move and failed to do so. She knew she was in shock. What he was proposing was evil! Bernice, to be handed over for indoctrination to someone like the Trescotts?

God help me! I can't breathe! If he were to take Bernice away from me . . . I couldn't bear it! And when I think what he could do to her . . .!

He saw he'd knocked the breath out of her. He smiled and withdrew his hand. 'Now, sit down and drink your wine till I'm ready to leave.'

I've got to keep going. I'll think about what he said later. Keep going. Keep moving. I'm not going to pass out. No.

Somewhat shakily, she managed to get to her feet a second time. 'Forgive me, but I must go to the toilet. Something I've eaten, perhaps . . . Leon, April. Please excuse me. Which way is it to the ladies'? I'll have to enquire.'

It was one of the most ancient of excuses but it worked. Cyril Trescott moved aside to allow her to leave the table. She forced herself to walk slowly and carefully across the room to the reception desk, and then slipped out of the door and on to the pavement outside. Taxis slowed and stopped, delivering more diners to the restaurant. She took the first and gave directions to home. She was trembling. Angry. Disturbed. And yes, feeling rather unwell. She hadn't made that excuse up. She wasn't going to be sick. No. But, she felt disconnected from the world around her. She felt hot tears on her cheeks. She brushed them away.

She was being stupid. No, she wasn't. That man was threatening everything that she had and loved.

Dear Lord, help me. Keep Piers and Bernice safe. Tell me what to do.

Bea let herself quietly into the house, silenced the alarm, and set her back against the front door. There were sounds of merriment from the living room. The scent of cheese and tomato advertized that a meal of pizzas had been dealt with. Piers' voice rose in triumph over some point won in the game, followed by a yell of 'My turn!' from Bernice. A game of some sort was being played?

Bea reset the alarm on the front door. She brushed more tears from her face. She couldn't join the others and pretend nothing was wrong. As she passed the half open door to the living room she called out that she was back but rather tired and going straight up to bed. She pulled on the banister to help her up the stairs. There was a sour taste in her mouth. The taste of defeat.

She dropped her evening bag and fell face down on the bed. And lay there. Immobile.

She hadn't the strength to turn over, or to put the bedside light on.

There were no more tears. She stared into the future. It was a dark pit, filled with crashing noises and a seething tangle of snakes. It was more real than her bedroom. It horrified her. She couldn't look away.

She couldn't even pray.

Someone came up the stairs, treading lightly. She didn't want to see him. She didn't move when he spoke her name.

'Bea.' He sat on the bed and gathered her into his arms. She didn't respond. Couldn't respond.

He held her close. Gradually the image of the snake pit receded. She could hear his breathing. Feel his warmth. She could breathe properly again.

He said, 'Take your time.'

She counted her breaths. In and out. Longer breaths. His arms were strong. She felt secure in them, even though . . . no, what that man had said was not true. Piers did love her. She could feel it. She knew it. Had known it for a long time.

Her pride, her fear that he would betray her again, had caused her to keep him at arms' length. But now?

She relaxed in his arms and worked saliva into her mouth. 'When did you last have another woman?'

'Mmm? What? Dunno. Four years ago, maybe? No, five. I looked at her and thought of you, and it just didn't seem worth it. I always hoped that you would let me come back.'

She nodded, fractionally. She tried to lift her head to see his face. Failed. She said, 'Yes. All right. If you still want it. No, what I mean is I'll think about it. You'd be better off running for your life than hanging around me. Cyril Trescott is . . . he wants to . . .' She couldn't say it. She turned her head away from Piers and tried to free herself.

He let her go, moving her up the bed, packing pillows behind her back. 'I thought you were dining with Leon?'

'Cyril Trescott and April came, too. I left Leon with them.

I shouldn't have done. I should have torn him away from them, somehow, and brought him here. No, I should have taken him to a doctor to see what's wrong with him. But they wouldn't have let me, would they? And he didn't want to leave. He's sick. Being spoon-fed by April, who's in cahoots with her brother. They were billing and cooing . . . ugh! It's so unlike Leon! He might be dead tomorrow. I feel so guilty, but what could I have done?'

She knew she wasn't making sense. She tried to push her brain back into gear.

Piers said, 'Cyril Trescott. The Silver Fox? He was there as well? What did he want?'

'To get me to toe the line. To make you paint his portrait. He's the great big wolf, and I'm the granny who gets gobbled up. Bernice is Little Red Riding Hood. He's going to take her away from me. I'm an unfit person to be her guardian. And you . . .? He thinks that yes, you'll come to heel, too, because everyone always does.'

He stroked her face. 'I'd paint him for you, but . . . no. That wouldn't work. Even if the urge to paint took over and I managed something halfway decent, I wouldn't do it. Because if he got to you by threatening me, then he'd do it again. You say he's threatened to take Bernice away from you? Hmm, he's got a nerve.'

She found a tissue and blew her nose. Wiped her eyes. 'I won't give in. I'm not letting Bernice go. Suppose she ended up as the ward of the Trescotts or their like? Heaven forbid! I do understand that if they bankroll high-flying lawyers and it goes to High Court, I'd be hard pushed to it to come up with an equal amount of cash. I can't compete with Trescott money. But I'll go down fighting, even if I have to sell the house and move out to the sticks and start up again there. If I can only keep her with me till she's sixteen or seventeen and on her way to uni, she'll have a fair chance of growing up straight and true. I wonder how much I could mortgage the house for? And I could sell the car. I hardly use it anyway. And the mews property. That might do it.'

Piers kissed her nose. 'I love it when you turn to fisticuffs. Count me in. I'm fond of the Brat, as you know. I'd hate to see her turned into another Evie.'

'What was that?' Bernice was standing in the doorway. 'I'm not turning into anybody but myself. Is that what Leon said? That I've got to go and live with the Trescotts? Fat chance!'

Bea reached out to the girl, who came and sat beside her on the bed. Piers laid his hand on Bernice's shoulder, and she didn't throw him off.

Father, mother, child. Not by birth, but through love.

Bea tried to explain. 'When I arrived at the restaurant Leon was already there with April Trescott hanging on to his arm. Leon's acting like Evie did when she first came here. Doped to the gills. I wonder if the Trescotts have somehow managed to get him on to the same drug? He's not an epileptic. He's never suffered from nerves. But now . . . he's not himself. She was all over him, and he was letting her pet him. Ugh! Horrible!'

Bernice said, 'Uncle Leon's never ill.'

Bea shuddered. 'She gives me the creeps. She's got her claws into Leon, and I'm so afraid of what she might do to him. I'm wondering if Trescotts aren't just interested in a merger with Hollands but are aiming for a takeover. If Leon falls victim to them, then that might well happen. Bernice, you are vulnerable because without Leon standing up for me, Cyril might well have you removed from my guardianship. I'll fight it, but . . .'

'I will fight beside you,' said Piers. 'Don't forget the foot soldiers.'

'Me, too,' said Bernice. 'I know I've been lucky to have landed up with you. Two fingers to the Trescotts. I'm not going to be handed around like a parcel.'

Bea managed a smile. 'Of course we'll fight them off. But meanwhile, oh, I realize I may be taking things too far, but I'd advise you two not to eat or drink anything offered you by them.'

'Ah-ha!' said Piers. 'So that's what that was all about.'

'What!'

'The chocolate, you mean?' said Bernice. 'Naturally, I refused to accept it. No great hardship. I don't eat much chocolate and I didn't want it hanging around in case Evie were tempted.'

Piers explained. 'It was while you were out, Bea. I was expecting the pizzas I'd ordered and instead the Trescotts' chauffeur arrived with an enormous box of chocolates for Bernice from Benjy with an orchid and a card—'

Bernice grinned. 'The card said I was bringing new interest into his life or something else equally ridiculous. Honestly, what a nerve! As if I'd accept anything from horrible Benjy. I told the chauffeur to take the stuff away and he said he couldn't do that, so I tore up the card and told him to take the orchid and the chocolates to the nearest refuge for battered women, and he went all pop-eyed on me. We watched him from behind the curtains in the front window because he didn't go back to the car but got on his phone. We suppose he was reporting back to Benjy. Then he took the orchid and the chocolates away with him.'

Bea said, 'A pity, in a way. If he'd left them, we might have had them tested to see if they contained some noxious substance.'

Bernice frowned. 'You think they were poisoned?'

Bea pulled herself more upright in bed. 'I'm looking at what has happened to Evie and what is now happening to Leon. Evie was sick with grief, and the aunt says that Leon has had some sort of medical problem. She doses them both and they start behaving like zombies. It's no great stretch of the imagination to think that they were given medication which rendered them helpless. Suppose, Bernice, you went down with a minor indisposition. Leon, acting under April's influence, might suggest you see the Trescotts' pet doctor, and you might be given something which removes the will to live.'

'I wouldn't take it!' Bernice did her frown thing. 'They'd have to force me. I know what I'm doing.'

Silence.

Bea said, 'If they could manage it so that your behaviour got out of control and you were sectioned, then you wouldn't have a choice in the matter. Evie didn't have a choice, did she?'

Bernice blinked rapidly. 'Evie's been off the pills for a while. Just now, when we were playing Monopoly, she was so sharp she almost had me a couple of times.'

Piers said, 'It's true, Bea. I thought playing Monopoly might give Evie a chance to show if her brain was working again, and it did. She was calculating the odds faster than I could, and almost as fast as Bernice.'

There was a tap on the door and Evie floated in. 'Talking about me?' She was wearing her new party dress and silver shoes. She held the skirt out and did a twirl. 'Have you a full-length mirror? Bernice hasn't, and I want to see myself. I feel like a new person in this dress. Isn't it lovely? And tomorrow I can have my hair done, can't I? And my nails? I've never been to a beauty salon or visited a hairdresser. What sort of tip should I give? Do you think I should have a pedicure as well?'

Bernice said, 'Drop that, Evie! This is serious. We know you're not really that stupid now you're off the drugs. We know you're feeding information back to Auntie, telling her everything we're doing, and it's got to stop.'

Evie stopped swaying about in front of the mirror. Suddenly she looked older and yes, sharper. 'You're only being nasty to me because I said Benjy loved me first.'

Bea drew in a deep breath. What was going on here?

Had Benjy really gone after Evie first? And then given way to Joshua?

Piers got off the bed. 'Evie, you've had a rough time. We all recognize that. But trying to hurt Bernice doesn't help.'

Bernice snorted. 'You think Benjy's trying to make you jealous by giving me things? No. Why would he bother? That's ridiculous.'

Evie's head went down, and her shoulders fell forward. Her hair fell over her face. 'I know. I'm sorry. I shouldn't have said that. You've been so kind to me.'

Piers led Evie over to the dressing table and made her sit down. 'You're confused and it's no wonder. Evie, look at me. That's better. There's a conflict of interest here. Your uncle Cyril is making things difficult for us and we're having a hard time working out what to do.'

Evie nodded. 'Yes, he wants you to paint him. Then later on, you'll paint me and Joshua. I don't see what's wrong with that.'

'I arranged to have the school holidays off, that's what.'

'Well, that's not so very important, is it?'

'Maybe not to you or to him, but I've worked non-stop since Christmas, I'd arranged to take a break and I'm not altering my plans for him or anyone else. That's annoyed him and he's made various threats to make me change my mind. Now, it's

understandable that you want to please your family. I know
they want you to stay here till the party, but I'm not changing
my mind about painting him, and if this is going to make things
uncomfortable for you, then perhaps you can think of somewhere
else you can go for a while?'

'You're throwing me out.' In a monotone.

'No. We wouldn't do that. Look, perhaps you should talk to
your aunt about this. She can't realize what a difficult position
you've been put in. She is your guardian, isn't she?'

'No. It's my uncle Constant who was my guardian. I don't
know who it is now he's dead.' Again, no signs of emotion.

There was silence while they all thought about that. Bea
wondered if Constant had made a will. He would have made
provision for Evie, wouldn't he? Or would he? His death had
been unexpected, so he might not have considered who should
take responsibility for Evie in the event of his dying before she
was eighteen.

Evie threw back her hair and straightened up. 'It's much
easier to take the pills and not to have to think. Thinking hurts,
here.' She held on to her head with both hands as if it might
fly off into the blue. 'I've been trying not to think for ages.
Sometimes I fear I'm going mad. They say this or that and I
say, "Yes, sir; no, sir. Three bags full, sir." It's easier to go
along with whatever they say, than to think about disobeying.
Naughty girls are taken back to the clinic where they have to
learn to behave themselves before they can be trusted enough
to go back home. Or to school. And after all, they do have my
best interests at heart, and I might really be ill and need the
pills. Only, as time went on and I didn't have any attacks, or
any attacks that I could remember, I began to wonder if I really
did have epilepsy . . . only thinking like that hurts. It really,
really hurts.'

Bernice looked shocked. Piers and Bea exchanged looks. So
was Evie really epileptic? Or was that the way they'd been
controlling a girl who would eventually come into a lot of
money?

Evie twisted a fold of her skirt and went on. 'Every now and
then I used to wonder what would happen if I stopped taking
the pills. I mean, if I had a fit, then yes; I was epileptic and I

must accept it. Only I was scared to try it. I knew the family would always look after me, no matter how ill I was. Just lately it occurred to me that perhaps I'd grown out of it and could do without so many pills. I told them so, and they were furious. I had to go back to the clinic and they gave me some new pills which I think were stronger than ever.

'Then one day I couldn't manage even the smallest sum in arithmetic, something I'd always been able to do off the top of my head. So I told Uncle Constant that I was worried about falling behind in my schoolwork. I said Daddy would have been so disappointed if he'd known. So Auntie arranged for me to go to the boarding school where I'm at now and because I had to have someone responsible to sleep in the same room, they arranged to give me Bernice as a roommate. And she's so alive! It made me realize how dopey I'd got. And I watched her, and wondered what would happen if . . . I didn't know if I could trust her, you see.

'I couldn't stop taking the pills at school very easily because the nurse used to give them to me twice a day. Sometimes I thought I could ask Bernice to help me, and sometimes I could see she was bored with me hanging around her and would have laughed if I'd asked her to cover for me. I could see she wasn't frightened of anyone at school, not even those girls who tried to bully the others. So that made me a bit braver. Now and then I faked taking the pills at night-time. I put them in my cheek and pretended to swallow them and the nurse didn't notice. I thought I'd get withdrawal symptoms but I didn't.

'I began to feel a bit more alive. I thought that one day I'd tell Bernice what was happening and ask her to help me. Then term ended and we were collected from school. Bernice even stood up to Auntie on the way back here! She didn't let her get her down, even then. So I left her a message and oh, I hoped and prayed that she'd understand, and she did, didn't she?'

Bernice looked at Bea, her eyes wide. Bernice was way out of her depth.

Piers said, 'I found your message and took it to Bea. We didn't know what to make of it.'

'I know,' said Evie. 'It was feeble of me, wasn't it? But then there was the most tremendous piece of luck. Well, not lucky for him. Uncle Constant died and Auntie sent me back here. I stopped taking the pills completely and nothing's happened. I know it's only been a couple of days, but I haven't had a fit, have I?'

'No, you haven't.' Bea was soothing. 'But Evie, how can we judge your medical condition?'

'Can you take me to a specialist? Let me take some tests? I mean, if I am ill then I'll accept it, but . . . please!'

Bea said, 'Oh, my dear! We can't do that. You're underage and . . . No, we can't!'

'Yes, you can, Bea,' said Piers. 'If Evie shows signs of a reaction to her medication, or if she has an accident or falls sick or whatever. April has given you the right to care for Evie while the girl is under your roof. At least, I think that's right. We can check the legal position tomorrow.'

Evie gulped air. 'If you won't help me, what am I going to do?'

ELEVEN

Monday, late evening

Bea said, 'I didn't say I wouldn't help you. Piers is right. We need to check the legal position.'

Bernice said, 'I promise we'll think of something.' She turned Evie round and led her out of the door and up the stairs. The door closed behind her.

Bea said, 'Bernice shouldn't make promises. She hasn't a clue what she's up against!'

Piers took his phone out of his pocket and read a text. He didn't seem to like what he saw. 'I'm ordered to be ready for collection at half eight tomorrow morning, when I'll be taken to the Trescotts to start work at nine. I think not!' He busied himself sending a reply.

Bea got off the bed and sat at the dressing table to take

off her jewellery and make-up. 'What are you telling them?'

'I'm texting that I'm leaving tonight for a vacation in Florida. Back in four weeks' time.'

'Evie will tell him otherwise.'

'Maybe. Maybe not. We need a council of war. A list of people to contact. Your solicitor's pretty good, isn't he? We need to fend off any attempt to remove Beatrice from your guardianship. Also, how do we rescue Leon? Who else do we know on the Holland board of directors? Surely they ought to know what's happening to the man? And can we work out what action Cyril is going to take next? We'll have to think up something soon or those two girls will do something silly and end up in worse trouble than they started.'

'I'm too tired to think.' She reached for the zip at the back of her dress, but Piers got there before her, and pulled it down. Slowly and with care. He kissed her bare shoulder. 'I'll put the cat out, make sure the grandfather clock's been wound up, the front door is bolted and the alarm on.'

She didn't have a grandfather clock and Winston would take care of himself but she was happy to leave shutting up the house to him. She took her time in the shower, and heard Piers use the one in the guest room. The girls were moving around on the top floor, calling out to one another. Also using the shower. They weren't planning to run away together, were they? No, of course not. Bea told herself she was overtired and imagining things.

She put on another of her best silk nightdresses. She wasn't quite sure why. Probably because it made her feel good.

When she emerged from her bathroom she found Piers sitting up in her bed wearing his new reading glasses and nothing else. He was tapping away at his laptop. She didn't know how to act. She thought of sweeping off to the guest room in a fit of high dudgeon . . . if only she could remember what 'dudgeon' meant. She thought of how comfortable it would be to slide in beside him, and have a cuddle.

She thought of the wound he'd dealt her so long ago and it was like being stabbed in her heart all over again.

He shut down his laptop and took off his glasses. 'You need a fighting fund. I can transfer you twenty thousand pounds straight away, if you'll give me your bank details. It will take a few days to get more. Just let me know how much you'd like.'

She blinked. 'You have that much to spare?'

'Small change. Most of my money is tied up in this and that but can be accessed as and when I need it. What do I need money for? I make Max and the grandkids an allowance. I pay my bills on time. I still earn more than I spend.' He set the laptop aside. 'I have this dream of being a white knight, riding to your rescue, saying something like, *Here's your enemy's head on a charger* . . . not that I'm absolutely sure what a charger is. It's not a horse, is it?'

'It's a kind of serving platter, I think. Piers, I'm not ready for you to come to my bed yet. There's too much going on. I can't think straight.'

He sighed and got out of bed. No, he wasn't wearing pyjamas. And he was ready for her.

Her body responded. She felt both shaken and stirred.

He said, 'I am your obedient servant, ma'am. But give me some hope. We'll make it legal as soon as possible. Right?'

She blushed and hated herself for doing so. She lifted the duvet and got in on her side. 'Possibly. Probably. But if you let me down again, I'll carve you into little pieces and throw them out into the garden for the birds to eat.'

'And I'll hand you the knife. Only, as I remember, your carving skills are not up to much. Perhaps I'd better buy you an electric carving knife. That should do the trick.' He held on for a count of five, but she made no move towards him, so he collected his laptop and glasses and left, turning out the centre light as he did so.

She was not going to cry. No. So many years had passed since they were last in bed together, and yet she remembered how sweet it had been. For two pins, she'd call him back.

No, not yet. A few more days wouldn't hurt.

We're turning into an old married couple. Darby and Joan. Tomorrow I must ring round and find out . . . Dear Lord, how good it was to lie with a man you loved and who loved you! My darling Hamilton, my loving second husband, I miss you so much. You put me back together again when

Piers betrayed me. If only . . . but there, we can't go back
in time, can we?

*Please, Lord: will you look after that poor child Evie . . .
and keep Bernice safe . . . and me. And Piers.*

*What will Cyril say when he hears Piers said he was going
to Florida? And what will he do when he finds out it's a lie?
Oh dear. I feel like laughing and I feel like crying and I don't
know which to do . . . so I'll do either.*

*Tomorrow . . . busy day . . . I have to learn how to forgive
Piers.*

Tuesday morning

Bea got up early and had a sketchy breakfast while making a
list of what she had to do.

Piers was nowhere to be seen and neither were the girls, but
Winston arrived, demanding attention on finding her alone and
at his mercy. Only, as soon as he heard someone opening
and shutting doors at the top of the house, he gave Bea a look
of reproach and vanished through the cat flap. He didn't usually
take against people, but it seemed that Evie was not on his
visiting list.

Bea waited to see if anyone else wanted breakfast at that
early hour but when no one appeared, she went down the stairs
into the agency rooms to switch on the lights and open the
office. There was still half an hour before any of her staff might
be expected to arrive, and she had a lot to do. She spread out
the list she'd made while having her coffee and got on with
it. Some of the people she couldn't contact till later in the
morning, but there was one particular person she needed to
contact immediately. If only he weren't out of the country or
on another job . . .

Staff trickled in to start the day and Bea worked on, putting
some people in the know, asking for help, sometimes giving
instructions, sometimes cajoling. She hadn't finished before
there was a clatter and Evie came tumbling down the stairs.
She was laughing but not as if she were amused. 'Can you
come, please, Mrs Abbot? It's Bernice. She's . . . oh, she's
mad!'

Bea abandoned her phone with a quick 'I'll call you back', and hurried through the office and up the stairs. In the living room she found a competent-looking, middle-aged woman with fashionably silver hair, dressed in expensive black. Botoxed, face-lifted, toned by hours in the gym. From the sour expression on her face, it looked as if something had disagreed with her.

Bernice, frozen-faced, had backed up against the big table in the window, her attitude indicating that she'd hit someone if they said the wrong word.

'Are you Mrs Abbot?' said the stranger, proffering her hand to shake. 'I'm Celia from Crystal's Model Agency. You've heard of us, I'm sure. You're her mother or guardian, aren't you? Thank goodness you've come. Perhaps you can talk some sense into the girl.'

Bernice was so stiff it looked as if she were vibrating. Her eyes were huge.

Piers came in from the kitchen. 'What's going on?'

Bea looked a question at the newcomer. 'Crystal's Model Agency? For fashion models? What have they got to do with us?'

Evie was bouncing up and down, flushed with a combination of pleasure and envy. 'They're offering Bernice a session with a top photographer and a six-month contract! Can you believe it? I'd give my eye teeth to be considered by them! The money! The places she'll go to! The people she'll meet!'

Bea didn't get it. 'What? But . . .! How on earth—?'

Celia pulled a file from a business bag and held it up. 'The pictures she sent in. Amateurish, of course, but they convinced us she had what it takes. What bone structure! What colouring! What a figure! She's just perfect! True, her eyebrows need attention, but she has that certain something we're always looking for and rarely find. We've booked her a first session with our photographer in an hour's time. That's for her portfolio, you understand. So, if you'll just glance over the paperwork . . . we'll need your signature, of course, as she's still a minor.'

Bernice almost spat. 'I didn't send you any pictures!'

Celia shook her head. 'Naughty, naughty! We know you dropped them by the agency the other day. I suppose you didn't tell Mrs Abbot in case nothing happened, but there . . . your secret's out now.'

'I didn't.' This seemed to be all Bernice could say. Her body was still rigid.

Bea tried to understand what was happening. If Bernice said she hadn't done something, then she hadn't.

Bea took the folder proffered by Celia and looked through a series of A4 size photos. Amateurish, yes. But they showed an elegant young girl with a shining mop of hair, clear skin and violet eyes in the act of dressing, looking out of a window, reading, taking a leap in the air . . . and then she was showing off her brand-new party dress and trying on shoes in a shop. At lunch with Evie. And lastly there was a delightful one of her asleep in bed.

The camera loved Bernice.

Bea said, 'This is a scam. No reputable agency will employ a girl who is under eighteen nowadays.'

Celia smiled widely. 'Oh, come now. She's nearly fifteen and looks older. She can easily pass for seventeen and who's going to ask when she looks like that on camera?'

Piers came up behind Bea. 'Her guardian would never agree.' He took the folder off Bea and riffled through the contents. He said, 'Most of these were taken at school. See, the clothes, the backgrounds. The next ones were taken when she was trying on the party dress in the boutique. The last few were taken by a different photographer when you were all having lunch together.'

'Yes,' said Bea. 'I see.' She went to Bernice and put her arms about her. 'There, there.'

The girl shuddered. 'Evie betrayed me.'

'Yes,' said Bea. 'How very sad. I suspect her family leant on her to provide them with the photos.' And she looked at Evie.

Evie was sullen. 'What if they did? It was just a spot of fun. They wanted to know if Bernice really was like her portrait, and I said I'd send them some pictures, because I've always got my smartphone with me, and they liked them and said they wanted some more, and then . . . and then . . .'

'And then,' said Piers, 'you told them where you'd be out

shopping, and they had someone come and take candid pictures of you when you were at lunch afterwards. You couldn't have taken those because they've caught you in the shots as well. You might not have known what they intended to do with the photos at first, but you knew what was going to happen when this woman arrived from the agency, right?'

'So?' Evie sulked. 'I don't know what all the fuss is about. Bernice ought to be pleased. Anyone else would be over the moon. She can be famous, and travel all over the world, and make a mint of money and never have to go back to school.'

Bernice laid her head on Bea's shoulder. She was trembling, but not as badly as before. Bea stroked the girl's sleek head. 'Hush, hush.'

Celia consulted the monster of a watch on her wrist. 'I hate to rush you, but the photographer won't wait beyond the time he's booked for, and we have to get the releases signed. So if we could just sit down and—'

Bernice murmured something. Bea bent her head to listen. 'What was that?'

'Tell her to go. That woman. And her. Evie, too.'

Bea looked at Celia. 'My ward is distressed. She feels her privacy has been violated. It was not her idea to put herself forward for a modelling career. I don't know whose idea it was but it wasn't hers. You knew how old she was, but you thought we would be tempted by the prospect of fame and fortune to ignore the rules. I wonder: have you really booked a session with a photographer, or are you planning to take her somewhere isolated, where she can be approached by a man who likes young girls? No?'

'How dare you!' The woman became icy. 'Of course this is a genuine offer! Don't you realize how many girls apply for a contract with us, and how few are selected? I understand my visit has come as something of a surprise, but when the girl has calmed down I'm sure she'll want to go through with it.'

Bernice shook her head and clung to Bea.

Celia said, 'What a stupid girl she is! But you, Mrs Abbot, as her guardian, must be able to appreciate what a rare opportunity this is for her.'

'I understand,' said Bea, 'that if I signed a release saying she was seventeen or eighteen, I'd be joining you in breaking the law. I am tasked with looking after Bernice's best interests and I'm not going to play your game.'

'Listen to me! She's a one-off. I know quality when I see it, and I don't see it often. Yes, we'd have to fudge her age, but I tell you that this girl's face will be on the cover of the world's most famous magazines. She will be on the A-list for parties, will be showered with couture garments to wear, the richest men will vie for her company. And you want to refuse her such a wonderful life?'

Bernice nodded. She didn't want anything to do with it.

'That's enough,' said Bea. 'Please, just go.'

Celia flushed with anger. 'I'm giving you one last chance to change your mind. You can't expect the agency to keep the offer open when so many others are pleading for attention. If I leave now, you can forget the whole thing. Now, let's hear it from the girl herself. She has a tongue, doesn't she?'

Bernice didn't react. She might not even have heard what Celia had said. Only her light, rapid breathing showed she was alive.

Celia said, 'Come on, girl! You can't be that stupid! Speak up for yourself. Are you really going to turn down this chance of a lifetime?'

Bernice lifted her head to look up at Bea. 'If she won't go, then I will.' She released herself and walked out of the room with her head held high.

Celia laughed, a sharp bark with no humour in it. 'I see how it is. She's playing for a better contract. Well, that won't wash. We're offering her the best she can hope for at this stage.'

Piers tore the photos of Bernice out of the folder. 'I suppose you have the originals. Our solicitors will be writing to your agency, asking that any photos of Bernice they have be destroyed, as they were taken without her consent.'

'And who are you, may I ask?'

Bea said, 'A friend of the family. For the umpteenth time, I'm asking you to leave.'

Celia turned on Bea. 'If you let that child get away with her tantrums, if you don't make her see sense and accept our terms, in a few days' time she's going to regret turning us down, and she's going to hate you forever.'

Bea said, 'I think I know who has put you up to this. Does the name "Trescott" mean anything to you?'

Celia's eyelids fluttered, but she set her lips in a firm line. She was not going to reply. She stuffed the empty folder back into her bag. 'I have no idea who thought the girl worthy of attention. I'm not on the board. I'm a talent scout, that's all.' And that was a lie. She knew of the name 'Trescott' even if she hadn't had face-to-face contact with them.

So the Trescotts had been behind this latest ploy.

Piers held the door open. 'Let me show you out.'

Evie collapsed on the settee, wailing, 'Oh, oh! It's all gone wrong!'

Bea rolled her eyes and went after Bernice, whom she found sitting on the garden bench in the garden below with Winston, the cat, in her arms. Winston was perfectly happy to be petted and stroked for a short while, so long as there was the prospect of food at the end of it.

The sun was full on the garden, mayflies hovered over the lily pond, pink and white geraniums spilled over the huge stone pots on the terrace, sweet peas climbed a trellis by the high, red-brick wall that enclosed this private space, and birds fought over the feeders at the end of the garden.

Bernice made room for Bea to sit beside her. Winston yawned, blinked at Bea and, knowing she was his most faithful provider, put out his paw to her while retaining his position on Bernice's lap.

Bea said, 'Piers is seeing Celia out. Evie is in tears.'

Bernice sighed. Bea was struck by the way the girl was growing up. The fine bones of her face were becoming more pronounced. Yes, she might well consider plucking her rather heavy eyebrows, but she was beginning to show the promise of the poised, elegant woman she would become.

Bea said, 'About Evie. Shall I tell the Trescotts to come and collect her? That we can't look after her any longer?'

Bernice went on stroking Winston, who decided that enough was enough. The birds twittering in the tree at the bottom of the garden were making inroads into his territory, and they needed to be aware that there was a cat on guard. He freed himself from Bernice with a leap, and shot up the trunk of the tree to send the birds flying.

Bernice relaxed, limb by limb. She sighed deeply, leaning back and closing her eyes. The sun was warm. A bee hummed, investigating a stand of lilies in the bed under the wall. 'I don't get it. What are they after? Why have they set Evie to watch what I do and report back? Why did they think I'd go along with it? I mean . . . ugh! Those pictures of me! Even when I'm asleep. How could she!'

'I assume she was under orders. You weren't tempted to take up a modelling career? Not even for a moment?'

Bernice shivered. 'At first I thought, "Wow"! Then I thought what a stupid way it was to spend your time, dressing up like a doll and not using your brain at all. That's not what I want out of life. You think the Trescotts arranged it? I don't understand why they'd think I'd go for it. First the puppy, then chocolate and an orchid and now this. Why are they getting at me?'

What could Bea say? She couldn't frighten Bernice with the notion that this was all a plot by Benjy to get her alone with him. Bea wasn't even sure that that was the motive behind his courtship – if you could call it that.

She said, 'You may be collateral damage. The Trescotts are talking to Leon about a merger. You will inherit voting shares. At the moment I hold them in trust for you. In the past Leon has always sent me a proxy form so that he can vote your shares as he thinks fit. That's presumably what will happen when the matter of the merger comes before the board. Because I control those shares on your behalf, I can see why there'd be a charm offensive to make sure those votes go the way they want.'

Bernice saw the flaw in that argument. 'They're targeting me, not you. If Evie were spying on you it would be a different matter. But it's me she's after, isn't it?'

Piers came down the steps to join them. 'Evie's gone up to her room in floods of tears, and with her phone jammed to her ear. No doubt to report on the failure of their plan B, or is it plan C? I lose track. Are you all right, Brat?'

Bernice nodded. She moved closer to Bea, so as to let him sit beside them.

Bea said, 'Let's recap what we know. If I'm right, there are several players in this game, each working on a different agenda. In the first place – and the most straightforward and easiest to understand – there is the desire by Cyril Trescott that nothing should stand in the way of the merger between the two firms. That's why he's pushing for closer relationships with us through the offers to Piers, the dinner in town and the invitations to us and to Max for the party at the weekend. His tactic is straightforward. When flattery doesn't work, he tries bribery and when that fails, he makes threats to remove me from Bernice's guardianship. Oh, and he thinks it would be amusing to be painted by Piers . . . but that's only one piece of an intricate puzzle.

'The next piece concerns Evie, whose future and considerable fortune is at stake. As far as I can make out, in her grief after her parents died she became ill, was diagnosed as an epileptic and put on some strong pills which make her sleepy. Bernice hasn't seen any signs of that illness and nor have I. Evie may well have grown out of a tendency in that direction. Now she's off the pills, she seems normal enough to me. Quite bright in some directions if not in others. Her aunt was perhaps overprotective in pushing her into an early marriage, and her Uncle Constant didn't care enough to interfere . . . well, that's all very understandable in its way.

'But then we got dragged in to look after her. Why? Well, what do we know for certain? Evie found her uncle dead in bed whereupon April drugged the child stupid and dumped her on us, saying it was important to get her out of the house so that the police wouldn't question her. April hinted that the girl bore some responsibility for her uncle's decease, although I can't think why. Can you think of any reason why Evie should have wanted her uncle to die? I can't.'

Piers and Bernice both shook their heads. They couldn't think why, either.

Bea went on. 'I would really like to know exactly how Uncle Constant come to die. We're told there was to be an autopsy. The aunt seems to think the verdict will be that he took an accidental overdose. If that is proved to be the case, I suppose we don't need to worry about it. But was he helped along the road to death? Did Evie have anything to do with his death? If she did, she is guilty of murder. If she knows that someone else was involved but doesn't speak up, then she's an accessory after the fact.'

Piers looked grim. 'You think that someone else in that family had a hand in the man's death? Not Evie. But you think she's a useful scapegoat? You think that they want to keep her sedated until she can't think for herself. That's "gaslighting". The victim is made to believe they are going mad.'

Bernice said, 'That's ridiculous! You can't make people believe any such a thing.'

Bea said, 'There's precedents for it. Especially if the victim is doped to the eyeballs and everyone keeps telling them they need to be careful or they'll be ill again and have to be sent back to the clinic. I'm ready to entertain the idea that this is what's happening. Evie's an heiress, due to come into a great deal of money in two years' time. They keep her in fear of what she might do. They tell her they'll always look after her. They control her every move. They—'

Piers completed the thought. 'With her guardian's consent, at sixteen she can get married. And that's what they've planned to happen, isn't it? She's being paired off with Joshua to keep the money in the family.'

'It looks to me,' said Bea, 'as if April is behind that scheme, which provides nicely for her eldest son's future. Let's move on to another part of the puzzle. Evie has been photographing Bernice and sending the pictures on to someone in the family. Evie has also been keeping that same person informed of our movements. I have to ask myself who would want the pictures and why?'

Piers said, 'I don't like the answer to that question.'

Bernice stared. 'I don't understand.'

Bea said, 'You're too closely involved to see it, Bernice. Let's compare what you and Evie have in common. You are both underage. You are both heiresses. And practically speaking you are both orphans in someone else's care. We are told that Evie is going to receive a proposal of marriage from her cousin Joshua at her birthday bash this weekend. She seems to take this as a matter of course. We're also told that Joshua has ambitions to go into parliament and eventually become prime minister. I'm not sure she'd be much good as the wife of an MP, or that he has the calibre to make it that far, but her money will undoubtedly help him climb the political ladder. So far, so good. Right?'

Bernice frowned. 'She says Benjy was her first boyfriend but went off her for some reason. She doesn't seem to me to be madly in love with Joshua, but what do I know?'

'Ah,' said Bea. 'Now we come to it. Benjy. The younger brother, ambitious and with a sense of entitlement. He aims to take over Trescotts. Possibly he will be able to do so in due course, but not yet because his uncle Cyril, the Silver Fox, is firmly in control at the moment. Benjy also needs money. I think he was looking around for another heiress when the Trescotts visited the Royal Academy and learned that Leon had a young great-niece who would inherit a goodly sum one day. The possibility of a merger with Hollands sharpened the Trescotts' interest in Bernice. At that point in time they had to find a better school for Evie, and it was a neat solution to their problem to send her to the same place as Bernice, and to suggest the pair might room together.'

'You're joking!' Bernice flushed.

'No, I'm not. One of the people I spoke to this morning was your headmistress, whom I was lucky enough to catch just before she flew off for her summer holiday. She confirmed that Mrs Trescott had approached her suggesting you were paired off with Evie because, she said, there was going to be a closer relationship between the two families. And, a clincher: it was April who suggested giving you a lift back here when she collected Evie at the end of term.'

Bernice rolled her shoulders. 'I feel like I've been used. I thought I was looking after her, and all the time she was spying on me and reporting to her horrible family? Ugh!'

'Exactly,' said Bea. 'Then young Benjy came to call with his brother one day. Why? Because they were passing and wanted to see their cousin? No. I think it was because he'd seen your portrait and was intrigued. To make sure he wasn't mistaken in his assessment, he asked Evie to send him photos of you. And what he saw, he liked very much indeed.'

Bernice flushed. 'I'm too young for all that.'

Piers sighed. 'I think he likes girls young. Remember, Evie said he was her boyfriend before Joshua took up with her.'

'That's sick.' Bernice lifted her shoulders to her ears. 'It makes me want to puke.'

Piers said, 'You're an attractive package, Bernice. Money, brains and looks. I know you've not had to think about this before, but Benjy's right in some respects: some girls of your age – and boys, too – think of nothing but sex.'

'Well, I don't. And I don't want to, either.'

'Agreed,' said Bea. 'Now so far Benjy has followed the family's usual method of dealing with their inferiors. He's tried charm. Then he tried tempting you to leave the straight and narrow in various ways. I must admit he is creative in his ideas. But next—'

'He'll move on to blackmail, if he can find a lever. And then, force,' said Piers.

'So,' said Bea, 'we have to take precautions.'

Bernice straightened her shoulders. 'The first thing to do is to get rid of Evie. I never want to see her again. Get her out of my sight or . . . or I'll do her an injury.'

TWELVE

Tuesday morning, continued

'Hold hard,' said Bea. 'I'd like to rescue the girl if I can.'

'After what she's done to me? Spying on me, telling tales and helping that . . . that turd Benjy to spy on me when we were having lunch together? I can't forgive that.'

Piers said, to no one in particular, 'Forgiveness comes with understanding. And remorse. And courage to look into the future and not back at the past.'

There was a long silence while Bea and Bernice thought about what he'd said. Bea knew he was reminding her that he was hoping she'd forgive him. There had been remorse on his side. She did miss him. Yes, she still loved him. She'd held back from forgiving him from a mixture of pride and mistrust.

Bernice would find it hard to forgive what Evie had done to her, too.

Bearing grudges hardened the arteries of the heart.

Forgiveness required courage. Did Bea have enough courage to forgive Piers and let him back into her life?

Bea avoided that subject by tackling something else that was bothering her. 'By the way, Bernice, has Evie learned the code for our alarm system?'

Bernice started from her seat. 'Oh! Oh! The sly cow! Yes. She said hers at home was her birthday and did you use mine and I told her! I told her!' She raised her fists in the air. 'Oh, I could kill her!'

Bea was amused. 'Don't beat yourself up. The child's not up to your weight. You are strong and have mental resources which she lacks. Think of it this way, that she's more sinned against than sinning. Think what it must be like to wonder every hour of the day if you are going to have another fit and do something silly that you don't remember afterwards. Think what it must be like to remember that your father used to say you were his little calculator, but that now you find the simplest sums beyond you. Think what it must be like to look in the mirror and see an overweight, unattractive lump looking back at you.'

'Well, yes. But.'

'Her family have trained her to accept the future they've laid out for her. But, as soon as she was paired off with you, she started to think for herself again. She began to cut down the number of pills she was taking. She reached out to you for help – rather ineffectively, I agree – but she did do so. Yes, she did go along with Benjy's idea of putting you under an obligation to him, but she did genuinely think you'd be pleased with the gift of the puppy and the prospect of a modelling career.'

'She wasn't thinking straight.'

'Agreed. But let's look what will happen to her if we chuck her back into the tender embraces of the Awful Aunt. She'll be dosed into imbecility, criticized till she thinks she's a worthless lump, and sold in marriage to Joshua . . . because that's what's going to happen, isn't it, if we don't interfere?'

'I don't see how we can interfere.'

'We can take precautions.'

Piers said, 'Bea, you know very well what to do. Divide and rule. Oh, and keep an eye out for boarders.'

Evie came down the outside stairs into the garden, looking washed out and lumpy. She'd been crying, and her hands were trembling as she held up her smartphone. 'I know what you must think of me. I know how it must look. But I didn't know what to do. I thought I could please my aunt and Benjy but it's all gone wrong, and they're furious with me. I didn't think . . . it's always best to do what they say. I didn't think Bernice would react that way. I'm so sorry. Please, help me!'

'You're a feeble-minded cretin,' said Bernice. 'Why should we lift a finger to help you?'

'Because . . . because I don't know what to do. Benjy's so angry. He frightens me. He says that if I don't . . .' She swallowed. 'He wants me to tell him everything you're doing, and everywhere you're going. I've got a bad feeling that . . . I don't want him to hurt you.'

'He won't,' said Bea, crossing her fingers.

Evie held up her phone. 'He says he's going to ring me every hour, on the hour, and I've got to be ready to give him the information he wants. What am I to do?'

Bernice sighed deeply. 'Where were you brung up? In a cave? I thought everyone knew what to do if they needed to lose their phone. Put it in your back pocket, go to the loo, and accidentally let it drop into the water. Phones don't work after they've been dunked in water.'

Evie's eyes were huge. 'But when he doesn't get through he'll think something's happened to me and will ring here.'

'No, he won't. I'll ring them on our landline and tell whoever answers what's happened. I'll say you're in a terrible state at having lost contact with them. I'll say we're going out later and will try to find you a replacement phone . . . which we may or may not manage to do today even though we try all sorts of places to get you one just the same. They can't be angry with you for that.'

Evie fleetingly managed a grin. 'Do I dare?'

Bernice said, 'Do I have to show you how to get dressed in

the morning? Come on. Let's do it.' She leaped off the bench and led the way up the stairs, with Evie following closely behind.

Piers tried not to laugh. And failed. 'Bea, may I commend you on your ward's education? Talk about "streetwise"! She could give me tips, any day.'

Bea couldn't help smiling, too. 'She really is something, isn't she? She listens, she watches, she learns. She thinks. I must admit I'm impressed. And now, we must take precautions to protect ourselves because I don't think the Trescotts are going to give up easily.'

'Talking of which,' said Piers, 'I've had another terse email, saying that as my plane seems to have been delayed and I am still in London, a car will collect me for work at fourteen hundred hours. Evie will have told them I didn't fly to the States last night. I suppose they're still hoping I'll toe the line. I've replied saying that I'm checking into a spa hotel for a fortnight, which I don't suppose will fool them but it will send a signal I'm not playing their game. Now, I don't want to leave you alone for any longer than I must, but I do need to get back to the mews to see what state my lodger has left the place in, collect my mail and some more clothes. Especially shoes. If I go now, this morning, I will hopefully be back by lunchtime to help you repel boarders.'

Bea examined in her fingernails. 'You might as well bring over what clothes and things you need for a while. The spare room is free and there's plenty of cupboard space. You could let the flat out again for a week or so, can't you?'

'Are you sure you want me to move back in? No, that's a silly question. You wouldn't say it if you weren't. But I hear the doubt in your voice. I don't think I could bear it if I moved back in, and you changed your mind.'

'I've thought about it a lot. If we take it slowly, I think . . . I hope . . . it will be all right.'

'Then the sooner I go, the sooner I'll be back.' He stood up and stretched.

She stood, too, saying, 'I'm going to have to change the code for the house alarm. I'm thinking I'll make it two eight six eight. That ought to be easy for you to remember.' She set off for the house without looking to see if he'd worked it out.

She heard him saying, 'Twenty-eighth of June, eighty . . .? Bea!' He started after her and she broke into an undignified run. She made it up the steps, laughing, with him pounding along after her.

On the twenty-eighth of June, nineteen eighty, they'd been married in a church in North Kensington, where they'd been living at the time.

Half an hour later, Bernice barged into Bea's office, to find her talking on the phone. Bea gestured that she'd be free in a minute. Bernice pushed the French windows wide open, and sniffed the air in the garden. Then, as Bea was still on the phone, Bernice pulled the visitor's swivel chair further away from the desk and amused herself by seeing how fast she could make it go round.

Bea ended the call and leaned back in her own chair. 'Where's Evie?'

Bernice stopped swivelling. 'I turned the telly on and dumped her in front of it, saying I'd be back in ten minutes to take her to the gym. She's stopped crying for the moment, anyway.'

'You destroyed her phone and reported the loss to the Trescotts?'

'Sure. I told Auntie the tale. She believed me completely when I said how clumsy Evie was and that she was in floods of tears, etc. She said she'd courier a replacement smartphone round to us straight away. I didn't think that was a good idea because Evie needs a respite from her, so I said we were organizing an Amazon delivery of a replacement to arrive this evening, as Evie was bereft without it. Auntie said that was very thoughtful of me, and to tell Evie to ring her the moment she'd got her replacement and she'd give me all the numbers to put into her phone for Evie. Meanwhile, she said, would I please tell her where we were going to be for the rest of the day. I said I didn't think we'd be going anywhere much as Evie had a headache and wanted to go to back to bed for a while.'

'She isn't going back to bed, is she?'

'No, but Auntie bought the lie because she thinks Evie's still taking her sleepy pills. I asked Evie what she'd told her aunt

that we were planning to do today and she said we were supposed
to be going to the gym in the morning and the hairdressers
in the afternoon. I had thought of seeing if my friend Mac – the
finance director at Hollands – might be free this afternoon. I
texted him and he said he'd make time for me today if I could
make my own way there and back. But it's some way out of
London, and I don't know what to do about Evie. Would she
be safe going to the hairdressers on her own?'

A chunky-looking man with a Mediterranean cast to his
features drifted in from the big agency room.

Bea rose to meet him. 'Here's your answer. Hari, bless you.
Dead on time. I don't know if you've met my ward Bernice
before?'

Hari was Maltese by birth and British by education, married
to one of Bea's old friends. He'd been a highly successful
bodyguard at one time but was now an independent security
consultant. He was a man who could slide through locked doors
faster than others could throw a peanut in the air and catch it
in their mouths.

Bernice was hesitant, looking him over. 'I've heard Bea
speak of you. You helped her out when she had a problem in
the past?'

He was assessing her at the same time. 'Kick-boxing? You
want to learn how to defend yourself against fresh young men?
Yes, I can teach you a couple of tricks.'

Bea said, 'Bernice, Hari has advised me of several things we
can do to make you safe and I'd like him to be your shadow
till we get this thing sorted. He can go everywhere with you.
He'll drive you where you need to go, he'll take you to the
gym or swimming or out to see Mac and he'll doss down here
at night.'

Bernice did her frown thing. 'I don't need a babysitter.'

Hari wasn't fazed by her rejection. 'No, I can see that. You
are a warrior, but you need some tools to help you defend
yourself in case of attack.'

Bernice shrugged. 'I suppose, if you put it like that. Can we
go to the gym this morning and then out of town for the
afternoon?'

A dark figure cut off the sunlight that had been streaming

into the room from the garden. Evie, looking unsure of herself. 'Oh, there you all are. Who's this man? What's he doing here? He's not come to collect me, has he?'

'On the contrary,' said Bea. 'Evie, meet Hari, a security consultant, who'll be looking after Bernice till things calm down. Hari, this is Evie Trescott, whom I've told you about.'

Evie said, 'Will he look after me, too?'

Hari looked to Bea for instructions.

Bea said, 'He can't be in two places at once and I don't think you're in danger at the moment, Evie. Or at least, not while you're under this roof.'

'Can't I stay here for good? I'm only just beginning to feel alive again. I could stay here for the holidays and go back to school with Bernice and if I work very hard, I could catch up on the schooling I've missed and—'

'And miss your birthday party and wearing your new dress and having a puppy and getting engaged to be married?'

Evie flushed. 'Can't I have them all? No, I suppose . . . but . . . Oh, I don't know what I want! Yes, I do!' She turned on Bernice. 'I don't want to be sat down in front of the telly and told to watch it like a toddler! I know you're all getting into trouble because of me, and I want to do something to help!'

Bea said, 'How about answering a couple of questions? Do you think that, if all else failed, Benjy would use force to get his own way?'

Evie's throat constricted, but she managed to say, 'Yes.'

'Second question: you said that everything hurt after your parents were killed and you had to be hospitalized. What was wrong with you?'

Evie's eyes widened. Every drop of colour faded from her face. She put out a hand to save herself from falling. She shook her hair over her face. And was silent.

Bea said, gently, 'Evie, have you ever had a monthly period?'

The shaggy head sank even further. 'Maybe. I don't know.'

Bernice pushed the girl into a chair, saying, 'That's enough. Hari's going to teach us some tricks and if Joshua ever tries to hurt you again, you'll be able to give him as good as he gets. Right?'

Evie nodded. Rounded shoulders, hair over face.

It wasn't Joshua who hurt Evie. It was Benjy. And Benjy's now turning his attention to Bernice.

Bea stood up. 'Right, let's get cracking. Hari, take the girls to a gym – not the local one in Church Street but another, not so close. Give them lunch when they've had enough. Get Evie a burner phone, and put this phone number on it so that she can ring me if anything goes wrong.'

I have to trust the girl not to contact her relatives today. They won't be expecting her to call yet, so maybe it will give her a respite from their demands.

'Next, Hari: deliver Evie to the beauty salon after lunch and then take Bernice on to wherever she wants to go. I think she wants to visit another school friend or something. She's got the details.'

Even though Evie says she wants to help us, I'm not trusting her with any more information than I have to.

Bea continued, 'Evie will be at the beauty salon for at least two and a half hours, maybe three. She's having the works: hair, manicure, pedicure, make-up. She'll call me on her burner phone when she's ready to come home, and I'll go to fetch her. You understand, Evie, that you don't get into a car or a taxi or go off with anyone else?'

'You mean if my family send someone to get me, I'm not to go with them?' She frowned a little, and in a tiny voice said, 'You think they might want to send me back to the clinic?'

'I don't know,' said Bea. 'I'm doing my best to cover all eventualities.'

Evie swallowed and nodded. 'All right. I'll wait for you to come. I trust you.'

'Good. Now, Hari, I'll give you a card for expenses. Oh, and I'm having the code on the house alarm changed, so when any of you return without me, you'll have to ring the doorbell to get in.'

Bernice tried it on. 'I'm sure I could remember the new code if you give it to me.'

'I haven't worked out what it should be yet.'

Hari said to the girls, 'We're leaving in ten minutes. Wear loose clothes, jogging trousers, trainers. Right?' He ushered them out of the door and turned back to Bea. 'Which leaves you here alone and unprotected.'

'Piers will be back soon, and I have someone coming in to check over my computers and alarm system. He can handle himself. And, I can always call on my office staff to help if necessary.'

'They're all women. No offence, but are they trained in hand-to-hand combat?'

'No, but I have to weigh up what are the most important things to do today, and those are to teach Bernice how to handle herself and to put her back in touch with Mac at Hollands' head office. Here's a credit card. I trust you with the number . . .' She wrote it down on a Post-it note and handed it over. He memorized it and tore the note to pieces.

Hari left, calling up to the girls to see if they were ready.

Bea sat back in her chair, running her fingers through her hair, wondering what problem she should tackle next.

Piers had said, 'Divide and rule,' and she was sure he was right. But how . . .?

There was a tap on the door and she turned to deal with her next visitor. This time it was someone in the family, so to speak.

Bea gave him a hug, partly to hide the fact there were tears in her eyes. 'Oh, Keith! Am I glad to see you! I didn't tell Bernice you were coming and I've got her out of the house for the day. You understand why I'm doing all this cloak and dagger stuff?'

Keith was a man approaching middle age with a comfortable girth and special IT skills. He had dark hair and beard, only slightly touched by grey, and the air of one contented with life. His marriage to Bernice's fragile mother, Dilys Holland, had transformed her from nervous wreck to contented wife and the mother of a bouncing baby boy. Keith was a man on whom you could rely.

Now he patted Bea's arm. 'We've always known you could do more for Bernice than we can. I'm sure you're right to keep my darling wife out of the Trescotts' sight. Bernice can come to us when this scare is over. We're planning to take a cottage down in Cornwall for a month and she could join us there for as long as she wishes . . . though what she'd find to occupy herself with, I don't know.'

'She wants to spend time with you, and so long as she has

Wi-Fi you can leave her to get on with her homework. Meanwhile, it would be great if you could find the time to help us keep the Trescotts at bay. They're making Piers' life hell already, and we don't want them starting on Dilys, do we?'

He seemed to find the situation amusing. 'I'm a tough guy and can cope, but you're right. Dilys doesn't handle pressure well, although she's getting better. Do you know, she even contradicted the woman who runs our son's playgroup last week? And she didn't even apologize afterwards! Was I proud of her!'

Bea laughed with him. 'Bravo, Dilys.'

'Now,' he said, turning to business. 'Hollands and Trescotts. That's a turn up for the books. And no, I wouldn't like to come between Leon and a business deal. As you say, it's best if I keep a low profile for the time being. No need to advertise what I'm here for. I'll start with a quick look at your computers to see if you've invited any strangers in recently, and then I'll sweep the house to see if you've grown any bugs.'

The front doorbell rang, and Keith gave Bea a little push in the direction of the stairs. 'You deal with that, and let me get on with what I'm here to do.'

Bea toiled up to the ground floor again, wondering which person of interest it might be. Leon or one of the Trescotts? And had Hari managed to get the girls safely away?

THIRTEEN

Tuesday, late morning

Bea opened the door to be faced with a man in chauffeur's uniform. Short-cut hair, fiftyish, with a solid, four-square figure. She'd seen him before. He drove the Trescotts around, didn't he?

Ah, he'd come to collect Piers, hadn't he? And, oh dear, he was double-parked in the road, holding up the traffic.

'I understand Mr Piers is staying with you? I have something to give him.'

'I regret. He's not here.' A small removals van was crawling along the road in the traffic. Piers often used a particular firm to move his bits and pieces around London, and this was probably him in the van now. An inopportune time for him to arrive?

The chauffeur didn't shift. 'I've been told to wait for him if he's popped out.'

'I have no idea where he's gone or how long he'll be.' Strictly speaking, that was true. Piers might or might not be in the removal van which was being held up in the traffic behind the double-parked limousine, but she wasn't going to tell the chauffeur that. Bea gestured to the gridlock in the road. 'You can't leave your car there.'

'My instructions are to—'

'Not to get a parking ticket, I assume. I'll tell him you called when he returns.'

'I'll find a parking space nearby, come back and wait for him.'

The chauffeur returned to the limo and drove off, being honked at by a stream of cars who'd been held up behind him. As if Bea had waved a magic wand, a car parked in front of Bea's house moved out into the traffic. The chauffeur stopped with the intention of moving back into that space . . . but lo and behold, the furniture van nipped quickly into the vacancy and the chauffeur had to move on.

Piers and a couple of men got out of the van, opened the back doors and started to hump cardboard boxes, a selection of bags and a dismantled easel along the pavement and up into the hall, followed by a number of canvases . . . and a couple of folding chairs . . . and a wooden crate filled with books . . . and . . . and . . .

Bea stepped back into the kitchen. She'd asked Piers to move himself back in for a while, but she hadn't thought he owned so much stuff. His belongings filled the hall, leaving only a small passage for people to pass through.

Keith popped up from the basement, eyed the clutter, and laughed. 'Running a hotel, Bea? You want a hand shifting this stuff, Piers?'

Piers paid off the men, helped them shut the van's doors, and edged his way into the hall, shutting the front door behind him. 'Hi, Keith. Good to see you again. Sorry, Bea. I hadn't realized I'd accumulated so much stuff. I'll have to find another studio to put my painting materials in. Shouldn't take me long. Perhaps a week or two.'

Bea felt rather faint. *A week or two?*

Piers said, 'We could dismantle the bed in the guest room and put everything in there. I can always sleep on the settee down here.'

Or in my bed! You rat! You sneaky, lying bastard! You could have taken most of this stuff and put it in store or left it in the mews, but you brought it here, thinking you could wheedle your way into my bed. Oh, just you wait . . .!

Keith was laughing. He'd known Piers for some time, and seemed to be on his side. Two men against one woman. What was she to do? Was Piers trying to smooth out a grin?

'I have it!' Bea said with a beatific smile. 'We don't use the small interview room at the back of the agency that much, and you can put some stuff down there. The rest can go into the guest bedroom for the time being. Now you can't sleep on the settee because Hari's going to be there, but I expect you can doss down on the floor in the sitting room on a lilo or something.'

Piers caved in. 'All right, I'll see about renting another studio this afternoon.'

Keith smoothed out a grin. 'Good try, Piers. By the way, Bea: someone's been trying to hack into your computers, but failed. Some foreign job. I'll strengthen your defences if you like.'

Bea said, 'Bless you. Now, as I told you, I'm at war with a powerful family called Trescott. Cyril, Constant and April are my generation; Benjy and Joshua are in their early twenties. As someone remarked earlier, the best form of defence is attack and I could bear to know more about their private lives. I've looked at Facebook and there's not much there but I know there's other sites they might be using. Can you check? April Trescott is divorced and reverted to her maiden name, and the two boys are hers.'

'You want me to hack into their private accounts? That's illegal. But there are ways round it. Let me see what I can do.'

The doorbell rang again.

'I'll go,' said Piers. 'I'm nearest.'

Bernice started to say, 'Watch it! It might be the Trescotts' chauffeur back . . .'

Piers had already opened the door.

The chauffeur was on the doorstep holding a phone to his ear. 'Good morning, sir. Are you ready to come with me now?'

Piers said, 'I regret. No.'

The chauffeur held out an envelope. 'Then my instructions are to give you this, sir. And to see you open it.'

Piers said, 'What?' He opened the envelope and stared at the enclosure.

Bea edged through the cases to see what he was looking at.

Piers said, 'This is a bearer bond for twenty thousand pounds? Is this supposed to bribe me into seeing things the Trescott way?'

'It now has your fingerprints on it, sir. I'm recording what you say so that Mr Trescott has proof that you have accepted the bond. Would you care to say a few words?' He held the phone up for Piers to speak into.

Piers glanced at Bea, standing at his side, and narrowed his eyes. Then he pulled her close to him and spoke with deliberation. 'On behalf of Mrs Abbot, I accept this money in consideration of the expense and trouble she has been put to while looking after Evelina Trescott, and in employing the protection needed to ensure her safety, and the safety of everyone in this house while the girl is staying here.'

In other words, Piers was accepting the money and using it to pay for Hari to protect Bernice and Evie against any advances Benjy might make.

Bea found herself holding the bearer bond. Piers had turned the tables on the Trescotts with a vengeance, and kept himself out of their clutches, too. Clever Piers!

The chauffeur looked at the phone. He looked back at Piers, and he looked at Bea. Did his lips twitch? Had he seen the humour in the situation? Yes, it seemed that he had. In a colourless voice, he said, 'I understand, sir. The money has been accepted by you for services rendered by Mrs Abbot.' He spoke into the phone. 'Did you get that, Mr Trescott? What would you like me to do now?' He listened for a moment, nodded, and put the phone away.

He said, 'Mr Trescott is not amused. I'm to report back to the house. But may I say, well done, sir.' He allowed himself a fleeting smile. 'And, my regards to Miss Evelina. Please remember me to her. I used to take her to and from her day school. Me and the wife, we were concerned about her, how she never seemed to pick up after her parents were killed. She's doing better now?'

Bea understood that the man was saying he wished Evie well. Bea said, 'She's having her hair and nails done. She's bought some new clothes. I'll tell her you were asking after her.'

He nodded and turned away. He took a step down towards the pavement, but turned back to say, 'It's good she's found a friend.' He hurried along the pavement to where he'd parked the limo.

Piers ushered Bea inside, and closed the door behind them.

Just inside the door, Keith was standing on a low stool, fiddling with the alarm system. He said, 'I enjoyed that. I was going to offer to pay half towards some security here for Bernice so it's a relief you've made them pay for it. Dilys and I are planning to up-size soon. We want a bigger house in a greener neighbourhood. Away from the pollution. Now . . . what is the new code you want put in?'

Piers recited, 'Two eight six eight. I need to lie down and have someone soothe my brow and bring me refreshments. All this thinking on my feet is wearing me out.'

Keith grinned. 'Could have fooled me.'

The two men did the high five thing. Keith said, 'I suppose we're related in some way, though I can't quite work out how.'

'We're in-laws of some sort, I suppose. Or will be when Bea and I make it official again.'

Bea wanted to say, Over my dead body! But didn't for some reason. On the one hand, she wanted to see Piers out of the house, and on the other . . . well, she didn't exactly dislike his moving in. It was . . . exciting.

She followed Piers along the obstacle course to the kitchen.

Piers went straight to the fridge. He sang out, 'Keith, do you want coffee, or some cake? I suggest we have a pizza for an early lunch, and then I'll shift my belongings downstairs except for what I can keep in the guest bedroom. Bea, I suggest you put that bearer bond into the bank immediately, if not sooner. I don't think they can cancel, but you might get burgled or something. Coffee first?'

Bea's mind was on the Trescotts' chauffeur. 'That man seems to have a soft spot for Evie. She said he was kind to her.'

'Divide and rule. A man in his position will know what's going on in that household even if he's not supposed to. Perhaps he can tell you what really went on when Daddy and Mummy were killed in that car accident.' He pulled a large pizza out of the freezer. 'This do us for lunch?'

Keith hove into view. 'Did you say something about coffee? I could do with a cup. So you two are going to get married again?'

Bea started to say, 'Not for a while . . .'

Piers got in first. 'As soon as they've got a slot. I could do with a best man. Would you care to oblige, Keith? I've hundreds of acquaintances but I don't have to explain anything to you, and you're already in the family, so to speak. Also, Dilys would like to be there, too, wouldn't she?'

Bea started to say, 'I really don't think . . .'

But Keith was nodding agreement and Piers was studying the kitchen floor. 'Is it clean? I really don't want to stain these jeans. They're my best pair. But, well . . . here goes.' He got down on one knee and held up his hands to Bea. 'Will you do me the honour, et cetera?'

'No, I . . .! Get up, for heaven's sake!' She flapped at him with a tea towel.

Whatever am I going to wear?

Keith was almost crying with laughter. 'Do I have to wear a penguin suit?'

'No, no!' Piers was horrified. 'Nor me! Best scruff, please!'

'Tell you what, I'll visit the charity shop on the way home and see if I can pick up a decent jacket. I tore the sleeve of my best last week. I suspect Dilys will want a new outfit, and we can't both afford to be dressed in designer gear.' He reached for some mugs. 'Do we toast the engagement with coffee or have we anything stronger? Bernice will love to be a bridesmaid.

Do we buy the dress for her for the occasion or do you? Etiquette's all over the place nowadays. However, you'll be glad to hear our little boy is too young to be a ring-bearer. If you asked him to carry a ring down the aisle, he'd probably put it in his mouth and refuse to take it out. He's into eating strips of newspaper at the moment.'

Bea hissed, 'No frills. No fuss. The moment someone asks about wedding presents or invitations, I'm out of here. Understood?'

Piers seated himself with an air of satisfaction. 'Ditto. Nice and quiet. Doing the dirty deed so quickly means it will have to be a registry office affair but we'll have a blessing in church later on. We'll invite a couple of old friends as witnesses on either side. Lunch or supper afterwards in the private room at the pub up the road. No honeymoon, because it's school holidays. Maybe in September we can get away for a bit. Pray for good weather. I do have one decent suit but it's a trifle on the tight side and if it rains, it might shrink, and then where would we be?'

Winston the cat landed on Piers' lap and put up a paw in begging mode.

Keith said, 'Can Winston be the ring-bearer?'

Torn between hitting them and laughing, Bea served up some salad to go with the pizza for lunch, and then left the men to it. She wasn't hungry and she needed some fresh air. She set off at a great pace to walk into the park and take her usual circuit . . . before finding herself for some reason back again in Church Street. Only then did she remember that she needed to put the Trescotts' bearer bond into the bank.

Once that was done, she turned into the church on the corner. Someone was practicing on the organ. Something reflective and peaceful.

Bea sat at the back of the side chapel. An elderly woman was already there, but soon left. The organ ceased to play. Quiet descended.

Bea thought about having a good cry. She was choked up with rage and tears and excitement . . . and oh, she didn't know what to think.

Dear Lord, I'm being railroaded into marrying this man

again, and I don't know whether I'm ready for it or not. Probably not.

I think you are.

But he's so pushy!

He's doing exactly what you want him to do, only a little faster than you expected. You could have stopped him at any point today, or yesterday. But you didn't.

What am I going to wear?

I'm not concerned with such things.

I'm worried about Bernice.

Yes, she is in danger.

I couldn't bear it if Benjy did to Bernice what he did to Evie. Or at least, what I suspect he did. Bernice thinks it was Joshua, but I'm pretty sure it wasn't him. It makes me feel sick to think about it. And what of the future for poor Evie? Is it possible that she will ever be able to lead a normal life? I can't see how it can happen.

Be vigilant. Watch and listen. A door will open.

I remember you said, 'Knock, and the door will be opened to you.' Well, here I am, Lord, knocking on your door.

She leaned forward and rapped three times on the chair in front of her.

Then she blushed and looked around to see if she'd been observed. Honestly, what would people think if they saw her going around and knocking on wood?

Her phone vibrated in her pocket. Evie was ringing from the hairdressers to say they'd finished with her and what should she do next? Bea told her to wait in the foyer, and she'd be right there. It wasn't far away. On no account was Evie to leave the shop till Bea arrived in person to collect her.

Better be safe than sorry. It wouldn't have taken much of an effort for the Trescotts to discover where Bea had her hair done. And she'd stupidly told the chauffeur what Evie was doing that day. Fool!

As Bea left the church, her phone rang again. She answered it as she walked along.

This time it was Piers. 'We're under siege here. Benjy arrived ten minutes ago, saying he was taking Bernice out into the country "to give her a driving lesson". He came in a red monster which he's managed to get parked outside. I said she wasn't here. He wanted to know where she was. I said I didn't know. He said I should tell her he was waiting for her and he'd sit outside until she got back.

'I've texted to warn her. She texted back to say she wouldn't be back till mid-afternoon if then. She added that Benjy should look out for traffic wardens. I haven't bothered to remind him about them. I hope he gets a whacking big fine. I can see through the window that he's still sitting outside, on his phone. The problem is that Keith needs to go soon but doesn't want to fall in with the Trescotts, which I absolutely understand. I'll have to think up some sort of diversion to allow him to leave unde-tected when he's ready to go.'

'I'm on my way to pick up Evie. I think we'll have lunch out. She's too fragile to have to meet up with Benjy at the moment.'

'Right. I'll hold the fort. I'm supposed to be looking at another studio flat this afternoon, but I'll wait till you're back.' He cut the call.

Bea walked into the salon and looked round for Evie, but there was no sign of her. Instead a stranger turned to meet her. Glossy dark hair in waves to her shoulders and she was unobtrusively but attractively made up, with shining, well-shaped fingernails. The stranger smiled, blushing at Bea's reaction.

'I look all right, don't I? Almost normal.'

'You look fantastic. Turn around and let me look at you.'

Evie rotated, pleased with herself and the impression she'd made on Bea. Had the girl lost weight this last week? Her figure seemed to have improved. The new bra helped, of course.

'Joshua will be pleased, won't he?' She sounded anxious about that.

Bea ignored that. 'Are you hungry? I'm famished. Bernice won't be back for hours. Shall we have a bite?'

They settled into the Italian restaurant nearby and ordered the chicken dish of the day.

Evie said, 'Auntie phoned the salon while I was under the drier. The receptionist asked me if I was there, and I told her to say that I wasn't. It was nice of them to lie for me, wasn't it? I wish I could go back to them every week to have my hair done.' She glanced at the mirror on the wall behind Bea and turned her head from side to side to admire herself.

'I thought you said you'd be able to do what you liked when you were sixteen.'

Evie bowed her head and didn't reply. But her head soon came up again. 'I suppose I have to go back and live with Auntie till we get married. Do you think it would it be all right for me to ask her for a dress allowance in future?'

'It depends who your guardian is now. It used to be your uncle Constant. Do you know if he made a will? It'll probably be in that.'

Evie's brow creased. 'I don't know. They say I don't need to bother my head with all that stuff.' She straightened her shoulders. 'But perhaps I ought to be bothered about it when I'm sixteen.'

Bea couldn't help herself. 'You said you were getting married and letting Joshua look after you.'

'And have a puppy and live happily ever after.'

'Will you have your own house? Learn to drive? Have children?'

Their chicken came. Evie made no attempt to start on hers, but repeated the word 'children' under her breath. She pushed her plate aside, untouched. 'I don't think Joshua wants children.'

Bea was hungry, so started on hers. 'Do you?'

'Yes. Oh yes!' A gulp. She was very pale.

Bea said, 'Some water?'

Evie tried to lift her glass and spilled some of it. She set it down again. She looked around the restaurant. People enjoying themselves. Normal people. Normal lives.

She said, 'I'm not normal. At least, I don't think so. I can't remember properly what they told me. It comes in flashes and then I think that was nonsense and it didn't happen. I suppose I don't want to know, really. It's better not to know. Better to have a puppy and get married and not care about anything.'

Bea's throat ached. 'Yes, my dear. I do see what you mean.'

Evie made another attempt to lift the glass, and this time she made it. She drank, set the glass down again, and straightened her knife and fork on the table. 'You know, don't you?'

'That it wasn't Joshua? Yes.'

Evie took a deep breath. 'Sometimes I think I'd like to run away and live by myself with a couple of dogs in a tiny cottage by the sea. Only I know that's a dream that won't come true.'

'I expect you could have your dream if you signed away your rights to Trescotts in exchange for a decent allowance. You must be hungry. Taste your food. It's good.'

Evie obeyed. She managed two bites before she put her knife and fork down again. 'I thought once or twice that I should go to a doctor, not the one at the clinic, to find out . . .' She swallowed. 'But I've been too afraid to ask. Growing up is hard, isn't it? It's a lot easier to let them have their way and not think. Thinking hurts.'

Bea was silent. The poor, poor child!

Evie drew herself up. 'Will you take me to a gynaecologist? I think I can bear to hear the truth if you come with me.'

'Don't you have a GP of your own?'

'The Trescotts don't have a GP. We're above all that. We go to specialists when we need attention. Auntie's pet doctor at the clinic says I'm a hysterical little girl who needs to take her medicine or she'll be in a wheelchair for life. What about your GP?'

'I'm not your guardian. I can't take you to a doctor without your guardian's permission. If it's going to be your uncle Cyril—'

'He'd say that my aunt takes care of all that, and she does.'

The waitress came by to ask if everything was all right. Bea nodded, and Evie picked up her knife and fork again. Bea got the impression that the child wanted to talk, but didn't know how to start.

Bea said, 'What was the row about, the night your uncle Constant died?'

'About my school report, and how much money my going to an expensive boarding school had wasted. Uncle Constant was always worrying about money although he'd no need to. He used to go around shutting lights off, turning the central heating down, querying the bills. But it was all noise, really. Auntie sees to the running of the two households. She says – used to say – that he was going soft in his old age.'

'She's organizing the birthday party for you?'

'Yes.' Evie pushed her plate away, the food almost untouched. 'I'm not hungry.'

'Your uncle was worried about the cost of the party?'

Silence. Evie kicked the table leg.

Bea said, 'My dear, I wish I could help you, but if you don't tell me what's wrong there's nothing I can do.'

'Won't you let me come and live with you and Bernice?' Her voice tailed away.

Wow! I didn't see that coming and I'm not sure I could cope with her. I'm panicking at the mere thought of it! Calm down, Bea. It's not going to happen.

Bea said, 'Unless you can show a very good reason for wanting to leave home, the courts wouldn't allow that while you have living relatives who want to look after you. Have you no other relatives you could go to for a while?'

A tiny shrug. 'Not now. No.'

April Trescott would be the obvious one to take charge of the girl. Having seen her at work last night, I'm wondering if she's in cahoots with the Silver Fox, or trying to catch Leon for herself?

Evie said, 'The row at supper was because Joshua told my uncle to lay off me, that it wasn't my fault that I'd lost so much schooling. My uncle asked, "Whose fault was it, then?" And Joshua said that if he was prepared to pick up the pieces and marry me, then it was no skin off our uncle's nose. Nunkie Cyril went icy cold and said that was the first he'd heard of marriage, and that I was far too young and immature to be married. Uncle Constant said that for once he agreed with his brother, that Auntie should have consulted him about it and he thought it was a crazy idea, too. He said that he was my guardian and he'd never agree to it.'

'Ah,' said Bea. 'He said he was against the marriage and that night, he died. And Nunkie said he heard someone arguing with Constant in the night?'

'He was dreaming. It definitely wasn't Joshua who took the whisky in to Uncle Constant later on, and made him take more than his usual dose of tablets. My window was open, and so was his, and I heard enough to know who it was. But of course I know that was all a dream and I mustn't tell anyone about it.'

It hadn't been Cyril. Cyril had agreed with Constant that Evie was too young to marry. Cyril didn't stand to gain anything by Constant's death. April and Benjy stood to gain because the marriage was going to tie Evie and her fortune down for good and if Constant, her legal guardian, refused permission, then it couldn't take place.

'It was either your aunt or Benjy?'

Evie finished off her glass of water and poured herself some more. 'Joshua has always stood up for me. He's promised he always will. If I marry him, I'll be free of my aunt, and we can live happily ever after.'

'I can see the attraction of getting away from your aunt, but marriage is a big step. Are you sure you're ready for it?'

A shrug. 'I have no choice. I'm not exactly a prize catch, am I? The pills I was taking turned me into a non-person, but if they find out I've stopped taking them I'll be whisked back to the clinic and have to stay there till I don't care what they do with me. It's Joshua, or nothing.'

Bea asked, 'Does Joshua love you?'

'Of course. I understand it's a bargain I have to make. He'll get my money in due course, but he's promised I'll always have enough to live on and we won't even have to share a bed. That's love, isn't it?'

Bea choked on the last nugget of chicken and drank some water. She pushed her plate away and tried to think clearly. 'No, my dear. It isn't. Love is more than friendliness. I know because I have loved twice and twice have lost the man I loved. I grieved bitterly each time, but now I have a second chance to be with someone I love and I'm taking it.'

Evie stared. 'But you're so old! I didn't think people your age could love.'

Bea felt herself blush. 'Well, you learn something every day. Piers and I married when we were very young. We were crazy about one another but he couldn't find work, I worked too hard and when baby Max came along Piers hadn't grown up enough to cope. So he played around with other women and I threw him out. Then I met and married my darling Hamilton, who was as different from Piers as you could imagine a man could be, but he loved me and he looked after me and he looked after Max, and I loved him back, as fiercely as I'd loved Piers. I was devastated when Hamilton died.

'Despite my age,' Bea said, with a touch of sarcasm, 'there have been other men who have wanted to get closer to me, but I could never summon up enough enthusiasm to take up their offers. And Piers kept bobbing back into my life. He's always kept in touch with Max, and lately . . . well, we're both older and wiser now. I'm going to marry him all over again. I'm excited and yet dreading it. I want it to happen tomorrow or not till next year. I think of him all the time. I count over his faults, and he has many. I remember his good points – and he has many of those, too. Warts and all, I want him to be with me for the rest of my life. Dear Evie, I understand where you are at, but I don't think entering into a loveless marriage at your age is your only option. Please, think carefully before you do so.'

'I have thought. For weeks and weeks. There's no alternative.'

'Yes, there is. It would require courage, but I don't think you lack that. You could go to the police, tell them you were raped and that your family covered it up.'

FOURTEEN

Tuesday afternoon

Evie shook her head with some violence. 'No, no, no, NO!' Bea said, 'The police would find you somewhere safe to stay. They'd have you properly assessed for the epilepsy which you seem to have grown out of, and a gynaecologist could put your mind to rest on the matter of having children in the future.'

'I couldn't do that to Joshua. He's my only friend.'

'It wasn't Joshua who attacked you, and you know it.'

'No, NO!' She put her hands over her ears and closed her eyes.

Bea said, 'Breathe deeply. In and out.'

The waitress came up. 'Anything the matter?'

Evie opened her eyes and took her hands away from her ears. She shook her head.

Bea told the waitress. 'We've finished, thank you. Evie, would you like a dessert or just coffee?'

Evie breathed the word, 'Coffee.'

Bea ordered for both of them. When the waitress had gone, Bea said, 'Evie, do you want to take one of your pills?'

Evie shook her head.

'Can you tell me about the day everything went wrong?'

'Do I have to?'

'I think it would be a good idea for you to acknowledge what happened before you can move on.'

Evie studied the top of the table. 'We were in the country house for the holidays. Daddy and Mummy went into Oxford, visiting friends. It was Carlo's – that's the chauffeur – day off, so Daddy said they'd take Mummy's runabout instead of the limo. If they'd taken the limo they'd probably have survived because it's so much heavier. Auntie was up in town that week but the boys were there, home from university. And Uncle Constant, of course. He didn't like London. He and I had a plan to play the boys at croquet that afternoon. The police came and said there'd been a terrible accident. Mummy had been driving and there was an oily slick on the road where something had been spilled, and they'd gone out of control and into a lorry coming the other way. And they were both dead. I couldn't believe it. Only that morning we'd been talking about where we'd go on holiday and what I was going to get for my birthday.

'Maria took me upstairs and gave me a sleeping pill. She sat with me till I dropped off to sleep. She was always kind to me.'

'Maria is your housekeeper?'

'She's married to Carlo. They have a flat over the stable block in the country, and separate quarters in the town house.'

'Maria put you to bed and stayed with you for a while. And then . . .?'

'Which version would you like? The one I've been taught,

or the one I imagined? Most of the time I can believe the one
I've been taught.'

'Give me that one, then.'

Their coffee came. Evie put three teaspoons of sugar in hers
and drank it off. The caffeine seemed to give her courage. She
gabbled through her tale. 'I was upset after my parents' death
and I had one of my fits and fell down the stairs and hurt myself
badly. Then I had my period and everything went wrong, and
that's why I don't have periods now and can't have children.
The family were all there and that's what they tell me happened,
and so I have to believe it.'

'And the version you imagined?'

A long silence. 'I try not to think of it too much. I get
flashbacks. Then I can't sleep unless I take a pill.'

'Tell me what you can.'

'I woke up. He was all over me. He had his hand over my
mouth, told me not to be stupid but to lie still. I tried to get
him off me. I screamed. He put his hands round my throat. He
threw me this way and that all over the room. He held me up
by my hair and hit me and hit me and then . . . I can't remember
the next bit . . . I suppose I went back to sleep. But when I
woke up, everything hurt and I couldn't see out of my eyes and
I couldn't talk because my throat hurt so much.'

It was worse than Bea had thought. She imagined it happening
to Bernice, and shivered.

Evie said, 'Maria found me when I didn't go down for supper.
She screamed, and that brought the boys in, and Uncle Constant.
I could hear their voices but I couldn't see them and I couldn't
speak, though I tried to do so. They argued about calling an
ambulance, but finally Benjy persuaded them I was making a
fuss about nothing and that I'd be perfectly all right in the
morning after a good night's sleep. So Maria helped me have
a shower and got me back to bed and put something on my
bruises and gave me some more sleeping pills, and I did go to
sleep, and I slept and slept.

'The next bit is weird. I woke and . . . I think I was hallucinating. I was in a black tunnel and there was no end to it. I
hurt everywhere. I was so hot and I felt so strange. I thought
I was going to die. I didn't care because if I died, it would stop.

I tried to cry out for Mummy and Daddy but I couldn't make any noise. I heard Auntie's voice, very sharp, and realized she'd come back. Then there was an ambulance and they took me to the clinic and I was there for a long, long time.'

Bea took Evie's hand in both of hers, and held it tightly.

The girl closed her eyes again. She breathed deeply, in and out. And finally, she opened her eyes and said in a normal voice, 'I've never told anyone outside the family before. They said I'd imagined it all. That I'd been hallucinating because I'd developed an infection. That bit was true. I did get an infection and that was why they had to operate, eventually. That's why there won't be any children.'

Bea said, 'You're a very brave girl. Thank you for telling me.'

Evie sniffed. 'I'm only telling you so that you will understand and take Bernice away for a while. Abroad. America, somewhere he can't get at her.'

Evie was now able to think how to stop Benjy hurting Bernice?

Bea said, 'I don't think that's possible.'

'I've only ever had one good friend before, but that was ages ago before . . . before everything went wrong. I know Bernice is a lot cleverer than me, but she's been kind when she didn't need to. I don't want her to have to go through what I did.'

'She won't. I've hired a bodyguard to look after her till she goes back to school.'

'You don't understand. He won't stop now he's seen her and she's rejected him. He can't. He'll stalk her and find a way to trap her in a lonely place. He won't stop even when she goes back to school. He's like that, you see. He can never bear to be beaten, at a game, or at school, or by a girl. He rather likes it when you say "no" because that's a challenge. And he needs the money.'

'Surely the Trescotts are rich enough that that's not a problem.'

'They're not. There's no money in having land nowadays. They rely on what the business brings in. It was my father who built it up, and when he died, Nunkie – that's Uncle Cyril – took charge of the firm. He's been married twice and that's cost him a pretty penny but he pays himself an enormous amount as chief executive of the firm so he's all right. Uncle Constant inherited this and that from grandfather but he never went into the firm or had a proper job. He lived on his dividends from the firm. He was always worrying how to make ends meet because he spent so much on his stamp collection.'

'Your aunt must have inherited something, surely?'

'Yes, she did, but it's never enough. The boys are so expensive, you see.'

'But their father . . . ?'

'Oh, he was lovely. I used to enjoy staying with them and I was so sad when they got divorced. For some reason Auntie didn't come out of it with any money and she'd never worked for a living, so she and the boys had to come back to live with the family. They'd both left school by then and Daddy saw them through their last years of university and offered to take them into the firm. Only, Joshua wanted to go into politics instead. He's working for our local Conservative association at the moment, learning the ropes, waiting for a seat to become vacant. It'll probably take him two or three goes to get into Parliament, but I'm sure he will in the end. Only, it helps if you've got money.'

'And Benjy? I thought he wanted to take over the firm.'

'Yes, he will, one day. It's just that . . . it's hard to explain . . . Auntie says that Benjy's too bright for Nunkie, who's stuck in the past and ought to listen to the young who have more progressive ideas.'

Bea couldn't prevent her eyebrows rising at this.

Evie shrugged. 'It's ridiculous. Nunkie wants Benjy to turn up at seven in the morning at some warehouse or other to see how it works. Just like any brainless boy from a sink estate who's left school without any exams. As if Benjy couldn't tell how things worked from what the foreman told him. Nunkie says he started in the business by learning from the bottom up but I don't think that's true as he started off in sales and never had to turn out that early in the mornings. Benjy says Nunkie is jealous of his brains, that he's afraid of someone like him, who has bags of flair, coming into the business. What's more, Benjy isn't being paid anywhere near his worth. How can he be expected to be nicely turned out and run a decent car if he isn't paid properly? Everyone knows he's going to take over the firm one day. Auntie can't help, so both boys have got to marry money. I don't mind about helping Joshua out with my money, I really don't, because he's never messed me around.'

'And Benjy has.'

A painful flush. 'He was just teasing, you know. Trying to kiss me and making silly suggestions. There wasn't any harm in it. At least, that's what I thought until . . . until.' A deep breath. 'Aren't I good? I managed to tell all that without taking a pill. I must be getting better, don't you think?'

If you were ever ill.

Bea said, 'I understand how it was, Evie, and I do see why you think it's a good idea for you to marry Joshua. Getting away from your aunt and Benjy is important, but may I ask if you've discussed a timetable with Joshua? How long is it going to be before you can get married? And where will you live afterwards?'

'He said to trust him for all that. And I do trust him. Of course I do.' She drank off the rest of her coffee and chanted, 'I had a fit. I fell down. I hurt myself. Benjy wasn't anywhere near me. I got an infection. There was an operation. There's not going to be any children. I'm going to marry Joshua and he'll look after me for ever.' She smiled brightly. 'There, aren't I a good little girl? I've remembered it perfectly, and I don't have to take a pill. Shall we go back now?'

Bea signalled they wanted the bill. 'I do understand your position, Evie. I have reservations about what you intend to do, and perhaps we can go into those at another time. But there's one thing I must ask of you, and that is not to tell your family what Bernice does every day or where she plans to go. I must try to keep her safe.'

'Safe? Nothing and nobody is safe in this world. But' – she darted a quick glance at Bea and returned to looking down – 'I will try to help her as much as I can.'

'You're a good little actress, Evie. You can play dumb if they ask you about Bernice. Remember your aunt thinks you're taking your pills. Act sleepy. You can do that, can't you?'

Evie nodded once. But she kept her head down while Bea paid the bill and they started back home.

Walking up the hill on the way home, Bea's phone rang. It was Piers. 'Bea, I have to warn you that Benjy's still sitting outside the house. A short while ago he rang the bell and said he didn't believe Bernice was out, and he wanted to come in and search the place. I refused, which didn't improve his temper. The thing is Keith has to leave now. Dilys needs him at home. The baby's developed a rash and she wants him to take them both to the doctors. He's checked out everything in sight and printed a whole lot of stuff off the internet for you to look at. Any ideas how to get him out unseen?'

'I'll be back soon. I'll think of something.'

'I suppose I could go out and engage Benjy in conversation while Keith sneaks out through the agency. Benjy doesn't know him, does he? If Benjy stops and questions Keith, he could always pretend he's a client, but we both think it would be best if he could get away without being spotted. Any other ideas?'

Bea said, 'We're less than five minutes away. Tell him to wait till our arrival. We'll distract Benjy so that the man can slip out unnoticed.'

Evie stopped walking. Her colour was poor. 'Benjy's come to get me? He'll be livid! He'll see I haven't taken my pills. He'll have me taken off to the clinic and I'll be dosed to the eyeballs and miss the party and Joshua proposing and I'd rather die!'

'No, you wouldn't,' said Bea, furiously texting Hari. 'Calm down, Evie. Act dumb, remember? Let me do the talking.'

Evie wailed, 'Benjy always wins!'

'No, he doesn't. He's not walking all over his uncle, for a start. Cyril's got his measure, hasn't he? Cyril's making Benjy learn the ropes at the firm instead of appointing him to some well-paid sinecure. Now, stand up straight. Look at yourself in the shop window. You are a stunner, dressed to kill, with hair and make-up just right. I doubt if Benjy will even recognize you.'

Evie glanced sideways at the shop front, and then turned to face her image. She pushed back her hair and lifted her chin. She liked what she saw. Almost, she smiled, but the smile soon faded. She said, 'You can't win against the Trescotts and you must realize you can't rely on me.'

'I rely on you to play the ugly duckling who's turning into a swan, and to answer all questions by saying that you don't know. You can do that, can't you?'

Evie enquired of her mirror image, 'Did you have a fit and fall down the stairs? *I don't know.* Did you hear who took Uncle Constant his nightcap? *No, I didn't.* Do you want to sign away your inheritance in exchange for your freedom? *Yes, I do.*'

She shivered. Then she started back up the hill. 'OK, let's get it over with. If you ask me whether or not the sun is shining, I'll say, "I don't know"!'

'Splendid,' said Bea. She held up her phone. 'There's a text just come in. Bernice and Hari are on their way back from wherever it is they've been this afternoon. We'll probably all meet at the front door.'

'You changed the code on the alarm. Are you going to tell me what it is?'

'Would that be a wise thing to do?'

'It would show you trusted me.'

'You've just warned me not to do so.'

Evie sang out, 'Testing, testing. What would Daddy and Mummy say if they could see me now?'

Bea thought she'd better play the game. Imitating the way Evie had spoken, she said, 'I don't know.'

Evie laughed. It was a weird, high laugh with a trace of hysteria in it. But she did actually manage to laugh.

Bea put her arm round the girl's shoulders as they crossed the busy road into the quiet street in which Bea lived. 'You'll do.'

'Give me the code.'

Bea weakened and gave it to her.

As Piers had said, there was a long, low, red car parked outside Bea's house. The sort of car which looks as if it would be more at home on a race track. The sort of car which didn't bother about speed limits and sneered at everything else on the road.

Evie stopped short. 'Benjy. I told you. He's come to get me.'

'No, he hasn't,' said Bea, urging her on with an arm round the girl's waist. 'He wants to take Bernice into the country for a driving lesson. Can you imagine her going with him? Anyway, he couldn't get you plus your new dress and all your belongings into that car. That sort of car doesn't have anywhere to put anything but a cigarette lighter or an internet connection. It must have cost a bomb.'

Evie's feet dragged. Bea could feel the girl trembling.

As they drew close, Benjy erupted from the car, saying, 'There you are, Bernice! I've been waiting for ever. I've come to take you for a drive in the . . . What! You're not Bernice! Evelina, is that you?'

Evie nodded, her breathing too rapid for speech.

Benjy didn't seem to know whether to be pleased or angry. 'Well, here's a turn up for the books. Has Joshua seen you now you're all tarted up?'

Bea guided Evie up the steps to the front door, delving into her purse for her key. 'Evie's looking good, isn't she? If you came with a message for her from her aunt, then please give it to her now. As I believe I made clear, you are not welcome in this house.'

As she'd hoped, Benjy followed to the foot of the steps. Now he had his back to the agency entrance.

'Oh, don't be so pompous!' Benjy threw a glance back at his car, then looked at his watch and took out his phone. 'I can't hang around all day. Get Bernice out here. Tell her I'm waiting to give her a driving lesson . . . Hello, hello?' he snarled into his phone.

Keith's dark head rose from the stairs leading down to the basement. Soundlessly he hove into sight, blew Bea a kiss, and disappeared down the street.

Evie had her arms around herself, still shivering. A rabbit caught in the headlights of Benjy's presence.

Benjy swung his free arm this way and that, concentrating on his phone. 'No, no! I said . . .! Yes, I know that, but I needed some time off. Yes, I'll deal with it. I said, *I'll deal with it!*' He shut the phone off. If he'd been in a bad mood before, he was now incandescent. He muttered, 'And who the hell does he think he is to order *me* about!'

Work? He should be at work and isn't? Someone's hauling him over the coals at work because he's gone AWOL?

Bea, key in hand, hesitated in the porch, giving Keith plenty of time to get away – which he was doing. Finally she put her key in the lock. 'Come along, Evie.'

Evie pointed with her chin. 'B-b-bernice . . .'

A large, expensive car with tinted windows drew up in the road and double-parked. There was a man at the wheel. Presumably that was Hari?

The back passenger door on the traffic side opened and Bernice stepped out into the road, but the car didn't move.

Ah, Bea got it. Hari had brought Bernice back in his car, but on seeing Benjy had decided that he would keep in the background to see whether or not Bea could get the girl inside the house safely. Hari wasn't going to drive on till she'd done so.

Benjy started towards Bernice. 'There you are, you little tease. I texted you hours ago to let you know I'd be giving you a driving lesson this afternoon, and I'm not in the habit of being kept waiting.'

Bernice was carrying her laptop. She ignored Benjy to look up at Bea. 'Sorry I'm late.'

Benjy opened his car door. 'Come on, come on. We're wasting time. We're off for a drive. I promise to let you take the wheel if you're good. Off road, of course.'

Bernice glanced at the car, said, 'No, thank you,' and started across the pavement.

Benjy grabbed the girl's arm, pulling her off-balance and hauling her round to face him.

Bea descended to the pavement. 'That's enough. Benjy.'

Bernice was icily polite. 'Let go of me, please.'

Benjy grinned, tugging on her arm. 'Come on, you know you want to—'

Bernice swung her laptop around in an underarm movement which caught Benjy amidships.

'Ack!' He doubled over, releasing her.

Bea, Bernice and Evie watched enthralled as Benjy bent over, tears shooting from his eyes.

Someone applauded.

Piers stood in the open doorway. 'I enjoyed that. Welcome home, ladies. I trust you had a good lunch and are now ready for tea and crumpets.'

The car which had brought Bernice rolled smoothly away. A man came sliding through the people on the pavement from the direction the car had taken, skirted their little group and dived down the stairs into the agency rooms. Bea blinked. Was that Hari taking refuge in the agency rooms? But, if he hadn't been driving the car, then who had?

As Benjy fought for control, a parking attendant arrived to give the red monster a ticket, which didn't improve its owner's temper.

Bea steered the two girls up into the house. Piers closed the door behind them and set the alarm.

Evie had a mild fit of hysterics. 'Oh, oh! He'll never forgive you. Oh, he's getting a parking ticket! He'll kill you, Bernice. He will! He can't bear to be crossed, and you've made him so angry! Oh, oh! How could you!'

'Easily,' said Bernice. She was showing the whites of her eyes and trembling, but otherwise in control. 'He laid his hand on me. I asked him to take it away. He didn't. I acted in self-defence.' She dropped her laptop, gave one small sob, and turned into Piers's welcoming shoulder.

'You're a brave girl,' said Piers, holding her tightly. 'And clever, too.'

Bea held out both her arms to the girl, who transferred herself to her guardian. She shook with nervous tension. Bea said, 'There, there. You managed that brilliantly.'

'Yes, she did,' said Piers. 'Now, let's have a cup of tea and get our diaries organized.' He pushed them down the hall to the kitchen.

Bea noticed that the stacks of Piers's belongings in the hall had diminished, though his easel was still there, occupying far too much space.

Piers switched the kettle on. 'Bernice, how would you like to be Bea's bridesmaid? Keith's going to be best man, and your mother says she's going to be a matron of honour though I don't think Bea wants frills and furbelows. But she'll have to put up with you being a bridesmaid though, won't she?'

'What!' said Bernice, rapidly recovering from her fright. 'Do you mean . . .?'

Bea said, 'Any more talk of a wedding, and I'm emigrating. Now, Bernice; who was driving that car which brought you back home, because I know it wasn't Hari.'

FIFTEEN

Tuesday afternoon

'No,' said Bernice. 'It was Mac, Uncle Leon's finance director at Hollands. Or rather, it was his chauffeur and Mac was in the back with me. We'd been talking about the possibility of Hollands merging with Trescotts. Mac says Uncle Leon had discussed it with him in general terms and that the idea has possibilities. He says Cyril Trescott is "a canny operator but perhaps not quite as sharp as he thinks he is".'

Her mimicry of Mac's dry tones was perfect.

Bea switched on the kettle. 'What does Mac think of Leon's present conduct?'

'He said he hadn't heard that Leon had been under the weather and assumed it wasn't serious, but he fingered his smartphone as he said it, and I think he'll check it out. I guessed it would be him who'd organize the digging into the Trescotts and the way the company worked, and he said yes, that he'd looked to see who the biggest shareholders might be and couldn't see any particular problem.

'I told him how Cyril and Leon were trying to push the two families into closer contact. I told him about Evie and the pills, and Benjy and Joshua and the Awful Aunt, and I could see he thought I was exaggerating. Then I told him that you'd hired Hari to look after me and he went all quiet on me. He seems to have a good opinion of you, Bea, and a high opinion of Hari.

'Mac had arranged for Hari to have lunch in the canteen while he and I had a sandwich in his office but after he'd heard what I had to say Mac called Hari in, and asked what your instructions had been. Hari told him. Then Mac asked us to wait a while and disappeared to make some phone calls. When he returned, he said he'd arranged to see Uncle Leon this afternoon in the City and he'd drop us off on the way. I said that wasn't necessary because Hari and I had come in a cab and would get another one back, but he insisted.

'As we came along the road we could see Benjy outside the house talking to you and Evie. Mac said he'd like to see for himself how Benjy acted when he saw me. I had to admit to him then that Benjy did frighten me a bit. Hari said he'd see me safely in but Mac said that Benjy couldn't do much to me in a street with everyone watching and it was a good idea to keep some crack troops in reserve in case they were needed later. He told Hari to stay in the car with him and they'd watch to see what happened next. If anything went wrong, Hari could leap out and come to my aid. If not, he'd drop Hari off at the corner and he could join us later. Hari agreed. I wasn't sure I could cope but they both seemed to think I could, so I went along with it.'

She swallowed hard. 'I wasn't sure I could hit anyone that hard, but he was hurting me and I reacted without thinking. Then Mac got his chauffeur to drive on, dropping Hari off on the way. I'm not sorry I hit Benjy. And, I'm famished. I only had a couple of sandwiches for lunch and I could murder a burger.'

Bea made tea in the biggest pot she had while Piers toasted crumpets and found the butter.

Evie slid on to a stool next to Bernice. 'Benjy frightens me, too. I think you were ever so brave.'

'I'm not brave,' said Bernice. 'I'm still shaking. But I'll live.' She looked Evie over. 'You look all right. Almost grown up.'

Evie managed a grin. 'Thank you.'

Bernice turned on Piers, mock ferocious. 'As for you, if you think I'm going to call you Daddy, or Pa, or Step-Dad or whatever, you've got another think coming.'

'Brat,' said Piers, without heat.

'Tom Cat,' she replied, with satisfaction.

They grinned at one another and did the high five thing.

Bernice turned back to Bea. 'So, what are you going to wear for your wedding?'

'I haven't given it any thought,' said Bea, who had actually spent some time thinking about it and come to the conclusion that she needed to go shopping again.

'And me?' said Bernice. 'Can I wear my new dress, the one we bought for Evie's birthday party?'

'Yes,' said Piers.

'Too formal,' said Bea at the same moment.

'Good,' said Bernice, 'I like that dress. Can I have something besides crumpets? A pizza, perhaps? Or a burger?'

'Help yourself,' said Bea. 'I'm out of here. I have some phone calls to make. Evie, you say your aunt was married for years until they got divorced and she reverted to her maiden name. Do you know why they went their separate ways?'

'No, I don't. There was a lot of talk behind closed doors and I asked what had happened and was told he'd behaved badly and I wasn't to ask about it again.'

'What was his name and where did he live?'

'George Kent. Uncle George. I don't know what he did wrong. He was ever so nice to me. He lived just outside Maidenhead. He had a garden centre which did some special kind of horticulture, trials for seed merchants, that sort of thing. He had acres of glass and poly tunnels and stuff. He grew plants for special events. I used to stay with him in the holidays and have fun with his niece who was a bit older than me, but an only child, too. I was sorry when I couldn't go there anymore.'

Bea left them to their food and went downstairs to check that all was in order in the agency. Which it was. Betty said that Keith had strengthened their computer defences and taught Betty how to use them. He'd confirmed there were no listening bugs in the house. He'd tried the Trescott business computer and found it well defended but said that the two youngsters Benjy and Joshua had taken only minimal precautions to protect their online accounts, and that he'd printed off some information for Bea to look at if she so wished.

And she did so wish.

Joshua first. According to his various online accounts, he was a serious young man. There were lots of shots of him taken with groups of boys and girls at different stages of his university life: politics, of course, standing in student elections, debating societies, and so on; graduation in a mortar board and gown; wearing a rosette; campaigning for a local election in Surrey; campaigning again for another ditto.

There were the usual semi-funny messages to accompany the photos. No girls appeared more than once in the shots. He wasn't into selfies. He was not seen with his brother in any of his activities. His political stance seemed to be mid-left of centre. He'd been hedging his bets as he climbed the ladder.

He gave the impression of being devoted to a career in politics but he lacked that spark which would have made him stand out from the ruck, and which carried people to the top.

Actually, he seemed rather dull. No wonder he needed Evie's millions if he was going to make his mark in life.

Benjy, now. Girls, girls, and more girls. All very young, judging by their photos. Yachts. Speedway racing. A number of different expensive cars. Selfies and staged photos.

Where did he get the money from for his cars? The red monster he'd turned up in today must have cost a fortune for a start. He'd got a first at uni. Medieval History, not something which would commend you to the business tycoons today. Or was it? Perhaps a study of Machiavelli might be considered useful?

Benjy had wanted to run the Trescott company, hadn't he? Ah, here was a nice photo of him standing at the shoulder of the burly man whom Bea recognized from his obituary portrait: Benjy's uncle Tom, the one who looked like a Smythe. Evie's father. So Benjy had indeed joined the firm at some point . . . yes, yes. But six months later and *before* Tom and his wife had died, Benjy was snapped being welcomed into a different, City trading company.

Why was that? Why hadn't he stayed with Trescotts?

Perhaps he'd been learning the ropes here and there . . . yes, three months later he's with another City firm . . . then holidaying in Cannes on a friend's yacht, and then . . . and then . . . another non-job. He'd been coasting along doing an internship here or there.

Ah, now here he was back with the Trescotts, being welcomed back into the fold by Cyril, the Silver Fox himself.

Bea seemed to remember that hadn't lasted either, had it?

Wasn't there something about Cyril suspending the boy for six months due to some bad behaviour at a Christmas do? But he was back with Trescotts again now, wasn't he?

It would be good to know how well he really was doing. The phone call he'd received that day while waiting for Bernice had seemed to indicate that someone, somewhere, was not pleased with Benjy. Evie's report on him indicated that Benjy was not being treated as the Golden Boy in the workplace, either.

Now, what about April, who'd produced Joshua and Benjy, these two paragons of society? There were no wedding photos of her marriage to George Kent. No divorce party, either. No blog.

Apparently life started after she'd divorced and returned home, and resumed the name of Trescott. From that time on there were a couple of photos of her with the Trescott family at different business functions. And that was that.

Bea accessed the internet to search for George Kent, divorced husband of April. She found a website devoted to an old, established company, which specialized in seeds and rare plants, internationally known, appearances at Chelsea Flower Show, Hampton Court and so on.

No family photographs. Early promotion material for the company included a shot of a rather beautiful Georgian house near Maidenhead, which looked well maintained. The family residence, presumably.

George Kent appeared in several professionally taken photographs. So this was the father of the Terrible Two? Fair of hair and complexion, but more like a burly Smythe than a fine-boned Trescott in build. He looked easy-going and yes, modest. Intelligent enough but not an intellectual. Not a Tricky Dicky.

Why on earth had this man married April Trescott? What on earth did they have in common? He hadn't needed her money. His seed business seemed to have been started by his father, from whom he'd inherited . . . and then he'd expanded, and so on.

Bea sat back in her chair to think about why George Kent might have married April Trescott. Well, April had the good bone structure of all the Trescotts. She would have been considered a beauty in her younger days when she'd had a bit more fat on her bones. She was blonde and 'county', which brought kudos in some circles. Yes, in spite of her sharp manner – which might not have been so strident twenty-odd years ago – she must have seemed an attractive proposition.

Why had *she* married *him*? Perhaps to get away from home? She had inherited some Trescott money, hadn't she? But there'd been no hint of a career. He was nice-looking and a neighbour; he had status in the community, and a beautiful house.

She'd probably thought she could manage him and maybe she had done so until . . . yes, what exactly had happened to break that marriage up and leave her with no alternative but to return home, penniless, with the two boys? Wouldn't she have been entitled to decent alimony after all those years of marriage? Yet, from what Evie had said, April was short of money and it was the Trescotts who had finished putting the boys through university.

Piers tapped on the door and entered. 'Joshua has just rung to say he's bringing round some stuff for Evie and is that all right? He seems to think you might bar him entry.'

'No, I wouldn't mind a word with him,' said Bea, frowning at her watch. 'What are we having for supper and are the children all right?'

'They're playing at dressing-up. By which I mean that Bernice has hauled Evie upstairs to change into something suitable to receive Joshua in style.'

Bea grimaced. 'She's probably going through my wardrobe as we speak. Do you know a man called George Kent? Specializes in rare plants and seeds, Maidenhead way.'

'George Kent?' He rummaged through his memory banks. 'Name rings a bell. Chelsea Flower Show? Have I painted him? No. Why do you ask?'

'He married the Awful Aunt and it ended in tears. I'd like to know why.'

'Mmm. Will think. Now, about my stuff. I know some of it's still in the hall but I've stowed some in the interview room next door, the one you don't use much now. I asked Betty if it was all right, and she said it was OK with her. I've got a line on another studio to rent and I was going to look at it this afternoon, but I don't want to leave you if another Trescott visitation is on the books.'

'That's fine. I appreciate it. Thank you.'

He came to stand next to her and peered down at the photographs Keith had printed off for her. 'Kent. A serious plants man? I don't think I've ever met him but I've heard someone talk about him . . . somewhere. Didn't she . . . yes, it was a she . . . she said he was one of those who talked to plants.'

He closed his eyes and concentrated. He lifted one of his hands as if he were painting. 'Now, who was I painting when she said that? Definitely a woman. Got it. She'd been mentioned in the Honours List for charity work.' He shook his head. 'I'll think of it in a minute.' He bent down to put his arm around Bea and kissed her on the temple. 'I'm rushing you, aren't I? Am I going too fast?'

She relaxed against him. She shook her head, not very much, but just enough to keep him beside her. She breathed deeply and closed her eyes.

He kissed her eyelids. 'I won't let you down again. Promise. Cross my heart and hope to die.'

'It was half my fault. I didn't understand how hard it was for you, without any work. We were too young.'

'Nice of you to take the blame, but it was my stupid pride that led me astray.' He stood up straight and wandered off to the door. Then stood still, hitting his forehead with the palm of his hand. 'George Kent. He was a near neighbour of hers. Lady . . . can't remember her name, it'll come back to me in a minute. Strong face, heavy eyebrows and chin. Interesting. I liked her. People often ramble on about whatever comes into their heads while I'm painting them and yes, she mentioned him because . . . now why was she concerned about him? Scandal? Something hushed up? When was that? Last year? No. Two years ago? She said I should look her up if I were down her way at any time. Not that that means anything with most people. But it's enough for me to give her a ring now.'

He disappeared into the little-used interview room next door, which was clearly about to become his domain.

Faintly from upstairs came the sound of the front doorbell. Bea went upstairs to let Joshua in – remembering to disable the alarm before she did so.

Tall, well-built, toting a carry-on case and an uncertain smile. Unsure of his welcome.

Bea said, 'You've brought some things for Evie? That's good of you. The girls are upstairs at the moment. I'll call them down.'

'I've brought some shoes for Evie. You don't mind if I . . .? I know you barred Benjy . . .?'

'Indeed,' said Bea, noting that the red monster had gone from outside, thank goodness. 'No great harm done.' She called up the stairs. 'Girls, Joshua's here.' And then, to her visitor: 'Come into the sitting room. Take a seat.'

He dumped the bag and selected a big chair in which to sit. He spread his knees, leaning forward on them. He was wearing a striped T-shirt and jeans. Good jeans. His hair had been cut by an expert recently. It wasn't quite so floppy in front. It made him look more solid. Perhaps, she thought, he was a little old-fashioned? He didn't look anything like his father. Yes, he was blonde like his mother, but he lacked the easy-going good humour which showed in the lines of his father's face.

Bea made conversation. 'Tell me about yourself. Do you get paid for working in the constituency or are you a volunteer?'

'I'm working as PA to the local party agent at the moment, and hoping to get another chance to stand at a by-election when one comes up.' He was off, parroting the party line. He'd learned his lines and he could deliver them well enough. He even looked the part of earnest, deeply concerned, young hopeful.

Bea wondered how much he was costing his family while he worked for nothing.

Bernice came in, looking amused. 'Evie's just coming. Hello, Joshua. I hope Benjy's fully recovered now.'

He half rose when he saw her, and then sank back into the chair, frowning. 'Er, yes. I mean, why wouldn't he be?'

So Benjy hadn't told Joshua that he'd been felled by a slip of a girl with a laptop and an attitude?

Bernice ironed out a grin. 'I mean, because he got a parking ticket.'

'Oh, so that's what put him in such a foul mood? He gets them often enough. Parking tickets, I mean. And Nunkie's been on at him about his timekeeping at work. Honestly, they expect him to carry out a junior temp's work and pay him tuppence for doing so. It's quite ridiculous. Mother says she'll have to talk to Nunkie again about Benjy's position in the business.'

Bernice opened her eyes wide. 'How ever does he pay for them? The parking tickets, I mean?'

Joshua looked puzzled. 'Well, naturally, Mother helps him out while he's learning the trade.'

Bernice picked up the tote bag Joshua had brought. 'Something for Evie?' Bernice plucked a pair of worn trainers from the bag, a pair of lace-up shoes suitable for a granny – not that Bea would have been seen dead in them – and a much-washed pink dressing-gown.

Bernice said, in a creamy tone of voice, 'I'm sure she'll be pleased to have them, Joshua.' Meaning that she thought they were only fit for the dump.

A soft voice spoke from the doorway. 'Joshua?'

He turned his head without rising from his seat. Then did a double take, and actually stood up. All the way up. 'Evie? Is that you?'

Evie enjoyed that moment. And yes, she was dressed in one of her newly bought outfits, a clinging white top and black jeans, with one of Bea's precious silk scarves draped becomingly around her neck. Her dark hair waved and curled to her shoulders, and she wore mascara and a pink lipstick which made her, for once, look her age. All in all, she was a very pretty package.

Joshua gawked. There was no other word for it. He gawked.

Evie lowered her eyelids, revealing that Bernice had used some silver paint as well as mascara to outline her eyes. Bea tried not to grind her teeth. She hated to think what her make-up table looked like at this moment!

'Evie?' Joshua wasn't at all sure that it was her.

Evie, eyes down, took a seat opposite him, lifting a tress of hair back to make sure it framed her face just as it should.

Bernice gave Bea a glance of much amusement and some embarrassment. Bernice knew she was going to get a rollicking for raiding Bea's things, but she didn't care. The result was stunning and Joshua was appropriately stunned. He resumed his seat with his eyes still on his cousin.

Bernice sat down beside Evie, saying, 'As you can see, Joshua, she's been shopping for things for herself. Don't you think she looks good?'

He nodded. Cleared his throat. 'Yes. Absolutely. Yes, I did bring . . . There's some shoes and some more of your medication. Mother made sure you had plenty. She said I was to stand over you, watch you take it.'

'Oh, I'm off that for a while. Just to see if I can cope.'

'But . . . I'm not sure that's a good idea. What does the doctor say?'

'I haven't seen him. Don't worry. At the slightest sign of any trouble, I'll yell for help.'

'Oh. I suppose that's all right. I'll tell Mother. No doubt she'll be in touch. Well, about the bag. Maria packed some shoes for you and put in a birthday card from her and Carlo, too.' He cracked his knuckles. He was not at ease.

Evie said, 'Maria's always been very kind to me.'

'Er, yes.' He cleared his throat again. 'Mother asked me to tell you. We've had to rethink the celebrations this weekend, because of Uncle's death. It wouldn't look right to throw a big party now. We've tried to fix a date for the funeral, but what with holidays and staff shortages, it's proved more difficult than we thought, and in fact they haven't released the body yet, so . . . but we hope we can bury him next week. I've had to spend hours on the phone, telling people what's happened and putting them off. So it will just be a quiet family dinner with a few friends this Friday night.'

'Oh. No fairy lights in the garden? No marquee with a band?'

'We've cancelled all that. We'll have a sit-down meal in the London house and you can wear your new pink dress. Mother says you can have a big party later on, perhaps at Christmas.'

'Will I still get my puppy?'

'I suppose so. I don't know. You must ask Mother.' He cracked his knuckles.

Bea and Bernice sat very still.

Evie said, 'There was going to be a fairy bower in the garden, covered with white roses and lit with tiny lights. You were going to ask me to marry you there. That's not going to happen?'

He shifted uneasily. 'Well, no bower, but we'll still do the

rest of it. After supper we'll break out the champagne, ready
for the toasts. I have the ring already. Or rather, Mother has it.'

'And then what, Joshua? How long before we get married?'

He relaxed. He knew this bit of his script. 'One month exactly.
The registry office has been booked already.'

'And a honeymoon?'

'Well, you're a bit young for . . .' He stopped abruptly,
realizing that the Evie he was now looking at was not too young
for a honeymoon. 'I don't know.'

Evie continued in the same quiet tone, 'I suppose you have
to ask your mother about that, too. And where will we live?'

Another restless movement. 'We'll still use our own rooms
at the top of the London house for the time being, and then,
when I get into Parliament, we'll buy a house somewhere in
the constituency.'

'That might take years,' said this new, quietly controlled Evie.
'How do you think I should occupy myself when we're married?'

'Well, I suppose you'll do what all young married women
do. Perhaps you can find a part-time job in a charity shop? That
would look good on my CV. Or you could come into the
constituency office and do some filing. I'm sure we can find
something for you to do.'

'Until we have children, you mean?'

Joshua reddened. His mouth opened and stayed there.

He knows Evie can't have children!

Evie continued relentlessly, 'Will you take me to a gynaecologist, Joshua, to see whether I'm able to have children or
not? It would be good to know that, wouldn't it?'

He gave a little cough. 'Well, why wouldn't you be?'

*He knows she can't have children but he's going to pretend
he doesn't.*

Evie stared at Joshua, and then through him. 'The night before
he died, Uncle Constant said he thought I was too young to
marry yet, and Nunkie agreed. I can't get married at sixteen
unless my parents or guardian agree to it. So who is going to
give consent to my marriage now?'

'Don't worry about that. It's all arranged.'

*He means his mother has arranged it. Nunkie said he didn't
think it was a good idea, before. Has he changed his tune?*

Who precisely has the right to decide this matter now? Who is Evie's new guardian? Did Constant leave a will, and what is in it?

Evie rose to her feet, and extended her hand to Joshua. 'Thank you for coming, Joshua. It's been good to have this little talk, hasn't it? We've known one another for ever, but we don't usually talk, do we?'

He held on to her hand. 'Evie, listen; you know I've always been fond of you.'

'Yes, I know that. Now I'm a little tired. Shopping is rather tiring, isn't it? But I'll have lots of time to shop when we're married, won't I?'

'Yes, but . . .'

'I'll see you on Friday at the party.' She pulled her hand away and walked out of the room, head held high.

Bea wanted to applaud. She exchanged an eye-roll with Bernice, and said, 'Yes, it was good of you to call, Joshua. Let me show you out.'

Joshua was not wearing the same calm, assured manner that he'd presented when he arrived. Joshua had been shaken and stirred. Joshua was having to *think*! With any luck, he was going to go back to his mother and ask a series of awkward questions.

And, he'd forgotten he was supposed to stand over Evie while she took her pills.

Bea opened the front door for him to leave. 'Do I understand that our invitations to the party have been cancelled? That there's going to be a small family affair instead?'

'What?' He was thinking about what he was going to say to his mother, wasn't he? Gathering what was left of his wits, he said, 'Oh, well. Yes and no. You and Bernice and the painter fellow are still expected. Leon Holland, of course. And that son of yours. He's a member of parliament, isn't he? Useful chap. It'll be just the two families.'

So Bea and Bernice and Piers were still invited to this much reduced party? Now there was food for thought.

Bea shut the front door on him and reset the alarm.

Now she had to face another problem. Joshua was going to tell his mother that Evie was off her tablets and asking about the future. Joshua would add that Evie was growing into an attractive young woman who thought for herself.

So what would April do about it?

SIXTEEN

Tuesday, late afternoon

Bea decided to go out into the garden and do some dead-heading. Giving your hands something to do helped the thinking process.

If Bea were right, April had planned for Evie to be kept in a semi-comatose condition through an early marriage until she could inherit and then the girl would be persuaded to transfer her fortune into Joshua's hands.

It would have been neater for Benjy to marry Evie. In some cultures, marriage compensated for an earlier rape. Not here, thankfully, but in some parts of the world, it did just that. But Benjy didn't want to marry Evie because . . . and here Bea had to think about it.

Think of his scarlet monster of a car. Think of the parking tickets. Think of all the different jobs Benjy had had so far. He's costing his mother a pretty penny and so is Joshua . . . but if Joshua marries Evie, then he'll be well provided for.

Benjy is the favourite. He is the golden wonder child who'd been brought up to believe he deserves a place in the sun.

Conclusion: Benjy had passed Evie on to his brother because he wasn't going to marry damaged goods. She couldn't have children and Benjy would want someone who would deliver children *and* money. Benjy was a cold-hearted whatsit.

Joshua had accepted the transfer. Why?

He knew what had happened to Evie but, although he wasn't prepared to go to the police about it, he was fond enough of the girl to want to make some amends for her treatment. Perhaps also he felt guilty about covering up what his brother had done to her? Also, her fortune was there for the taking. He probably considered – as far as he had thought about the matter – that she'd continue to be a pliable little girl when they were married. He might well imagine she'd allow him to have affairs on the side and she, being so thankful that he'd rescued her, would pretend not to notice.

Um, no. Joshua's really not that sex-orientated, is he? Not like Benjy.

Let's look to the future through April's eyes. She would want grandchildren and money to keep the family in the style to which she was accustomed. Joshua's marriage to Evie would bring him money but not children. Had April suggested that he should marry Evie, wait till she had control of her fortune, have her sign it over to Joshua and then get a divorce? At that point he'd be a wealthy man and free to marry again. Next time he would marry someone who could bear him children.

What would happen to Evie once she'd married Joshua, inherited and made a will in his favour?

Oh. Dearie. Me.

Bea decided she wouldn't insure Evie's life for tuppence. But perhaps . . . oh, my! Would Auntie insure the girl's life? Joshua wouldn't, would he?

No, he's not that devious. He'll be a failure as a politician.

Piers drifted into the garden, looking lost. He saw Bea and brightened. 'I spoke to her. Lady Whatsit who I painted a couple of years back. I explained about Evie staying with us and that we were worried about her. My lady wouldn't tell me exactly what went wrong in George's marriage because she says it's not her secret to tell, but it seems to have been a shocker. She's going to ring him, see if he'll talk to us.'

He stood there, staring into space.

Bea recognized the symptoms and sighed. 'You want to set up your easel somewhere? What about the studio you were going to look at today?'

Piers said, 'I haven't been able to leave the house to look at it. I'll set up at the top.' He went back into the house. Bea didn't need much imagination to follow his progress. He would pick up his easel and climb the stairs. He wouldn't stop at the first floor but continue on up and up. He was going to set up in the girls' room at the top of the house, wasn't he? Not much space but lots of lovely light. He'd done that once before.

The girls would be furious at having their territory invaded, but when the spirit took hold of Piers to paint, that was what he had to do.

Bea stifled annoyance. Piers would do nothing, see nothing, hear nothing else but what he was painting for the foreseeable future, just when she could have done with his help.

She sighed. Bea thought she could see exactly what April Trescott would do next. As soon as she heard from Joshua that the girl was off her pills, April would shove Evie back into the clinic and knock her out with medication so that she couldn't start thinking constructively about anything. Then on Friday evening, still drugged to the eyeballs, she'd be produced at a family gathering and commit herself to marrying Joshua.

How could Bea prevent that? Could she take the girl to the doctor's herself? Or to the police? She could say that Evie was a visitor on strong medication for her nerves but had this strange story to tell about abuse and death in the family. No, even if Evie backed her up, Bea would be laughed out of court.

Surely it was better for Evie to be married off to Joshua than living in a drugged state with nothing to look forward to except getting a puppy? It would be a compromise but perhaps that was the best the girl could hope for. Bea wondered about Joshua's idea of the future. Had he allowed himself to think about Evie making a will in his favour once she inherited? And if so, had he planned for that to be followed by her early death?

No, no. He seemed to think they could live happily as brother and sister forever.

Er, could he afford to wait that long? He needed money now or in the immediate future, didn't he? Marrying Evie was a long-term plan. Bea couldn't see how marrying her now would be to his advantage unless he planned to insure her life and arrange for her to meet an early demise. No. Joshua wouldn't do that. Would he?

Well, there was one thing Bea could do right now, and that was to tear Bernice off a strip for making free of her guardian's wardrobe! Oh, and make sure she knew the new code for the house alarm. Hari, too. And, she must update Hari on what was going on.

Her smartphone rang and at the same time a noisy lawnmower next door broke the peace and quiet of the garden. Bea went back into her office and shut the French windows in order to take the call. The agency staff were packing up for the day. Bea raised an eyebrow at Betty, who smiled and shook her head. Nothing to worry about there.

It was Max on the phone, Bea's self-important member of parliament son.

Max was saying, 'Just touching base. I sent my wife and the kiddies up north to the constituency today. I'll be joining them after the party, of course.'

Bea waved goodnight to Betty. 'The party at Trescotts? Yes, Joshua dropped by to say we were all still invited.'

'Cyril asked me to let you know that the venue will be at the town house, and not out at Maidenhead as originally planned. Too many sad memories there, and now it's a smaller party, it makes sense to hold it in town.'

Bea already knew that. So why was he ringing? She sat in her big chair and swivelled round to look out on to the garden, which was glowing in the late-afternoon sun. 'I'm doubtful about attending what is meant to be a small family party.'

'We will all be one big family when this merger goes through. Leon says he told you how important it is to him, and to me personally, that you attend.'

'How do you come into it?'

'Oh, this and that. Business. You wouldn't understand.'

'Try me.'

'Well, we've a small problem back in the constituency, factories closing down, competition from abroad . . . I told you that you wouldn't understand, but there's an opportunity for a new Trescott plant to move in, which would bring in two hundred and fifty jobs, and that would—'

'Please the electorate and keep you safe in your job? How much does your future depend on the merger going through?'

'Well, clearly, there is much to be explored . . .' He went on, using as many big words as he knew.

'I understand,' said Bea, feeling rather sick. 'If the merger

goes through, you will be flavour of the month with the electorate for bringing jobs to your constituency and that will keep
you in parliament. Tell me. When you first introduced Leon to
the Trescotts at the Royal Academy, who was in their party?'

'Cyril, of course. His sister and one of her sons.'

'Joshua or Benjy?'

'Benjy.' A sly laugh. 'He was very taken with Bernice's
portrait. Likes them young, apparently.'

'I believe he was suspended from the Trescott family
business for a while. Do you know why?'

'Oh, some boyish prank or other. He tried to get a date with
someone's daughter at a Christmas party. Got a little physical.
Stupid boy. Cyril's told him to take six months off to grow up,
and then allowed him back into the business.'

*Max seems to be very close to Cyril, calling him by his
Christian name, and speaking of family matters to him.*

She said, 'Benjy likes them young? Did you know that he's
now after Bernice?'

'Is he?' A fat laugh. 'Well, she can take care of herself, can't
she? Stroppy little madam. I was telling Cyril only the other
day how difficult life is for you, having her thrust upon you
just when you could be giving your own grandchildren a spot
of loving care and attention.'

*Oh, Max! How could you! I've suggested meetings often
enough, I've offered to babysit at weekends, but you always say
you've got a good nanny and the children need to socialize with
their own age groups. Your excuses hurt me!*

She said, 'I fear for Bernice. Benjy's been sending her
presents, trying to get her to go out with him in his car, making
his interest very clear. Max, she's only fourteen!'

'Well, well. Boys will be boys.'

Bea rubbed her forehead. She didn't dare ask if Max would
sacrifice Bernice if it meant bringing much-needed jobs to his
constituency because she thought she knew what his answer
might be.

Max was at his perkiest. 'So, all ready for the jolly, are we?
Make sure Piers has something decent to wear, and that the
dumbo is clean and tidy. It's good of young Joshua to take her
off the family's hands. Quite a responsibility, that one.'

Bea wanted to hit him. 'Evie is no dumbo. She is a lovely girl who's been through a bad patch.'

She spoke to thin air, because he'd put the phone down.

Bea went upstairs, trying not to care that she was at odds with Max. The hall had been cleared of Piers's belongings. Some things were no doubt in the spare office downstairs, and the rest . . . She went up to check – yes, he'd put the rest on the bed in the spare room.

Where did he think he was going to sleep that night? With her? Well, perhaps. She hesitated about going up to the top. When inspiration struck, he would neither hear nor see her. She wondered who he was painting now? Someone he'd sketched in a spare moment? One of the Trescott boys, perhaps?

In the kitchen she found the two girls concentrating on Bernice's laptop.

Bernice said, 'Mac gave me a problem to solve. He says one of the Holland companies claims to be doing well but isn't. He's challenged me to find out which from the balance sheets and annual reports. Evie thinks there are two companies which don't look right, but I can only see one.'

'Bully for you,' said Bea, thinking that Evie was coming on a treat, wasn't she! Dumbo, indeed! She said, 'I gather Piers has started work on something?'

Bernice said, 'He's in our sitting room upstairs. We yelled at him to get out because it's our space and we'd left our new clothes there, but he didn't seem to hear us. He's paining some woman's portrait. Dunno who.'

Bea reflected that he only painted people he'd met and studied. Not one of the Trescott boys. April Trescott, perhaps? No, he hadn't met her, had he?

Anxiety returned. April was plotting her next move. Bea was sure of it. Could she get Evie out of London for a bit? But who would take her in?

Back to basics. What were they going to do about supper?

And then . . . Where does Piers think he's going to sleep tonight?

And then . . . If Piers works through the night as he sometimes does, I'll be sleeping alone again anyway.

Wednesday morning

Piers came to her bed in the early hours. He didn't even try to kiss her, but lay down beside her, yawned mightily, settled his length beside her and was dead to the world.

In the morning she left him asleep and was halfway down the stairs when her phone rang. It was April's ex-husband, George Kent, who apologized for the early hour. He said a neighbour had given him Bea's number and suggested he call her about a family matter. Perhaps she would like to drop by his place sometime?

So he'd agreed to talk?

She settled on a time for that morning and hurried into the kitchen only to find a full-scale row going on.

Hari didn't shout. That wasn't his way. But he was coldly furious with Bernice who had slipped out of the house early without telling him, in order to put in an hour at the gym down the road.

Bernice didn't mind shouting when it suited her. Colour rising, she yelled at Hari that she'd go where she wanted, when she wanted, because she wasn't a child any more, was she!

Evie tried to be a peacemaker. 'But Bernice, you know that—'

'I know what I'm doing!'

'No, you don't,' said Hari, quietly.

Bea entered the fray. 'No, you don't, Bernice. Any time you walk out of that door without protection, you are placing yourself at risk. Evie, can you convince her not to be rash? Can you bear to tell her what Benjy did to you?'

Evie went scarlet. She bent her head so that her hair fell over her face, and clutched herself. 'I c-can't.'

Bea patted the girl's shoulder. 'All right. I know. It was a big ask.'

Evie threw back her head, and let her arms fall to her sides. 'All right. I'll try. I can tell that nothing else will make her see sense. Bernice, when the police told us about the car crash and my parents dying I went to pieces. Maria gave me something to calm me down and put me to bed. I fell asleep and woke to find him on me. I tried to scream and he put his hands round my throat. I tried to fight him off. He did it to me. Horribly.

He beat me up. I blacked out. Maria found me. She cleaned me up, put me back to bed. I blacked out again. I was bleeding but they didn't call a doctor for ages. Perhaps days. I don't know how long it was. Until Auntie came and realized I was really ill. An infection. I nearly died. They took me to a private hospital for treatment but it was too late, and in the end they had to operate. So I probably can't have children now.'

Bernice stared at Evie, the colour draining from her face.

Bea stroked Evie's hair. 'You are a very brave girl.'

Evie was breathing hard, but she wasn't as shaky as when she'd first spoken of the rape to Bea.

Hari nodded his approval.

Evie wasn't finished. 'Bernice, don't go anywhere he can get you alone. He thinks he's irresistible, that there's something wrong with you if you don't want to have sex with him. If you resist, he loses control. I couldn't bear it if he did that to you.'

Bernice stared at her friend. 'Why didn't you go to the police?'

Evie shook her head. 'When I eventually came to after the operation, they told me I'd had an epileptic fit and fallen down the stairs and that that's what had caused my injuries. I tried to tell them about Benjy but they said I'd been in shock due to my parents' death, that I'd had a fever and been hallucinating, and that the fever had triggered an epileptic fit. They said I was out of my mind and would have to be sectioned if I continued to talk like that. And when I persisted, I was sedated and transferred to the clinic, the one I told you about. At the clinic they said that due to my epilepsy, I would have to be on strong drugs for the rest of my life, but that they would keep me safe and once I'd stopped hallucinating I'd be able to rejoin the family. It was made clear that if I stopped taking the drugs after I went home I'd have to be sectioned and taken back to the clinic until I was stable again.'

Bernice was aghast. 'Didn't the doctors at the clinic realize what had happened?'

'One of my mother's cousins was epileptic and had to live a very restricted life. I suppose it wasn't unreasonable to think I might have the same thing. Auntie told me there'd been incidents in his past which had had to be covered up. They said they thought I'd grown out of it, but clearly I hadn't done so and look what had happened to me! Also, the clinic was in need of money and Trescotts gave them a huge donation for refurbishment.'

'But you're not an epileptic.' It was a statement, not a question.

Evie hesitated. 'I might be. I can't tell. They say I am. I can't remember it ever being mentioned when I was growing up, when Mummy and Daddy were alive. But if I was, well, I stopped taking the tablets completely when I came here and even though so much has happened this week, I'm still all right, aren't I? I think I've grown out of it.'

'Or never had it,' said Bernice, her eyes reflecting the horror of what she'd heard. 'You can go to the police now.'

'No,' said Evie, shaking her head vigorously. 'I can't. You don't understand. You've no idea how scary it is to be me and trying to think. These last few days have been like coming out of a darkened room into the light, but the light is hurting my eyes. At times I just want to curl up in a dark place and die. If I speak out and they give the police my medical history, I'll be sectioned again. So I won't, and you can't get me to say I will.'

Bea said, 'It takes two doctors to section anyone.'

'They wouldn't find that a problem at a clinic funded by Trescott money,' said Evie. 'I've only told you what happened because Bernice didn't understand the dangers of the situation. If you tell the police what I told you, then I'll deny it and they won't take any action because my medical history proves I'm not a reliable witness. No, I'm going to be a good little girl and keep my mouth shut. I'll marry Joshua and be safe forever.'

Bea doubted that but decided to break the tension. 'Well, now we all understand where we're at. Evie, I've just had a phone call from your uncle, George Kent.'

Evie produced her rare, beautiful smile. 'Have you? How lovely.' The smile vanished. 'Oh, but I'm not supposed to have anything to do with him now. They said he'd behaved very badly over the divorce and that's why Auntie and the boys have no money nowadays.'

Bea heard the echo of April's words. 'Perhaps it might be a good idea to hear his side of the story?'

Evie struggled with this novel idea, but finally nodded. 'I suppose so. Provided Auntie doesn't hear about it.'

'You remember him well?'

Evie smiled, widely. 'Oh yes. I used to stay with them at weekends quite often. I liked that because it was a bit lonely at home by myself if Mummy and Daddy went away on business, and my cousin Natalie and I got on like a house on fire even though she's not a Trescott but from Uncle George's side of the family. We used to run wild through the greenhouses and play hide and seek and all those other silly childish games in the old days. Later we'd play Snap or games on the Xbox. She was such fun. She must be quite grown up by now. Seventeen or eighteen? I'd love to see her again.'

Bea said, 'I explained that you were staying with me while recovering from a long illness. Mr Kent said he was surprised to hear from any of the Trescotts, but he agreed it might be good for us to meet and have a chat. He said that if we can get to the garden centre by eleven this morning, he'll make time to show us round. We'll take my car. Hari can drive the three of us. Yes, Bernice, that includes you, too. I'm not leaving you here by yourself. You can't count on Piers knowing which day of the week it is when he's working. You can bring your laptop with you if you like, but you must stay with us all the time. Understood?'

George Kent's kingdom lay in a green and pleasant part of the countryside not far from London. The manor house itself stood back from the road while a sign directed visitors to the shop, cafe and car park off to one side.

As they got out of the car, they saw that poly tunnels and greenhouses in regimented lines covered a considerable area of land to one side and beyond the manor house. The place was neat and tidy. There were no potholes in the driveway and no weeds on the grass verges. A well-run, successful business?

George Kent met them at the entrance to the car park. He was instantly recognizable from his publicity photographs. He was now, perhaps, fifty years of age. Tall and well-built with clear, light-grey eyes in a weather-beaten face and thick, fair hair turning grey. And yes, Bea considered that, with his easy-going, slightly self-deprecating air he would be perfect prey for someone like April who knew how to work on people's weaknesses.

Bea liked him. She approved his handshake which was firm, and of the way he held Evie at arms' length and said how great it was to see her, before giving her a hug.

Evie abandoned whatever misgivings she might have brought with her and hugged him back. 'Oh, Uncle George! How good it is to see you again. And Natalie?' Evie was as excited as Bea had ever known her to be.

'Yes, she's here. She's looking forward to seeing you.'

Bea nudged a sulky Bernice forward. 'And this is my ward, Bernice.'

'Delighted,' said Mr Kent, and seemed to mean it. And to Evie: 'We live in the carriage house now. This way.'

He led the way through an archway into what had once been the stable yard of the manor house but which had been converted to single-storey living quarters. A ramp had been installed leading through the first door into a large open living area with wide archways opening on to more rooms on either side. There was a wooden floor and a young woman with fair hair sitting in a motorized wheelchair.

Evie hesitated. 'Natalie?' Hoping it wasn't, and knowing it was.

Natalie lifted her arms towards Evie. 'I wasn't sure you'd recognize me.' Her smile was painful.

Evie crashed down on her knees beside Natalie and hid her face. Tears? Yes. 'What happened? Why did nobody tell me? It wasn't . . . oh, say it wasn't him!'

Natalie cried, too. 'It was Benjy, yes. He didn't do it to you, too, did he?'

Evie wept. 'Yes. I can't have children. I thought I was going mad. They've turned me into a zombie!'

'A zombie?' George Kent looked to Bea for an explanation.

'Gaslighting,' said Bea. 'Keeping her sedated. Making her believe she'd got epilepsy and had done all sorts of things which she hadn't. Messing with her head till she does as she's told.'

Mr Kent was horrified. 'But . . . how could Benjy . . .?'

'April. She's the one with the brains. She arranges for Trescott money to go into a private clinic which is happy to treat Evie as required. She covers up for whatever Benjy does. What's more, he's now set his sights on Bernice here, who's only fourteen.'

He looked Bernice over. 'Is that true?'

Bernice nodded. 'I said I'd bite him, but I'm not sure that would stop him. So I'm taking self-defence lessons.'

He winced. 'At least you're taking him seriously. I wish to God I had. Oh, do sit down. Do you want coffee or something? I'm afraid I'm not . . . raking this all up again . . .!'

Bea urged Bernice to take a seat beside her on a settee. 'Don't bother about coffee. Can you bear to tell us what happened?'

He clasped and unclasped big hands. 'Natalie and I have talked of nothing else since my friend rang me last night. Yes, if it will help, we will tell you what we know.'

Natalie nodded. 'We don't know if you'll believe us . . .' She shrugged, but her eyes pleaded for understanding.

George Kent said, 'It was the summer holidays. Natalie had just turned fifteen. My sister and her husband had long since divorced and money was tight, so she'd rented a house nearby and taken a job in an office so she could send Natalie to a good school. Joshua and Benjy were home from university.'

He winced, the memory painful. 'I was always a disappointment to April. I've always loved this business but it didn't bring in enough to give April the life she wanted or to send the boys to good private schools. She got the Trescotts to pay their fees. It was . . . difficult.' He stopped, not knowing how to explain how April had chipped away at his self-confidence.

Bea said, 'We've had first-hand experience of how April operates.'

'The boys were brought up to think that . . . Benjy in particular made it clear that I didn't measure up to . . . My small successes in the gardening world meant nothing to them. As they grew up, they thought it only right that they should have sports cars, holidays on yachts. Joshua did listen to me sometimes. I'd always hoped he'd come into the business after me, but . . . Well, Benjy . . . He kept getting into debt. I paid up twice but the third time I suggested he took a job in the holidays to keep him out of trouble. April was furious. She said I should be proud to support him.'

Natalie broke in, 'As Uncle says, Joshua was all right, sort of, but Benjy was horrible to my mother and me, just because she had to work for her living. It's no shame not to have money, so when I was fifteen I asked Uncle if I could have a holiday job here, and he agreed.'

Mr Kent beamed at her. 'She wanted to learn about everything. She humped compost and learned to pot up seedlings and asked questions all the time. I was thrilled.'

Natalie smiled, too, remembering. And then lost her smile. 'That's when Benjy started to chase me around. I didn't like it. Uncle told Benjy to cool it and he did, for a while. But one day he caught me in the far poly tunnel, the one that's not open to the public. I fought but he was too strong for me. Blessedly he knocked me out before he raped me. When I came to, I found he'd left me dangling over a bench. I couldn't move.'

Mr Kent said, 'He'd crushed her vertebrae. Broken her back. Joshua found her and raised the alarm. I called my sister, Joshua phoned for an ambulance and we took Natalie to the hospital, where she was shot straight into theatre. Joshua stayed with us all that night. He was terribly upset. He told us he'd gone looking for Natalie because Benjy had said she was a cock-tease and he'd had to teach her a lesson. Joshua kept saying he didn't know what had got into Benjy. Me, neither. I couldn't believe that my own son . . .! And yet, deep down I knew it was true.

'Natalie survived the operation but remained unconscious. In the morning we sent Joshua home but my sister and I stayed on. Natalie opened her eyes late that evening and knew us, praise be! The doctors said the damage had been so severe that she might be able to use her arms again at some point, but was not likely to walk again.'

Natalie slapped the arm of her chair. 'Come on, now! What do we say? "Never say never!" I'll walk again one day, just you wait and see!'

Mr Kent managed a pretend smile. 'Yes, there's hope. There's always hope. New inventions, yes, yes. You will. Of course you will.'

Bea said, 'You called the police?'

Mr Kent shook his head. 'By the time my sister and I felt we could leave Natalie to go home Joshua had changed his story. He denied that Benjy had ever said he'd touched Natalie. He said she must have been attacked by one of the part-timers we'd taken on for the summer. Natalie was too fragile to be questioned for a long time. When she was able to speak of the matter, she confirmed it had been Benjy who had raped her but by that time everything had gone pear-shaped. Benjy swore he'd been with his mother all day and April agreed. She attacked me for daring to accuse our son of rape. She demanded I apologize to him for doing so. She brought up every sin I was supposed to have committed in our married life. She packed up and took the boys back to her people. And that was the last I saw of any of them.'

SEVENTEEN

Wednesday morning, continued

Bea said, 'But there was a divorce? And you survived?'
'After a fashion. The Trescotts believed April's lies and welcomed her back to the fold. She resumed her maiden name and filed for divorce, demanding everything I had. My family solicitor was Natalie's godfather. We laid the facts before him, and he advised us that since Joshua had changed his story, we were unlikely to get a conviction against Benjy if we went to the police. But he also said that if April didn't get realistic about a divorce settlement, we could threaten to do just that and to involve the newspapers. He thought the mere threat of that would make the Trescotts back off – and it did. I didn't ask for any Trescott money, and she left me my home and the business.

'Then we had to decide what to do in the future. I felt guilty that I hadn't stopped Benjy somehow. My poor sister aged overnight. She lost her job, couldn't function. The doctors said Natalie would have to stay in hospital for good unless we could fund private care for her. There was no way my sister could meet those bills, so I felt it only right that I stump up. The business was doing well enough but not bringing in enough to pay for what Natalie needed by way of private care. Also, the manor house was totally unsuitable for someone who needed nursing, so I decided to downsize.

'I rented out the manor house and converted these outbuildings so that Natalie could live here as soon as she was able to leave hospital. My sister moved in with us. She died last year. Cancer. Since then Natalie and I have had a series of carers, some living in and some coming in by the day. Incredibly, she's managed to keep up with her schooling, and has even had some offers from university, but she's decided to go into the business with me. And we're thriving! Positively thriving! Do you know, she's already taken over some of the office duties from me?'

Natalie boasted, 'You should see me swanning around the site to check on everything, working on the computer, and telling everyone what to do!'

Her uncle agreed. 'She's an absolute whizz kid. I can't keep up with her. She understands more about the finance of the business than I do, and it's she who's pushing me to expand all the time. And she's great company. We're down to part-time carers twice a week now, and regular visits from the physiotherapist. This wonderful niece of mine is even learning to cook for us both. How about that, eh! She's a little soldier and I'm very lucky to have her.'

Bernice turned horrified eyes on Evie. 'Evie, you've got to go to the police. Benjy has got to be stopped, or he'll go on attacking girls and getting away with it.'

Evie's teeth chattered. 'You know I can't. I daren't. They'll have me back in the clinic again. My only hope is to marry Joshua. He'll protect me.'

'Joshua is a broken reed,' said Bea. 'You know that. His loyalty is to Benjy and not to you. He could have stopped his brother after he attacked Natalie, but he didn't, which meant that Benjy was free to go on to attack you. And now he's got Bernice in his sights.'

Evie wept. 'I know I'm a coward! I can't help it! You can't expect me to stand up to them.'

Bernice was brutal. 'Joshua's only marrying you for your money. You know that, don't you?'

Evie cried out. 'No, no! You mustn't say that. It's not true. He loves me . . . sort of. He has a fondness for me.' Her voice ran down like a toy with a flat battery.

Bea said, 'What if Benjy insures your life once you're married? And then gets Joshua to look the other way while you meet a fatal accident?'

Evie was shaking so hard she could hardly get the words out. 'You're just saying that to make me give him up. He's not like that. He wouldn't insure my life and then . . . No. You're quite wrong!'

Mr Kent was shocked. 'Mrs Abbot. That isn't a possibility, is it?'

Bea said, 'At this very moment I've got my staff trying to find out if insurance has been taken out on Evie's life and if so, by whom. They're ringing all the major companies today to check. It's a time-consuming job. Betty said she'd ring me if they found anything. So far, they haven't.'

Evie curled herself into a tight ball, with her hands over her ears. 'I can't bear it! Please, make it go away!'

Bea's phone rang. Was it Betty with news for them?

No, it was Piers. 'A couple wearing some kind of paramedic gear have arrived with paperwork to collect Evie and take her to the clinic for a check-up. They didn't come to the front door. They got in through the agency rooms and came up through the house searching for Evie. I told them she'd gone shopping with you. They said I should tell you to bring her back straight away, and that they'll wait till you do so.'

Bea looked at her watch. She stood up, holding on to her phone but addressing the others. 'I'm sorry to break this up, folks, but there's been a development back home. Some paramedics have arrived to take Evie back to the clinic. I wondered if April would try this.'

Evie squeaked, and curled herself into a ball.

Bea made a calming gesture. 'It's all right, Evie. It's not going to happen.' Back to the phone. 'Piers, any idea how to get rid of them?'

'I asked them to leave. They said their instructions were to wait for Evie if she'd gone out. I said they could wait if they wished to do so, but not in the house. I said I'd get the police to remove them if they didn't shift themselves. So they're sitting outside in a private ambulance and I hope they get a parking ticket. Any comment?'

Bea said, 'They'll give up after a while. We're in no hurry to return. I'll let you know when we're on our way back.' She clicked off the phone.

Evie shot to her feet and looked wildly around. 'I'd rather die than go back to the clinic. I'll run away. You'll give me some money to get away with, won't you? Oh, but where can I go that they can't find me and take me back? I don't have a passport or a cheque card or anything.'

'No need for histrionics,' said Bea. 'Yes, an ambulance has come for you but you're not there so they can't take you.'

Bernice put her hands on her hips and appealed to Bea. 'We aren't going to hand her over, just like that!'

Bea said, 'I'm struggling with this, Bernice. No, I don't want to hand Evie over. But I'm not her guardian. She's underage. I suppose we could try Social Services, see if they'd take her into care, which would keep her out of circulation for a bit. But legally, if her aunt is now her guardian . . .'

Bernice said, 'We don't know that.'

Bea was conflicted. 'True. If we could only find out which member of the family is now responsible for her . . .! I think we need a solicitor, and a doctor.'

Evie gulped. 'That will take too long. Days. And meanwhile . . .' She threw herself at Natalie's feet. 'Can't I stay here with you? I'd feel safe here.'

Bea consulted Mr Kent. 'Could she . . .? You're family still, aren't you?'

She could see the whites of George Kent's eyes. He'd lived a quiet life since April had walked out on him. He could imagine only too well what April would say if she learned he'd taken Evie in. He blenched. And then . . . and then Bea saw him decide to take a stand.

He said, 'Yes. Not for good, because she's got to go back and get this matter sorted at some point, but for tonight, yes.

Evelina, could you face going to the police, if Natalie and I come with you?'

Evie sobbed. 'They'll say I'm mad, and the clinic will back them up. Joshua is my only hope. He'll save me.' Defiant, stifling seeds of doubt.

Bea was brutal. 'It's Joshua who's dropped you in it this time. The Trescotts were happy enough to leave you with me till you told Joshua you'd stopped taking your pills.'

Mr Kent rubbed his chin. 'Ah. So what can we do? Mrs Abbot has suggested consulting an independent doctor. Let's do that, shall we? Suppose I see if we can get an appointment to see our family doctor as soon as possible? You remember him, don't you, Evie? He stitched you up when you cut your leg and gave you antibiotics when you got earache. He can take blood samples and whatever else it is they do and see if we can clear up this business of your having epilepsy or not. You'd like that, wouldn't you?'

Evie relaxed a notch. 'Yes, I don't mind doing that. I think I've grown out of it and if that is so, I was right to cut down on my medication. But how long will it take? Won't they have to send samples away and wait for the results? And where can I go till then? I won't go back to Kensington because they'll come for me there and no one will be able to stop them. Please, help me.'

Mr Kent waggled his eyebrows at Bea. 'We do have a spare room and we can find her a toothbrush, I suppose. What do you say, Natalie?'

Natalie said, 'Sounds good to me. We can have a real girly time together.'

Bea hesitated. 'It's only a temporary solution, but I like it. The only thing is that if the Trescotts serve me with an injunction to produce you . . . oh, that's for another day.'

Evie said, 'It only has to be till the party. Joshua and I will exchange our vows in front of everyone, and then I'll be safe forever.'

Bea looked around her. 'Mr Kent, what if the Trescotts work out where she might be? Will you be able to keep her safe till Friday morning?'

Mr Kent grinned. 'You've no idea how many precautions

against theft we have to take in this business. There's a high fence all round the perimeter, and a dog patrol at night. Alsatians. I'll make sure the men know to watch out for trespassers. Now, shall we have some lunch in the cafe here, and I'll show you around the place?'

Bea mentally reorganized their schedule. 'That sounds good. All right. You get an appointment for Evie to be checked out by your doctor. Hari will take Bernice and me back to London this afternoon. Somehow or other we'll stave off the Trescotts till Friday, when Hari will come back to collect Evie. The girls are due to have a last-minute titivating in Kensington in the morning: hair, nails and make-up. It will be too late for the Trescotts to do anything by then. We'll get Hari to take us all to the party. After Evie has had her little chat with Joshua, she can decide what to do next. Does everyone agree?'

Mr Kent had been thinking. 'I wonder . . . You mentioned insurances. April always went to one particular insurance agent to cover holidays, her jewellery and so on. I'm still using him because he finds us the right insurances for all the different policies we have to have here; for health, for covering the work force and the public. I'll see if I can track him down this afternoon and ask if April's still using him. And now, let's eat.'

Wednesday, early evening

Hari drove Bea and Bernice back to town. Bernice got in the back with Bea. She was tired. They both were. It had been a long and difficult day.

Bernice had invested time and energy in Evie. They had shopped and played together. Evie had seemed to value Bernice's friendship, and yet, at the first hint of danger, Evie had turned away from Bernice to Natalie.

Bernice had said little after it was decided that Evie should stay with the Kents. She hadn't snapped at her, or shown that she was hurt – but Bea sensed that this was so. Bernice laid her head on Bea's shoulder, and closed her eyes. Bea put her arm around her ward, and laid her own head against that of Bernice.

Bea wondered if she were glad or sad that responsibility for

Evie had passed into other hands. She rather thought she was relieved. Yes, that was the right word for what she felt. With an undertow of anxiety, for the affair was not over yet.

True to his word, Mr Kent had made an appointment for Evie with their family doctor for the following morning. He had also managed to speak to his insurance agent, who confirmed that yes, he was still acting for April.

Mr Kent said that once he'd told the agent that he had Evie staying with him, the information he needed came tumbling out. Yes, someone had indeed taken out insurance on Evie's life recently.

Evie couldn't allow herself to believe it. 'No, no. Joshua wouldn't—'

Mr Kent said, 'Joshua didn't. Hold on to that. It definitely wasn't him.'

Evie hiccupped into silence. She pushed the hair back from her face. 'My aunt?'

'Yes.'

Evie took a deep breath. 'I want to live. I really, really do.'

George Kent said, 'And so you shall. Mrs Abbot will know what to do.'

Bea reflected that George Kent might be a whizz at raising plants from seed but he was only too happy to let others deal with April Trescott.

Mrs Abbot herself wasn't so sure that she could ensure Evie's survival but she smiled and said, 'Of course! Leave it to me.'

And then she'd wondered how on earth she was going to do that. She'd hardly thought of anything else while they had a light lunch in the pleasant cafe and were shown around the place.

She hadn't even thought of anything helpful by the time she and Bernice got back in the car and were being driven back to London. Her brain kept slipping sideways. She was overtired. Overanxious. She would ask Hari if he had any ideas . . . but not when Bernice was there, listening in.

Bea thought Bernice had behaved very well that day. She thought Bernice might need to know how much her conduct had been noted and appreciated. She said, 'You managed that very well today. It's hard, growing up, having to accept that no one's perfect.'

Bernice said, 'I kept thinking how lonely Evie must be. No one in that family loves her. I mean, Mr Kent and Natalie do, but they're not in her everyday life. I see why Evie *wants* to believe Joshua loves her, and why she can't give up her dream. If I were her, I suppose I'd want it, too.'

'We all want to be loved for ourselves.'

'You and Piers love one another that way. Properly. Deeply. Not going on about it, but needing one another. I've watched you. When Piers comes in, he looks for you first off. And you lift your chin and smile when you hear him coming. He matters to you, and you matter to him.'

'Not when he's got the painting bug.'

Bernice grinned. 'No, not then. But when he comes out of it. He's not finished yet but I think he's painting Evie as a ghost. It's weird, a bit unnerving. I've been thinking that there are worse crimes than murder. What the Trescotts have done to Evie makes me want to vomit.'

And what they'd like to do to you, too.

Bernice said, 'What if the Trescotts ring and want to talk to Evie tonight? What will you do?'

'Lie, I suppose. Any ideas?'

Bernice shook her head. 'You'll think of something.' And then: 'Did Piers sleep with you last night?'

Bea smiled, but didn't reply, and Bernice didn't insist on an answer. The girl relaxed, made as if to lie down. Bea helped the girl to lie across her lap. She reflected that Bernice and Evie had probably stayed up till all hours the previous night, talking about this and that. Bernice had had a rotten childhood and survived. It had equipped her better than Evie to cope with life.

Bea closed her eyes, too. It had been a tiring day.

By the time they turned into Bea's road, they had both dozed off.

'Here we are.' Hari drew up, double parking outside the house. 'I'll take the car round to the mews and be back in a trice.' He got out to open the back door for them to leave.

Bernice stumbled out of the car, yawning. She turned back to collect her laptop and set off across the pavement and up the stairs to the front door.

Bea shuffled across the back seat to follow her.

'There she is!' A well-built man in a yellow high-vis jacket and jeans darted up the steps behind Bernice and grabbed her arm. 'Well, missy, I suppose you thought it was funny, keeping us waiting all this time. Now, you come along with us!'

The people from the clinic? Bea had forgotten about them.

A bulky woman in a paramedic's tabard who had been sitting in the porch, scrambled to her feet. 'About time, too! Where have you been, eh?'

Bea was halfway out of the car. 'Hari!'

'Get off me!' Bernice tried to bring her laptop round in the same move which had felled Benjy, but the man was ready for that. He twisted Bernice's arm behind her back so that she dropped her laptop with a cry of pain.

Bea cried out, 'You! Let go! Now!'

The woman ignored Bea to concentrate on Bernice. 'Now, now, dearie! Don't make difficulties. You come quietly, and we won't have to tell the doctors how naughty you've been.'

Hari was out of the car and halfway up the steps before Bea stopped him with a gesture.

'You, there!' said Bea, pointing at the man. 'Take your hands of my ward!'

'You keep out of this! We've got our orders and there's nothing you can do about it.'

Bernice cried out, 'You're hurting me!'

Hari cracked his fingers. 'Let me at 'em!'

'No need.' Bea produced her smartphone. 'I have the police on speed dial.'

The man said, 'Police? What? Why? We've got every right . . .' But he loosened his hold on Bernice so that she could stand upright.

Bernice was incandescent with fury. 'Let go of me, you . . . you ape!'

The woman put her hands on her hips and looked at Bea. 'You don't understand, dearie! We're only doing our job. We have papers to collect the girl and take her back to the clinic where she needs urgent medication. If you involve the police, they'll tell you to get lost.'

Hari leaned back against the railings at street level. He looked amused. He trusted Bea to extricate Bernice from the situation.

'See!' The woman waved a piece of paper at Bea.

Bea hesitated, lowered her phone and took her time to extract her reading glasses and put them on. Every second that passed was defusing the situation. And yes, the man had released his painful grasp of Bernice's arm, although he still loomed over her in a threatening manner. Bea inspected the paper. 'Yes, this is the right address. But you've made a mistake. This girl is not Evelina Trescott.'

'What?' The woman swivelled to look at Bernice. 'What do you mean? Of course it's her. She's the right height, dark hair and eyes. She's living here. You're having me on!'

The man was losing it. 'Get the sedative! That'll sort her!'

Bernice bit out the words. 'I am not Evelina Trescott. My travel pass is in a pocket of my laptop case. It has my name on it, and a picture.' She pulled away from the man and leaned forward to pick up her laptop.

His confidence had been dented. He let her go.

Bea tried for a conciliatory tone. 'I see what it is. You've made a mistake. You really cannot go around kidnapping young girls from the street.'

The woman hesitated, and then firmed up her resolve. 'This is the right house. This is the girl, and you can't prevent us from taking her.'

'Wrong!' Bea stowed the paper in her bag. 'You've got the wrong girl.'

Bernice produced her travel pass from her laptop case and held it up. 'See this? Now you'd better apologize before my guardian sets the Rottweiler on you.'

Both man and woman blenched. A Rottweiler could do considerable damage to an intruder. Not that Bea had ever owned a dog – but they weren't to know that.

'We-e-ll . . .' said the woman, grudgingly forced to accept they were in the wrong. 'You can see how it happened.'

Piers opened the front door. 'You two troublemakers still here? I thought you'd gone ages ago. Come on in, Bea, Bernice. All's well at this end. No messages from the office. Betty's finished for the day, locked up and put everything to bed. I've finished for the day, too.'

Bernice stepped into the house, followed by Bea. They rushed round to the living-room window overlooking the road in time to see Hari return to the car and drive it away followed by the stream of traffic which had been held up by the double parking.

The man and the woman from the clinic returned to their vehicle, arguing with one another and producing phones, presumably reporting on their failure to collect Evie.

Piers put his arms about them both. 'Well done, both of you.'

Bernice was trembling. 'I froze! I forgot everything Hari has been teaching me! If you hadn't been there, they'd have got me!'

Bea said. 'Hari would have rescued you if necessary but I wanted to avoid fisticuffs on my doorstep and arguments about who'd hit who first. As Piers said, you did good there, Bernice. You kept your head, and you didn't try to hit him till after he'd laid hands on you. Now, restoratives needed. Tea. Come on. Let's see what we can find to eat in the kitchen.'

Bernice couldn't relax. 'They'll be on to the Awful Aunt to complain. They'll be back. Suppose they'd got me when I was by myself! I'd be locked up and drugged and . . . I couldn't really believe it before, but Evie was right to run away.'

Bea went straight to the cake tin in the kitchen. 'Carbohydrates needed. Come on, Bernice. They didn't get you, they didn't get Evie, and she's safe where she is.'

Bernice said, 'But for how long?'

'Tea with sugar all round?' Piers was on to it.

The landline shrilled. They all looked at it. Bea said, 'If that's the aunt, then it's about time she had a taste of her own medicine.' She took her time to pick up the phone and switch it to speaker mode so that they could all hear April's sharp voice.

'Mrs Abbot, what is going on! The clinic has just rung to say you stood by and encouraged my niece to attack them when they arrived to collect her and—'

Bea hyped herself up to sound outraged. 'I was on the point of ringing you. What is going on? A couple of strange people attacked my ward on the very steps of my home, in broad daylight! What did they think they were doing! I'm just about to report them to the police,' said Bea, sinking into a stool and accepting a mug of tea from Piers.

'What!' quacked April, at the other end of the phone. 'What was that? The police! But . . . you say they attacked your ward, but . . . there was obviously a mistake. They were there to collect Evelina, who has had a small relapse and needs to be treated at the clinic before she does anything else criminal.'

'You mean you sent those two goons to remove a vulnerable girl whom you had placed in my care? And they had the nerve to attack my ward by mistake? I'm not going to stand for this. I'm having them for assault and attempted kidnap of a minor.'

'Well, I'm sorry, that was a mistake. But you don't seem to realize how ill Evelina is and—'

'Don't you think you ought to have advised me of your intentions before you acted so high-handedly? I am outraged. My ward is in shock! Heaven only knows the damage you've done to her psyche!'

Possibly that was going a little far, but April deserved it.

Bea continued, 'As for that niece of yours that you've foisted off on to me . . . Well! All she can talk about is getting engaged to her cousin, and will he think her pretty in her new dress. Oh, and the puppy. I gather you're giving her a puppy for her birthday. I can't work out whether she's fonder of the puppy or her cousin, but that's not my problem and I can't wait to hand her back to you on Friday. Now if you'll kindly get off the phone, I am about to ring the police to report the assault on—'

A shriek. 'No need for that! I told you, it was a mistake.'

'A mistake which will cost them dear. Bernice's arm is badly bruised and she is very much shaken by this entirely unprovoked attack,' said Bea, sipping her tea with relish. 'I am also contacting my solicitor on her behalf to demand damages to cover the cost of counselling for—'

The line went dead. Piers proffered the cake tin, saying, 'Splendid. The best defence is always attack.'

Bernice recovered enough to laugh and lift her own mug in a toast to Bea.

Bea felt smug. 'She didn't even get round to asking where Evie was.'

'Not that we'd tell her,' said Bernice.

'That depends,' said Piers, 'on who her legal guardian is now. I think I know who might have that crucial piece of information. Ten to one, Leon will have found out who it is. We must ask him.'

Bea said, 'We can't do that. He's gone over to April's side.'

Piers grinned. 'He doesn't know the full story, does he? I got his phone number from Betty and I've invited him round tomorrow morning for a chat.'

Before Bea could object further, Hari slid into the room, saying, 'All clear. No strangers on the premises.' He beckoned to Bernice. 'Come out into the garden and I'll show you how to deal with the move the paramedic put on you.'

Bernice flushed. 'I was stupid. I froze. When will I learn?' She followed him out through the French windows and down the outside stairs into the garden.

Piers put his arm around Bea. She tried to smile. A poor effort. He kissed her temple and let his head rest against hers. 'All right?'

She didn't answer. She sighed, and let her body relax against his.

He said, 'We'll get through this together, and be stronger than before.'

But what can you do against people like April? How can you deal with Leon?

EIGHTEEN

Thursday morning

Bea dreaded hearing what Leon would have to say when he arrived. Bernice, on the other hand, looked forward to his coming.

Piers didn't seem to have a care in the world. Nor, it seemed, did he have the need to paint this morning. Instead, he happily played at being a house husband, putting the breakfast things in the dishwasher and giving the cat a treat.

When the doorbell rang, Bernice said, 'Uncle Leon?' And ran off to the hall to let him in.

Bea followed, slowly. She had a fondness for Leon and it hurt that he'd chosen April before her. Oh well. That's life. She silenced the alarm because Bernice had forgotten to do so.

Leon lifted Bernice in the air in a hug. 'My, how you've grown!'

He put her down, and she chattered away. 'Did you hear they tried to kidnap me, thinking I was Evie? I tried to hit the man but I didn't know how and Bea was wonderful and they went off with their tails between their legs.'

Bea had last seen Leon canoodling with April and allowing the Silver Fox to order everyone about. Leon had been heavy-eyed, then, and slow in his movements.

Today he was bright-eyed and bushy-tailed, immaculately dressed and polished to the nth degree. Had he been acting then, or was he acting now?

She held out her hand to shake.

He said, 'No kiss for an old friend?' He kept one arm around Bernice but with the other drew Bea to him, and kissed her cheek. Then led them both into the sitting room.

Bea looked back into the kitchen hoping that Piers would join them, and yet fearing what would happen if he did. She couldn't get her head round Leon and Piers getting together. The mind boggled, it really did. If Leon tried to put Piers down by pulling rank and money how would Piers react? And how would Leon react if Piers openly laid claim to Bea?

Bernice had continued to chatter throughout this. 'And we went to see the Kents and heard about what Benjy had done to Natalie. Wasn't that awful? Oh, but I don't suppose you even know about the Kents, do you?'

'Slow down!' Leon guided Bernice to sit on the settee beside him. 'Of course I know about the Kents.'

'Oh!' said Bea, collapsing into her own big chair. 'Of course you do. You researched all the Trescotts, but I thought—'

'You thought I cared more about the merger than about safeguarding Bernice? That wasn't very clever of you, Bea, now was it?'

'No,' said Bea, meekly. 'I'm sorry. I should have trusted you. The other night . . .'

'Ah, that was a revelation, was it not?'

Bernice jiggled at his side. 'You aren't going ahead with the merger?'

'Oh yes. It makes good business sense. On my terms though, not theirs. Where's this man of yours, Bea? I don't think we've ever met, though I've heard a lot about him over the years.'

Piers came in, looking amused. He held out his hand to Leon. 'I've heard a lot about you, too, over the years.'

Eyes and hands met. Both men maintained calm, friendly expressions. No fireworks, then.

Bernice dug Leon in his ribs. 'Don't stop now! What have you found out? Start at the beginning. Bea thought there was something dicey about the way Evie's parents died. Were they murdered?'

'What a bloodthirsty child you are,' said Leon. 'No, it was a genuine accident. There was an oil slick on the road, they lost control of the car, ran into a lorry and that was that. It was all properly investigated at the time.'

Oh? Bea was sorry about that. She'd been toying with a scenario in which the Awful Aunt had done away with her brother and sister-in-law for some ghastly reason of her own. Ah, well. Bea reflected that she couldn't get it right every time.

'What a shame,' said Bernice, who'd obviously been thinking along the same lines. 'But you do know what happened to Evie?'

Bea said, 'Hold on a mo. Let's go back to the beginning. Leon, were you thinking of a possible merger with Trescotts before you met, or was it a chance meeting at the Royal Academy which brought you together?'

'It was purely by chance that your son Max and I met in front of Bernice's portrait. The Trescotts joined us, Max made the introductions and it was immediately clear that we had interests in common. Trescotts have the rights to certain mineral deposits we need and we have the technology to process them and expand the market.'

'What did you make of the Trescotts?'

Leon patted his fingertips together. 'It is unusual to find a woman with the killer instinct. I thought April Trescott had more of that than Cyril, who is a bully but not a killer. He tried to impress me with the old-school-tie talk, the upper-class accent and the "little" place in the country but didn't have any of the relevant figures at his fingertips. I thought he enjoyed the power of heading up a big company but hadn't the ability to take it any further. April is a different matter. I thought her . . . interesting. She introduced her son Benjy, saying he was working his way up in the business. At that point I saw Cyril wince, and it made me wonder if she'd spoken the truth. I asked the lad to tell me about himself. His air of consequence failed to convince.'

Bea added this up. 'So you thought Trescotts were ripe for the plucking. You thought you could easily get round Cyril, who acted big but didn't know enough to manage a fish and chip shop. Ditto Benjy. So you entered into negotiations with Trescotts, using April to grease negotiations? My guess is that she did that well. But it also worked in the other direction. She got round you on the social front, invited you to various functions and tried to make herself indispensable to you?'

He admitted it. 'Correct. Naturally I had taken the precaution of asking Mac to research the Trescotts for me. Cyril has been married and divorced twice and is childless. The two divorces have cleaned him out and he's coasting along as head of Trescotts, enjoying the prestige of heading up an international company and drawing an extortionate salary for doing very little. I thought I would arrange for him to receive a hefty pay off and perhaps get him put on an Honours list so that he could retire happily with a good pension, which would leave the combined companies to me to run.'

Bernice bounced in her seat. 'Get to Benjy.'

'He has his mother's sense of entitlement, but it's all on the surface: good schools, Oxford university and friends in expensive places. I heard his Uncle Tom had given Benjy a job at Trescotts straight from uni, but suspended him after a few months for "inappropriate behaviour". He seems to have had a series of internships, none of which led to an offer of permanent employment. Then Tom was killed and Cyril gave Benjy another chance, only to discover that the boy's attitude hadn't improved.

I understand he's on his final warning at the moment. The word is that he's lazy, doesn't turn up to work if he doesn't feel like it and skimps whatever task he's asked to perform.

'On the personal side, I've heard he'd had to pay off a girl when he was at university. No one wanted to say why, but that report left a nasty taste in the mouth. He's currently in debt and likes fast cars. My conclusion: I wouldn't employ him in any concern of mine.'

Bernice said, 'What about Joshua, the older brother? Did you meet him, too?'

'A couple of times, later on. A hollow man, a puppet, spouting the party line. No ideas of his own. People in the know said he worked hard, but they didn't see any great future for him.'

'Poor Evie,' said Bernice. 'She thinks he's going to be prime minister one day.'

Bea said, 'I understand that my son Max helped the merger along, hoping the new consortium will open a plant in his constituency which will bring hundreds of jobs in, and therefore please the electorate.'

'Max is pushing his own agenda, yes. I get that all the time and can discount it. But April . . . I must admit I was . . . intrigued. Gossip says she married beneath her but waited till the two sons had grown up to divorce her no-good husband.'

'Well, we know why!' cried Bernice.

Bea said, 'Go on, Leon. How did April get to you?'

'I have always been attracted to powerful women, as I was to you, Bea.' Here he dipped his head in tribute to her. 'I suppose April studied me as I studied her. I don't have any women in my family who care for my wellbeing. No one asks if I need a scarf when I go out on a cold day. That sort of family life has never been mine. I never thought I wanted it, but she . . . yes, she really seemed to care if I were cold or hungry.

'I don't have much time for a social life. April knows how to put on small dinner parties with interesting people; people in the media, household names. She got your son Max to invite Cyril and myself to dine at the House of Commons. I could have got these invitations myself if I'd thought of it, but I hadn't. And I was flattered. She went to a lot of trouble to please me.'

'She was playing you as you thought you were playing her.'

'I suppose so. She had brains and looks. She took an interest in my health. She bought me a special muesli which she'd mixed for me herself.'

'She drugged you with whatever it was she'd put in the muesli?'

He grimaced. 'I thought I was going down with something. April wanted me to see her doctor—'

'I'll bet she did!' said Bea, grimly. 'But you fought her off?'

'On Monday she suggested I invite you out to dinner so that she could get to know my old friends better. To my surprise Cyril joined us.' He frowned. 'I didn't care for his behaviour towards you, Bea. I'd been feeling under the weather, struggling to concentrate . . . and then you made that remark about poisoning. And, I began to wonder. I made some excuse about feeling too ill to go on to her friends' party as arranged. April insisted on accompanying me back to my flat. Once there, she offered to put me to bed and bring me a nightcap and . . . well, that's not what I wanted.'

Almost, he blushed.

Bea refused to let herself smile. Leon had always been a loner. He'd always slept by himself, even in the years when he'd had a long-standing partner. April hadn't taken his fastidious nature into account. 'So you got rid of the muesli and rethought your priorities.'

'I purged myself and have sent the muesli off for examination.'

'Good. We must bring you up to date on what's been happening here, but before we do that, there's something I must ask. Do you know who Evie's guardian might be now that her uncle Constant is dead?'

He frowned. 'You keep mentioned the name "Evie". Do you mean Evelina, April's niece? She's special needs, isn't she? It's lucky they have enough money to look after her.'

Bernice threw up her hands. 'You don't know anything!'

Bea put a calming hand on Bernice's shoulder. 'What have you been told, Leon?'

'April shared with me all about her family, the tragedies that have visited them, the cruel deaths of her brother and sister-in-law and the crushing death duties, not to mention Evelina's poor health.'

'Oh, three choruses of hearts and flowers,' said Bernice.

Bea hushed her. 'Leon, I'm talking about hard facts, not sob stories.'

'Well, naturally I needed to know what percentage of the shares were held by various Trescotts. Tom Trescott held ten per cent, a very large holding for such a big corporation. It meant, basically, that he controlled the company. His shares and all his private property are held in trust for his daughter Evelina, who will inherit when she's eighteen. Tom's younger brother, Constant, was named in his will as Evelina's guardian. I could see why Tom didn't choose Cyril, who has no interest in anyone but himself, and wouldn't have bothered to look after an orphaned child. I never met Constant. April said he was an old woman, but harmless.

'Then Constant died unexpectedly and it changed the picture again. I'm glad you gave me the heads up about that, Bea, because none of the Trescotts had mentioned it and I needed to know whether or not his death might skew negotiations. Constant had owned some Trescott shares but never attended meetings and always gave his proxy vote to Tom or Cyril to deal with. Apart from that he had a nice little portfolio of stocks and shares plus a stamp collection to make the mouth water. He'd made a will years before and that will now goes forward for probate. He left everything to his niece Evelina without specifying who her guardian should be in his place, or giving the age at which she would inherit. Which means that, as she's under eighteen, there'll probably be a court case to decide who should be responsible for the care of a very wealthy young lady.'

Bernice whistled. 'So that's why her life has been insured and she's being handed over to Joshua, who will no doubt strip her of everything she owns.'

Leon frowned. 'As I understand it, the girl is not of sound mind and someone will need to look after her. April is the obvious choice.'

Bernice was disgusted. 'Evie's fine when she's not been drugged to the eyeballs. And now she's got away from her appalling family, she's as bright as you or me, although dead scared of what they can do to her.'

Leon said, 'You mean, she's taking heavy drugs? Cocaine and the like? She's an addict as well as being half-witted?'

Bea intervened. 'It's about time we brought you up to date, Leon. You've been looking at the family from one perspective, but we've seen it from a different point of view. Let's start at that fateful meeting at the Royal Academy and with what you observed then. My son Max introduced you to the Trescotts because it's his business to make connections. You worked out that the men in that family all needed money, and that April was a clever, manipulative woman.

'Quite by chance, this meeting took place beside Bernice's portrait. You and Max claimed kinship with her, meaning no harm. As you soon learned, April's sons needed money. For reasons of their own, Joshua had already been chosen to marry Evie, so he was provided for. Benjy wasn't. He hadn't held down any job for long, he has expensive tastes, he's in debt and, as we learned later, he likes his girls young.

'Benjy was intrigued by her portrait. April arranged for Evie to attend Bernice's school and to room with her. Benjy asked Evie to send him some photos of Bernice. Come the holidays, and he made an excuse to come here to meet the girl. He liked what he saw. He made a play for her, young as she is, and was rejected. He's accustomed to getting his own way and he is, I'm sorry to say, ready to use force when things don't go exactly as he wishes.'

Leon said, 'Oh, come now. You think April is encouraging him to woo Bernice for her money? Is that why you've been trying to stop her attending the Trescotts' party? She doesn't have control of her money for four years, so what would Benjy gain by courting her now? I see no harm at all in her being invited to a family party with a limited number of guests.'

Bernice said, quietly, 'Benjy's horrible. You don't know what he's done to Evie and Natalie, and maybe others—'

Leon leaned forward to pat her hand. 'My dear, I don't know what you've heard, but April told me that her niece Natalie was tragically raped by a casual labourer. April's husband got some stupid idea into his head . . . anyway, that event ended what had been a dead marriage for some time, and April was forced to move back to her family. As for Evelina, I agree with April that the best possible outcome for a girl like that is to be in the care of a man who loves her and is sworn to look after her. And, if you find young Benjy's attentions too much for you to handle why, you've only got to say so and he'll back off.'

Bernice pulled her hand away from under his, and said, 'You don't understand!'

No, he doesn't. He's been brainwashed by April and won't hear anything we say.

She looked across at Piers, who had seated himself at the far end of the room, listening. Making himself invisible. As if he'd been waiting for her to turn to him, he got up, rescued an unframed canvas from under the table, and propped it up on a chair for them all to see.

Bea caught her breath. This was no finished painting, but a sketch in oils, hastily executed, but full of life.

Piers had painted Evie as a ghost, slumped in a chair, gazing out of the picture with unfocused eyes. Rising from the seated, semi-transparent figure of Evie was another girl, painted in vibrant colours. This girl was wearing one of her new outfits, her hair shone and her eyes were bright. She was looking out of the picture, directly at the viewer. She was leaving the shadows behind her, though they still reached out to claim her.

Leon said, 'What! Who is this?'

Bea explained. 'That's Evie. Piers has painted her as she was when she first came to us, dulled by drugs, badly dressed and unkempt. Then he's painted her rising from her old self. You can see how different she looks now, all bright and hopeful, but still fearful of the future. She's been off the drugs since Saturday evening, she's had all sorts of frights but she hasn't had a fit.'

Bernice took over. 'When I was asked to look after her at school, she wasn't capable of adding two and two together. Now she can add up and subtract almost as quickly as I can. But it's been drummed into her that if she tries to think for herself, she'll be taken back to a private clinic which is funded by her family and kept sedated till she doesn't know which day of the week it is. That's the threat they hold over her. Stay

drugged and compliant or be sent back to the clinic. She looks
at the future and can only see one way out, and that's to marry
Joshua. She thinks he'll take care of her forever but she hasn't
allowed herself to think what life with him is going to be like.'

Bea picked up the story, 'We've discovered that April has
taken out insurance on Evie's life. Why? The girl is sixteen
tomorrow. Can it be that April is expecting Evie to meet with
a fatal accident? We told Evie about the insurance policy. She
refuses to believe Joshua has had anything to do with it, and
actually I don't think he has.'

Leon didn't like this. 'You're accusing April of plotting the
girl's death? That's ridiculous.'

Bea said, 'Look at this way. Both boys need money. Evelina
is due to inherit her father's estate, but not till she's eighteen.
She's also due to inherit her uncle Constant's money much
sooner. But that won't happen for at least six months as it will
have to go through probate. So as of this moment, she's not
worth anything. The only way anyone can gain from her death
now is if she is insured and meets with a fatal accident. We've
discovered that April has insured the girl for a hefty sum. What
I'm trying to get at is that the courts shouldn't appoint April
as Evie's guardian, because she's taken out life insurance on
the girl. Evie currently has no one looking out for her
interests—'

'Except Joshua,' said Leon. 'Young as he is, he could probably make out a case for being appointed to the job.' He got
out his smartphone and took a couple of pictures of the portrait.
'I suppose the critics will say this is a depiction of how puberty
changes a young girl into a young woman.'

Piers said, 'When Evie first came here, Bernice asked if I'd
want to paint her and I said "no" because there was nothing
there. But she changed, and as she changed, I did itch to paint
her. I only paint what I see. This is her as she was, and as she
is now.'

Leon went and stood in front of the fireplace, his eyes still
on the portrait. 'It's a powerful piece. Is it for sale?'

'It's not finished. I'll give it to Evie for a birthday present.
If she's handing herself over to Joshua for safekeeping, then it
will be a reminder to him of what she's like when she isn't

drugged to the eyeballs. It won't be a comfortable reminder because he's connived with his mother to control her through drugs. I suspect he'll probably destroy the picture.'

Bernice said, 'Uncle Leon, you don't know the half of it. Benjy's out of control. He raped Evie when she was sent to bed after her parents died. He beat her up and impregnated her and persuaded everyone else to let her sleep it off. So instead of receiving the medical attention she needed, they left her to develop an infection and only when they realized how ill she'd become, did they whip her off to hospital for emergency treatment. And, as a result, she's infertile.'

Leon was not perturbed. 'A terrible story, if true. I've heard different.'

'Oh yes. That story. Yes, she tries to stick to it when she can. They told her to say she fell down the stairs and that's what made her infertile. Unbelievable! And what about her cousin, poor Natalie Kent? Raped and left in a wheelchair! I mean, get real!' Bernice made a sound like a kettle boiling.

Bea put her hand on her ward's arm. 'Steady, girl. April Trescott has been telling him a different story, and he's reluctant to look any closer in case it jeopardizes his merger.'

Leon had the grace to colour up. 'Come on, Bea. That's not fair. Evelina had a nasty fall, suffers from nerves and epilepsy, and has needed to be on drugs ever since. Natalie Kent played around with a casual worker and got burned. It's a tragic tale, of course, but you mustn't go round spreading rumours which could blight the careers of two promising young men . . . one of whom, I must remind you, is prepared to take care of his cousin for the rest of her life.'

'A life,' said Bernice, 'which will be very short if the family's need of money increases faster than his fondness for Evie. Will there be a small item in the papers in a few months' time about a girl who, befuddled with the strong drugs she's been taking, fell from a high building and died? How sad, people will say. But how convenient that the family had taken out some insurance on her life.'

Leon narrowed his eyes. Was he taking it in? He looked as if he were. And then, he looked at his watch and said, 'You have a fertile imagination. Now, I really must be off. I have a meeting in the City in half an hour. Bea, you'd better have a word with young miss here. Make sure she realizes the penalties for slander.' He took one last look at the portrait and turned away. 'Yes, a powerful piece. But, a fantasy. By the way, where is this Evelina today? I thought to meet her here.'

'Upstairs,' said Bernice, eyes cast down. 'Having a nap.'

Was Leon convinced? He pretended to be so, anyway. He said, 'I understand we'll all be meeting up again tomorrow evening at the Trescotts, when I hope we shall remember our good manners and enjoy the birthday toasts. Bea, will you show me out?'

So he wanted a word in private with her? She followed him into the hall and shut the sitting-room door behind her. She said, 'Leon, promise me you'll be careful? I do care what happens to you. I do think you're wrong about Evie but . . . no, don't let's part on bad terms.'

He jerked his head at the sitting room. 'You're not serious about Piers?'

'Yes, I think I am.'

He fiddled with his watch strap. 'I always thought that perhaps one day . . .?'

She put her hand on his arm. 'No, you didn't, Leon. You don't want a wife. You want a dinner companion when you have the odd evening to spare, and a good friend to listen to you now and then. No matter if we disagree about this or that, I will always be your friend.'

'Aren't you afraid Piers will let you down again?'

'No. I don't think he will. We're supposed to be getting married again next week. Would you like to give the bride away?'

He laughed. Shook his head. And then nodded. 'It's a deal. Let me know when and where. I'll see you tomorrow at the Trescotts'. With both girls in tow, right?'

Bea let him out and made sure the alarm was switched on.

NINETEEN

Thursday afternoon

Back in the sitting room, Bea found Bernice pacing up and down, emitting squeaks of fury. 'Is he blind and deaf? Well, if he won't help Evie, maybe . . .'

Hari appeared at the open French windows. 'Bernice, fancy practicing some moves in the garden?'

Bernice started to dance around. 'I have it! I have it! I know how to deal with that piece of filth! I'll lure him to come here and as soon as he tries it on, we'll hand him over to the police, because I personally am prepared to testify against him.'

Oh, no! She can't possibly think that she can deal with Benjy by herself, can she?

Bea said, 'No. I forbid it. Absolutely NO!'

Bernice grinned. 'You can't stop me.'

'As your guardian—'

'Are you going to lock me up? Shove me in a clinic and drug me into imbecility?'

Bea was silent. Of course she wasn't going to do that.

Bernice went into overdrive. 'The evil that he's done lives on in the lives of the girls he's damaged, and nobody seems prepared to do anything about it. If we can't be bothered to do anything, Evie's going to end up in a coffin, right?'

Hari said, 'You propose yourself as bait? An interesting thought. The police would put in a ringer. Some woman who's trained to deal with predators. Let me see if I can find someone.'

Bernice laughed in his face. 'No jury would convict if Benjy said he'd expected to meet me, and someone else turned up instead. He'd argue that was entrapment.'

Hari didn't give up. 'No need for you to put yourself at risk. We find out where he usually goes and put a trained girl in his way. It might take some time to set up—'

'We haven't got time,' said Bernice. 'Tomorrow evening Evie

commits herself to marrying Joshua in front of witnesses and she passes out of our lives for good.'

Bea said, 'I honestly don't think Joshua means her any harm.'

'No, but his mother does, and it's his mother who calls the shots, isn't it? If she says "jump", he'll jump. Evie will be back in the clinic in no time and then there'll be an unfortunate mix-up with her drugs and she'll get an infection and die. Oh, I'm sure the Awful Aunt will give Joshua some of the insurance money to console the grieving widower, and to keep him quiet. Would you take a bet on her being alive to reach seventeen? I wouldn't.'

Hari sent a narrow glance to Bea, which she interpreted as meaning that he didn't think the girl could take Benjy. Bea didn't, either.

Neither did Piers. 'Bernice, your idea is not without its attraction, but I don't see how you can pull it off. For a start, what makes you think you can get Benjy to attack you?'

'Evie still hasn't got a smartphone, but I have. I've already rung the aunt once, remember, when I told her that Evie had lost her original phone. She won't be surprised if I ring her again. I'll say Evie's still not got a phone of her own but that one's in the post to her. I'll say she's fussing about some jewellery she's supposed to be wearing at the party and can her dear auntie have it ready for her to wear when she arrives. I'll complain that Evie can't think of anything else and that she and Bea are planning to spend all day tomorrow at the beauticians which is dead boring for someone like me and that I'm looking forward to some quiet time by myself when I can get on with my homework. I'll complain that my laptop isn't working properly but I can use Bea's computer when the agency closes at midday. It's a bit tight because the party's in the evening but if he knows I'll be alone in the house all afternoon, I reckon that he'll come. He won't be able to resist an opportunity of finding me alone and unprotected.'

Hari scratched his chin. 'He might, I suppose. But I wouldn't like to take odds on it.'

No!' said Bea. 'No, and no and NO!'

Bernice came and sat beside her. 'I have to try! Think of it this way. Benjy's not going to give up, is he? You can keep me safe this week, but what about next month? Whenever I step outside the front door here or walk to the gym, whenever I leave the school buildings, wherever I go by myself I'll have my chin on my shoulder aware that he's going to be out there one day, waiting for me. Quite frankly, I'd rather get it over with than live all my life in fear.'

Bea's voice cracked. 'He's too strong for you. What if he actually succeeds in . . .'

Bernice put her arm around Bea. 'Then you will see to it that I get the best treatment possible. I understand that being raped is terrible, but it's not necessary to die of it. I learned that from the book *Candide* which we did in school last term. You'll be there to watch me and you won't let him get that far. Attempted rape should be good enough to get him sent down because there's no way I'll keep quiet about it. Maybe Natalie and Evie will speak up then.'

'But what would Evie do without her white knight?' asked Bea.

Bernice grimaced. She'd already worked that out. 'Live with the Kents and go to a good day school nearby. She needs something a boarding school can't provide. She needs to be with people who love her. Even more, perhaps, she needs to be with people she can love. And she does love the Kents.'

But she didn't love Bernice? No. Brave words from a girl who'd thought she'd made a good friend and discovered that friend preferred someone else.

Hari said to Bea, 'We won't leave her alone, not for a minute, and she'll wear a wire. They come in small sizes nowadays. I can find her one that looks like a brooch or a pendant and I can set up my equipment in the kitchen. Wherever she goes in the house or garden, I can record what he says but she can't leave here, even to go to the gym.'

'Agreed,' said Bernice. 'I wouldn't do this if you weren't around to keep me safe. Now, before I lose my nerve, I'd better go and phone Auntie with the news.' Off she went with a smile fixed to her face.

Hari reassured Bea, 'Don't worry. Nothing will happen. But, just in case, I won't leave Bernice's side. We'll ask the Kents to bring Evie back here tomorrow instead of my going to fetch her.'

Piers was not convinced. 'That kid's got nerves of steel. I see her uncle Leon in her. I think her scheme is foolhardy but she's right about one thing: if we can deal with Benjy now, it'll save us all from months of anxiety wondering when he might strike. We can't protect her twenty-four-seven, even for a week.'

Bea managed a stiff nod. Piers was right, but a little voice at the back of her head cautioned against stirring Benjy into action.

Dear Lord, look after her, please.

Bernice was fitted with a wire, which looked a pendant on a chain round her neck. She and Hari exercised in the garden.

Nothing happened.

Nothing will happen . . . will it?

Bea wore herself out, worrying.

Supper time. Nothing happened.

Of course nothing will happen. Surely Benjy would see sense and abandon his attempt to get hold of Bernice? Won't he?

Friday morning

It was Evie's birthday and the day of the party.

Everyone's nerves were stretched to screaming point. Everyone pretended nothing was going to happen.

Nothing did.

George Kent brought Evie back to Kensington. Over coffee, Evie displayed the pretty trifle of a bracelet and a blue pashmina which the Kents had given her. There was colour in Evie's cheeks and she was on a high, looking forward to the party.

Bea gave Evie a locket on a chain, and Bernice gave her a blue silk evening bag. Piers gave her a fine leather handbag which she declared she was going to take to bed with her and never be parted from as long as she lived.

George Kent was preoccupied. He said he'd an appointment in the City and went off while Bea took Evie and herself off to the hairdressers for a last-minute titivation.

Piers went out to meet with his agent, who wanted to kiss and make up, and to discuss future arrangements.

Hari took Bernice into the garden for a workout.

They were all back in Kensington in time for a snack lunch. Nothing had happened.

Bea told herself that nothing *would* happen, at least until after the party. The boys surely wouldn't jeopardize that.

Evie went upstairs to put on her party dress. She said she knew it was too early, but she was so excited that she couldn't wait. Bernice was in T-shirt and jogging trousers but said she'd change at the last minute and settled herself down in the living room to work on the problem which Mac had set her of locating the underachieving Holland company.

Bea went down into the agency rooms to deal with some agency matters which Betty had set aside for her.

Piers said he was going to catch up on some business and cloistered himself in the little used interview room next to Bea's office.

Hari took himself off to the garden to bask in the sun. It was a fine, warm day, and the scents of the garden drifted in through the open French windows.

Five of the clock and all was well.

Someone pressed the doorbell.

Friday afternoon

Bea hard the bell. She raised her head and mentally checked over who would answer it. Five o'clock and the agency was packing up for the day. Betty was pottering about, turning lights and computers off. She called out, 'I'm off, then, Mrs Abbot!'

Bea heard the agency door to the street shut as Betty left.

It wouldn't be Benjy at the door. He wouldn't try anything now, so near to the party. Nevertheless Bea hastened through the big office and started up the stairs to the living room – just as she heard Evie came clattering down from the top floor.

Bernice called out, 'Evie, it's a huge bunch of flowers. I suppose it's for you. I can't see who's carrying them. Let's get Hari to open the door.'

Bea paused, halfway to the stairs. Hari would deal with it . . . whatever it was.

Then she heard steps above, running to the front door. 'Flowers for me?' That would be Evie. 'I'll just shut off the alarm . . .'

No, she mustn't do that! She mustn't open the front door by herself!

But she did. Bea heard a choked cry of alarm.

Then feet, more than one pair, as someone – or more than one person? – pounded into the hall and slammed the front door to behind them.

There was a muffled shriek from Evie.

Benjy? No, surely not!

Piers came to the door of his office, eyes wide. 'What . . .? It couldn't be . . . could it?'

Bea brushed past Piers to fetch Hari.

He was standing on the lawn, hand over eyes, peering up at the living-room window.

Piers made for the inside stairs.

Bea shot out to join Hari in the garden. Looking up, trying to see what was happening.

Why had she ever told Evie the code? Fool that she was! If Evie hadn't cancelled the code, the alarm would have gone off and the police would have been alerted.

Idiot! Bea ground her teeth.

The French windows which led from the living room out on to the balcony were open. Bea heard a man say, 'Back, bitch! Back! Joshua, don't just stand there. Put a chair under the handle of the inside door. We've got to wait till the cab goes round the block and then we'll be off, but we don't want anyone disturbing us.'

Bea breathed, 'It *is* Benjy! Hari, can you . . .?'

Hari started for the outside stairs.

Benjy's voice rang out loud and clear. 'Now, lock the French windows and pull the blind down.'

As Hari reached the balcony, the French windows slammed to, and the blind within was pulled down.

Hari tried to open the doors. Failed.

The transom window above was open and Bea could hear

what was said – and registered the sound of a strong, hard slap.

Evie's voice, whimpering. 'Benjy, no! Why . . .?'

Another slap.

Bea shivered. Whatever had possessed her to trust the girl with the code to the alarm!

Hari took something out of his pocket and bent to the lock, starting to work on it.

Evie shrieked, 'Joshua, tell him to stop!'

Joshua bleated, 'Benjy, there's no need for that.'

Piers darted out of the house into the garden, shaking his head. 'I tried getting in, but they've jammed something against the inside door. It's too thick to break down. I've phoned the police.'

Bea put her finger to her lips. 'Speak softly. The boys don't know we're here. They're waiting for their cab to go round the block before they leave. We mustn't spook them into doing something silly. Call the police again. Say it's a hostage situation. They'll take ages to get here through the traffic, but so will Benjy's cab.'

Piers bent to his phone, swearing under his breath. 'Come on, come on!'

It was no use urging Hari to work faster. He was doing his best.

Bernice's voice floated out. 'Benjy, you were told you are not welcome here. You can't just come in and beat Evie up. I must ask you to leave—'

Another slap. Bea winced. Her nails bit into the palms of her hands.

Hari got on hands and knees to try another key.

Benjy's voice. 'I'll deal with you in a minute. We're taking the two of you out of here for a nice quiet time together and if anyone wants you back, they'll have to pay for what's left of you!'

Evie's voice was thick with tears. 'But why, Benjy?'

'Nunkie called us in this morning to say the party's off and he's reporting us to the police. Leon Holland's calling off talks about the merger till Nunkie can prove . . . It's nothing but lies, and where did they come from? You, of course! You've been talking, haven't you? Don't you realize what you've done now? Ruined us, that's what! And now you're going to pay for it!'

'But I haven't said . . .!'

'Who else? Nunkie's even had our fool of a father in to give his version of what happened to that slut Natalie. He's brought up that lie about Joshua giving me a false alibi, and he's asked Carlo and Maria what they knew about your illness. Now he's getting on to the clinic, asking questions about "inappropriate medication" and what they've been supplying us with to keep you quiet. He's had our mother in, asking about some insurance fraud or other. Now he wants Evie to tell him what she overheard when Mother was giving Uncle Constant his extra pills the night he died and I'm not having it, do you hear?'

'Yes, but I did hear Auntie forcing Uncle Constant to take more pills.'

'No, you didn't! He'd have come round and agreed to let you marry Joshua in the end, if only . . . Mother just helped him to have a good sleep, that's all.'

Evie wept, 'I didn't say anything about that. I didn't!'

Benjy took no notice. 'Every single thing the three of us have done for the good of the family is going to be raked over and misunderstood. I've been sacked from Trescotts, and Uncle's going to make sure Joshua loses his post. We've been told to get out of the house and never come back. Mother, too! My car's been repossessed and I've had to use the last of my credit cards to hire a cab to take us out of here! We're ruined, and you're to blame!'

Bea put her hand to her head. Leon had thought over what Bea had told him, talked to Mac who'd witnessed Benjy's behaviour to Bernice, and reconsidered his view of April's attentions to him. He'd been sufficiently persuaded of the truth to tell Cyril that the merger was off until the girls' stories had been investigated, and now Benjy was bent on revenge.

Cyril, for all his faults, had refused to fast-track his unsatisfactory nephew through the organization in the past, and had tried to ensure he learned the business. Cyril didn't give a toss about the family. Cyril wanted that merger to go through and if his no-good nephews and difficult sister were found to have upset that dream, then goodbye to them.

Piers drew close to speak in Bea's ear. 'The police say I'm to stay on the line. They're on their way. Can't Hari break the glass?'

Bea whispered, 'Special toughened glass. New locks, supposed to be burglar-proof. I thought at first we should shout out that we're here and listening to everything they say. But I'm afraid that might set Benjy off. He might even kill the girls. We can't risk it.'

Hari crouched ever lower, working on the lock.

Lord, be with them. Lord, help them. Oh, dear Lord . . .

Benjy was talking again. 'Right, you two. When the cab comes back for us, you're going to walk out of the front door and get into it without making a fuss. We're off to a little place I know of in the country where we won't be disturbed. We need money, and your families will have to come off with a hefty ransom if they want to see you again. What's left of you when I've finished, that is. As for my little peahen here, when I've finished teaching her who's master, I'm going to re-arrange her face so that she'll remember me every time she looks in the mirror! Joshua, watch out for the cab!'

Bea crept up the stairs, followed by Piers.

Hari's breathing was slow and regular. He refused to panic. He tried another key.

Evie was pleading. 'Joshua, you can have everything I've got! Just don't let him hurt me anymore!'

Hari's shoulders relaxed. He looked down at Bea and nodded. The French windows opened inwards. He pushed at them, and they opened . . . but only a few inches. The blind inside had been pulled down and impeded his efforts.

Bernice's voice came through, loud and clear. 'That's enough and more than enough, Benjy. While you've been beating Evie up, I've been texting the police. They're on their way, now. You'd better get out while you can.'

Bea almost shrieked. That was unwise! It would provoke Benjy into action!

A confused sound. A chair overturned?

Another shriek from Evie.

Benjy, shouting, 'Bitch! Either you walk, or I'll carry you out of here!'

Hari managed to push the window open widely enough to reach for the blind. He tugged at it, trying to get it to retract.

Finally, he succeeded and shot into the room, only to be brought up short.

Bea pushed in after him, with Piers at her elbow.

Joshua saw them and panicked. 'Benjy, we've got to go!' He made a grab for Evie's arm but she slithered away, falling to the floor.

Benjy concentrated on Bernice, who had taken refuge behind the big table. 'Come here, bitch!'

Evie caught hold of Joshua's leg, and clung on. He threw her off. She landed in the fireplace. She pulled herself up, holding on to the clutching the mantelpiece, scrabbling around for something, anything, a weapon . . .

Bea shouted, 'Stop!'

Joshua screamed, 'Benjy!'

Evie's hand ran along the mantelpiece.

She found Bea's snowstorm globe, the one Piers had brought back from abroad. Panting, half blind from the beating she'd received, she threw the ball with all her might across the room . . . at Benjy?

Joshua got in the way. He shrieked and clutched at his arm.

Benjy was intent on catching Bernice.

He feinted to the left.

Bernice, eyes wide, went the wrong way.

He reached out to grab her arm.

She caught his hand and slowly, gracefully, with apparent ease, she cart-wheeled him into the wall.

Hari had taught her a thing or two, hadn't he?

Benjy made feeble movements, trying to ease himself away from the wall.

Hari took a flying leap and landed on Benjy, flattening him to the floor.

Evie's throwing of the globe activated its music. A sweet tinkle of a tune filled the room.

Bea stepped round Joshua and reached for Bernice. 'It's over. Thank God.'

Evie crumpled to the floor, weeping. Both eyes were closing, but she was laughing, too. Sort of.

Piers said, 'Hari, don't hurt him too much. We don't want any bruises. Don't give him a chance to say we attacked him.'

Bea held Bernice close. 'You wonderful girl!'

Bernice shook so hard Bea could hear her teeth chattering. One cheek was bright red, and puffy. 'I had to let him hit me, otherwise the police wouldn't believe he attacked me.'

Bea looked over at Hari. 'Bernice did activate her wire, didn't she? You did get a recording of what was said?'

Hari said, 'Teach your granny.' Which presumably meant that he had. He bounced on Benjy, causing him to groan.

Piers picked Evie up off the floor and guided her to a seat. 'You're safe now.'

Evie wept, 'It was my birthday. It was supposed to be the best day of my life.'

Bea pulled Bernice down to sit beside her and Evie. 'You are two brave girls!'

Bernice leaned over to take Evie's hand. 'You've got a future now. They can't hurt you anymore. You're going to learn self-defence, too. And one day, when we're both grown up, we'll be meeting across the table as partners in Holland and Truscott, and if we find any more rotten apples in the barrel, we'll know how to deal with them.'

Evie gulped, and nodded. 'You think so?'

Bea reflected that Bernice took after her uncle Leon in manipulative skills.

Bea feared that Evie might never fully recover from what had happened to her. Too much had been taken from her. But with care, she might grow up to be a thoughtful, caring woman who would use her money to help others less fortunate than herself. Well, it was a nice thought, anyway.

Bea didn't think Evie would ever be up to Bernice's weight. Evie might even come to hate the girl who had survived while she'd gone under. And as for the firm, by the time Evie inherited her chunk of it, Leon would probably be in complete control of the merged businesses.

Ah, Leon. Bea freed one hand to get at her phone. She texted Leon. 'Pull a sickie. Police on way.' He'd know now not to turn up at the Trescotts.

Max! Her son intended to part of the birthday celebrations,

too. He was supposed to be picking Bea and the girls up. Well, if she'd time, she'd text him, too.

But here came the cavalry, police with marksmen prepared to deal with a hostage situation which had already been defused.

Piers removed the chair from under the door handle and went out to advise the police that the worst was over bar the shouting.

Bernice went limp against Bea and breathed deeply and slowly. Bernice had her own way of dealing with stress.

Evie tried to tidy her hair. Her party dress, created by a master, had suffered less damage than her face.

Benjy found his voice and started to mouth threats against the girls, their families, their lives, his brother and the universe.

Hari said, 'Shut up, or I'll bounce on you again.'

Joshua moaned. 'For pity's sake! My arm's broken!' And yes, it did look odd.

Bea said, 'Joshua, you'll get a lighter sentence, or maybe just probation, if you say Benjy frightened you into helping him.'

Joshua stopped rocking. He'd heard her. Now he had to consider his options.

Evie followed Bernice's lead. 'Joshua, I did hear Auntie arguing with Uncle Constant that night. She was making him take more and more pills. I can tell them that now. And about the rape. There's no way Benjy can avoid a long term of prison. But you could . . . if you told the truth.'

Benjy screamed, 'Joshua, don't listen to her. You and I hang together, don't we?'

Three large policemen and an even larger policewoman walked in and took charge.

Bea counted how many of them there were, and how many cups of tea would be needed to keep them going. She tried to calculate how long it was going to take to explain what had happened, and whether or not they'd all have to go down to the police station to make statements. She also wondered whether she could get the blood out of Evie's dress . . . such a pretty dress . . .

The morning of the wedding

Piers said, 'I'm panicking.'

He didn't look as if he were panicking. He'd brought them up an early-morning cup of tea, and gone back to bed with his laptop and his expensive, rimless glasses.

Bea had had a shower and was wondering which of three outfits she'd wear that day.

She said, 'It's me who's supposed to have pre-wedding nerves, not you. Having second thoughts?'

'We never discussed how we were to live before we dived into marriage before, and we haven't discussed it now. Do we set up a joint account for household expenses, going half and half? I don't need to change my will because I made one ages ago leaving a small amount to the grandchildren and the rest to you. But what about my work and yours? Here I've been drafting my schedule for the next year without consulting you. And you haven't said anything to Betty about a change in your working practices, either.'

'I gave Betty a rise. She's to do more of the interviewing in future.' The silver outfit, the dark blue or the grey? The silver outfit was the one she'd bought at the boutique. Would it be a good omen for herself and Bernice to wear dresses bought for another occasion?

Piers said, 'Do we go on as we have been doing, with me renting a studio somewhere, and coming and going as I please?'

'Why not? I suppose we can synchronize our watches now and then. Find more times when we can go off together by ourselves.' She held the silver outfit against herself, and then the grey.

He wagged a finger at her. 'You are not taking this seriously. Marriage is a solemn affair, not to be undertaken lightly. I've been trying to get back into your bed all these years, and now I've succeeded, instead of being light-hearted and joyful, I'm worried in case you won't let me have one of those rising television sets at the end of the bed. They go up and down, up and down, till they send me to sleep.'

Bea grinned. 'There are other matters which may occupy your mind when you're married.'

She knew he was babbling about unimportant matters to hide his nerves. Strangely enough, she felt serene.

He said, 'Am I doing the right thing? Tell me, what made you think I could be trusted this time round?'

'You learned how to care for Bernice.'

They raised their heads as a door swung to on the floor above. Bernice was up and going to have a shower. At the weekend she was going up north to stay with the new friends she'd met at school, and Piers and Bea would go off somewhere – it didn't matter where – for a few quiet days by themselves before they all went to France for a holiday.

Piers said, 'It came easily to love Bernice. She's a great kid. Max is a different matter. I took a long time to learn how to be a father to him, and now he's angry with me for messing up his deal with the Trescotts.'

'Give him time. The deal will go through eventually. Leon will see to that. I only hope they get April for conspiracy, if they can't make a charge of her murdering Constant stick. Fortunately Leon now agrees with me about her. I think finding some strong drugs in his muesli has hardened his dislike of her tactics. She's going to have to sell him her shares in Trescotts to pay for some expensive legal representation for herself and the boys. I thought that was natural justice.'

Piers said, 'Benjy will definitely go down for attacking the girls. Joshua turning Queen's evidence will see to that. I doubt if they will even need to put Natalie and Evie in the box, but both girls have agreed to testify. And Bernice. What a witness she'd make in court! Wow! Those boys are toast!'

Bea held the silver up against her. Would it be better than the grey? She couldn't decide.

Piers said, 'We must look to the future now. George Kent applying for Evie's guardianship is a step in the right direction. I feel happy about that. I suppose Joshua will only get a suspended sentence but his prospects in politics look bleak . . . which is as it should be.' He set aside his laptop and swung his legs out of bed. 'You'd better wear the silver. I've got a silver tie to wear with my best grey suit. I can't think when I wore it last. Let's hope it hasn't any gravy stains on it.'

MWIN 03/20
3rd July '21

Windsor Library
Bachelors Acre
Windsor SL4 1ER
01753 743940